HEIST AND *SEEK*

Other Five Star Titles
by Amy Sandrin:

Got Mick?

HEIST AND *SEEK*

Amy Sandrin

Five Star • Waterville, Maine

First Edition
First Printing: October 2004

Set in 11 pt. Plantin by Al Chase.

Printed in the United States on permanent paper.

Library of Congress Cataloging-in-Publication Data

Sandrin, Amy, 1961–
    Heist and seek / by Amy Sandrin.—1st ed.
      p. cm.
    ISBN 1-59414-179-7 (hc : alk. paper)
    1. Government investigators—Fiction.   2. Bank robberies—
Fiction.   3. Hostages—Fiction.   I. Title.
PS3619.A55H45 2004
813′.6—dc22   2004043259

To Don and Anthony,
for making laughter a big part of my life.

Acknowledgments

It's impossible for this author to critique her own prose, so thanks to Ann, Terri, Lynda and Maggi for doing all the dirty work. And to Russell Davis: there isn't a better editor out there. Thanks for all your support, enthusiasm, and belief in me, and my stories.

Chapter 1

"Robyn Jeffries, you need to get a life." Ignoring her own words, Robyn continued dancing with the mop in her hand to the beat of the rock music blaring through the Walkman's earphones.

"Men," she muttered. "Who needs them?" She held the cleaning instrument out in front of her. "You are more reliable, a better dancer and . . ." She cocked her head sideways and studied the dirty white rope-like material springing in a hundred directions like unruly dreadlocks. ". . . you're better looking than most of the losers I've been stupid enough to go out with."

A loud banging noise drew her attention away from her stick partner. With one hand, she tugged the headset away from her ears. "What's the matter, Charlie?"

The United Financial Bank's security guard rubbed a hand over his chin, his thick, bushy white brows drawn together in frustration. "It's this dang-blasted contraption again." He tapped the glass on the security monitor. "It's the third time this week it has gone out. I'm about ready to take my gun out of the holster and shoot it." He glared at the monitor as if that alone would make it shape up.

Robyn bit her bottom lip to keep from laughing. "Charlie, in the two years my company has been cleaning this building, I've never even seen you so much as touch that gun. Tempting as it is, I don't think you're going to use it on the stupid monitor."

He turned toward her, a shameless grin on his face. "You've got me on that one. Where's your apprentice to-

9

night? I thought Doug was glued to your side."

"Believe it or not, he asked for a personal day, so I gave him the night off. I think he had a date with a little blonde he's been trying to hook up with. And Doug is not attached to my hip. He's just young, eager and willing to learn. I'm very lucky to have him. Who knows, one of these days I might even take a vacation and then you'll be glad he's so fired up to learn as much as he can. Most high school kids don't even have an attention span, or a hint of motivation, so I feel quite fortunate."

"Yeah, I guess you're right." Charlie threw the monitor another evil look over his shoulder. "I'm gonna take a stroll around the building—make sure everything's okay." He turned toward Robyn. "Will you be all right while I'm gone?"

"Of course I will." She paused a moment, leaning on the end of the mop, a hand on one hip. "Do you think the bank will miss a measly couple hundred dollars?"

Charlie laughed, his weathered skin creasing into a sea of wrinkles. "I wouldn't do that, Miss Jeffries. I'd be required to frisk you and my wife might get a tad upset."

A breathy sigh escaped her lips. That's what she wanted, dreamed about—a man who placed his woman above the duties of his job. Someone who had the wherewithal to hang around the same dame for forty years and still be happy about it.

Charlie was older than her own grandfather. Forced to work past retirement age, to make up for what his pension didn't cover, he'd taken a job as a security guard at the bank's Denver branch. They'd become like family to each other in the years they'd worked together.

"See the red button here?"

Robyn nodded, one eyebrow arched.

"If anything funny happens while I'm gone, push it."

10

"Funny as in ha-ha, or funny as in weird?"

He shook a finger at her and walked away without saying a word.

They'd had this exact same conversation too many times to count. She pulled a metal file out of her pocket and fixed a nail that had developed a snag. "Yeah," she snorted to Charlie's retreating back. "What are the odds of that happening?"

Either Killian Hart had been an FBI agent too long, or he needed to get a life, because at that exact moment the curve and heft of the Glock .45 felt more familiar against his palm than the gentle sway of a woman's hip.

He cursed himself. Why was he thinking about women now—when all hell could break loose at any second?

He shifted position from his crouched stance behind the bank's counter, easing circulation into his cramped legs. He'd been on this particular case for months, taking two frustrating steps back for every tiny step forward. When reliable information had leaked to the Denver Field Office's Special Agent in Charge that this bank was tonight's target, they'd moved quickly. He was beginning to wonder if they'd been a little hasty.

With their inside tip, bagging this piece of scum would be easy this time, unless Killian decided to let his mind wander, again, to the forbidden territory of females. Forgetting women, he refocused his animal-sharp senses, listening to the absolute stillness of the darkened bank lobby.

There, he heard it again, the distinct ping of metal against metal. Faint, but detectable to the trained ear.

Adrenaline shot through his veins. Every time he thought about quitting, about settling down to a normal life, he remembered this rush. A white picket fence existence, no matter how appealing, would bore him to death after the first week. Without the FBI he was nothing—had nothing. He'd do well to remember that.

When he stood, his knee creaked from an old bullet wound. He shook the discomfort away, then on silent feet clung to the shadows, steadily closing in on the noise. His heart pumped faster than rounds of ammunition from a machine gun.

When he reached the north wall, he looked at the ceiling. The noise came from the ventilation duct.

Killian smiled. For once it was too easy. As a rule, McKnight was one step ahead of them. They thought they'd had him in Vegas. Dan Stevens, his partner, had him cornered, but by the time Killian had come on to the scene, the bastard had gotten away. Not this time. This time McKnight was his.

Killian touched a hand to the tiny earphone nestled inside his ear. "Dan," he whispered to his backup, "we've got action."

"Do you need me to move in?" Static laced through his reply.

"Negative. Wait for my call."

"Ten-four. Out."

Careful to remain hidden, Killian followed the path of what sounded like a body crawling through the metal network overhead. Outside the plate glass windows to his right, cars zoomed by on the busy street. It was another part of his job he loved. Here he was in the middle of civilization and he felt as if he was in another dimension, another world—isolated from reality. An exciting world that called for every bit of mental cunning he possessed. He'd never felt more alive than when he was in the middle of action going down.

His knee stiffened, reminding him of how very real the danger—and bullets—could be. The crackle of the radio in his ear gave him the assurance he wasn't alone. Backup was a radio call away if he needed it.

The grate above him shifted and he flattened against the wall.

A figure dressed in black from head to toe dropped to the ground, with just a whisper of sound, through the overhead opening.

Killian jumped into action, his legs in a wide stance, his weapon raised in front of him. Adrenaline pumped like fire through his veins. "FBI. Freeze!"

The stocky form spun around. Catching sight of the barrel of a gun aimed right at his chest, McKnight dropped a rope, a bulging gunnysack and a flashlight to the ground and raised his arms to the sky.

Through a pair of black panty hose covering his head, the thief eyed Killian.

Prey sizing up the predator.

Killian stared back.

Predator sizing up the prey.

"I've finally got you, dirtball. For once we were one step ahead of you. How does it feel to have the shoe on the other foot?"

A door burst open. A woman walked through, the words to Alanis Morissette's "Ironic" dying on her lips.

Killian shifted the gun from the suspect to the woman, who stood staring at them with wide-eyed surprise. "Who are you, lady?" All the information the FBI had cultivated suggested this particular bandit worked alone. Had McKnight changed his MO?

Killian loathed complications.

"I repeat, what are you doing here?" He'd been assured that all personnel had been informed to stay out of the building. Not waiting for an answer, he called for backup.

"Dan, move your team in." No answer. "Stevens?" Jesus Christ, where was his backup? What the Sam hell was going on?

The woman ripped a set of headphones off her ears and left them dangling around her neck. Her gaze shifted nervously from Killian to the man in black. "Hey, look, I'm just the cleaning service. I know nothing. I see nothing. I'm gonna turn around"—she jammed a thumb over her shoulder, her voice shaking—"and leave and we can pretend this conversation never took place. How about it?"

"Don't move, lady." McKnight's voice rippled with the kind of intent that got people killed.

Killian's gaze flitted to the mop in the woman's hand, then back to his prey's eyes. McKnight was getting shifty. All Killian's instincts told him the dirtbag was ready to make a move. The last thing he needed was civilian involvement.

"Back away from here, ma'am."

She stood frozen to the spot, confusion evident in her eyes. Before she could respond, the thief grabbed a gun from his back waistband, reached out and hauled the woman toward him.

Killian remained where he was, his heart thumping in his chest. The tiny brunette struggled against the tight grasp, her dark eyes open wide. Her jerky movements propelled the suspect forward. She wielded her mop like a weapon, lashing it back and forth in front of her in a panic-stricken frenzy. When the pair stumbled closer, the mop swung an unexpected wild arc to the left, knocking the gun out of Killian's hand. He lurched toward it.

"Don't even try it, Hart."

Helpless, Killian froze and watched his only form of defense spin across the linoleum floor out of reach. How did

McKnight know who he was? Had he been expecting him?

"Ah, I can see by your eyes you're surprised I know your name. I know every move the FBI makes, Hart. Don't you forget it."

When McKnight attempted to move back a few steps, the woman kicked her feet out in another effort to break free from her captor. Her gym shoe connected with Killian's groin. In agony, he doubled over. Stars swam before his eyes as pain engulfed him. He longed to curl up on the floor in the fetal position, but knew he'd be as good as dead if he did. He forced himself to remain standing.

"I'm one of the good guys," he managed to wheeze.

"I'm sorry . . . I'm sorry. It was an accident." She gave her captor a wide-eyed glance over her shoulder when he squeezed her tighter, then put the barrel of his gun to her temple. She muttered something unintelligible before she lapsed into frightened silence.

Killian sensed the moment she went from fear to anger. The flashbulb look left her eyes and her jaw clenched. It was as if she thought she wasn't going to make it out alive and had nothing to lose. He groaned internally, knowing anything he said at this point would fall on deaf ears.

"Do you want to lighten up your grip, mister? You're hurting me," she growled.

The suspect obviously squeezed tighter, because a glimmer of pain crossed the woman's face and she winced. "Lady, I have a gun and I'm not afraid to use it." McKnight's eyes took on a crazed, wild look.

"Yeah, well, you big jerk, I have PMS, the hammer's cocked and the safety is off. Top that."

Killian knew she wasn't thinking coherently. People in their right frame of mind cried, went into hysterics, begged for mercy even, when held at gunpoint. This feisty brunette was slinging insults at her captor. He had to stop her before someone got hurt. "Ma'am, what's your name?" he asked, making sure he kept his distance so he wouldn't spook her captor.

"Robyn." Her bottom lip trembled.

"Well, Robyn. This isn't a movie, this is real life. The man holding on to you is one of FBI's Ten Most Wanted." He kept his tone smooth and even. "He's the bad guy, Robyn. He's wearing black."

She looked Killian up and down, her eyes wide with fright again. "So are you," she pointed out.

He glanced down at his black battle dress uniform and Goretex Rocky boots. Standard FBI issue. "Yes, but my black has FBI written on it. His black"—he nodded toward the man behind her—"is a fetching pair of L'eggs nylons."

Okay, so the agent had her on that one. But it was dark in the lobby, and everything had happened with lightning speed. He couldn't blame a girl for trying to defend herself, could he? God, she'd never been so frightened in her life. Suddenly, she had to go to the bathroom as if she'd downed a gallon of water in thirty seconds.

She tried to take several deep breaths. Mr. FBI's Ten Most Wanted's tight grip around her middle made it difficult. It didn't help her bladder situation, either. She closed her eyes for a second. *Calm down. Calm down. Calm down.*

"We're going to go for a little ride," the thug behind her informed them, "before your backup arrives."

Backup. Charlie! She'd forgotten about him and his orders regarding the red button. She wiggled in the man-in-black's tight hold. If she didn't push the red button, Charlie would be disappointed in her. Could it be possible he'd even think she was in on the crime? The bank wouldn't fire him for trusting her, would they? It didn't matter. None of this mattered if she didn't survive. She went slack.

"I don't want to go for a ride right now," she squeaked.

"I'm not asking you, I'm telling you." He picked up the bag of money and, with one hand, dragged her toward the door. "Hart, you walk in front of me. If you make any sudden moves, I'll blow her pretty little head clean off."

Robyn's throat went dry. Tears pricked her eyes. In an instant she went still. She was dead. This was the beginning of the end. She had heard that one's life flashed before her eyes in moments of crisis. Not until this moment had she ever believed it. Every miserable date she'd ever had paraded before her eyes in rapid succession—and there were a lot of them. She was almost thirty years old and she'd never found Mr. Right—never would now.

The FBI agent circled around them, a muscle ticking in his neck. His gaze locked with hers. The brief contact reassured her for a moment. At least she wasn't going alone. Small comfort, but it was all she had, so she held on to it for dear life.

A portable radio clipped to the agent's belt emitted a bunch of static, then a voice called out, "Four-eight-nine, what is your position?"

The agent looked at the man in front of him. "I have to answer this. If I don't they'll send people in after me."

"Hurry up, and don't say anything stupid."

Hart grabbed his radio and held in the button with his thumb. "I'm code 41."

"Copy, 489, code 41."

The bad guy reached out and yanked the radio out of the agent's hand. He threw it on the ground, then stomped on it. The crunching noise reverberated throughout the lobby as loud as the crack of doom. "I'm not a idiot. I know code 41 means a hostage situation. You just placed yourself in more danger."

As big and burly as this government agent was, what could he hope to accomplish without backup or a gun? Guilt flooded her cheeks. A gun Robyn had accidentally disposed of for him, thank you very much. Now they were in even more danger.

Cold steel jabbed hard against her temple. "Walk."

Robyn kept her eyes trained on Agent Hart's solid back. Woodenly, she followed him. She was surprised to find herself still standing on legs that felt no more supportive than the rope mop she'd held moments earlier.

"Go out the doors, Hart. Parked to the right you'll see a black van. Open the back doors. I'm warning you, no false moves." His warm breath brushed against her cheek, and Robyn suppressed a shudder.

"Charlie, where are you?" Robyn muttered.

"That old man can't help you now."

She was afraid to ask—didn't want to know if Charlie's wife was now a widow. "What'd you do to him?" She bit her lip to keep it from trembling.

"I didn't kill him, if that's what you're worried about. But I could have. Just shut up. Typical female. You ask too many damn questions." His hot breath grazed her cheek. "Shut up, before I decide to get rid of you right here, and then go back and finish off the old man."

Robyn squeezed her eyes closed and clamped her lips together. She always chattered when she was nervous or scared. Right now she felt like talking a blue streak. Maintaining silence took every ounce of willpower she possessed.

She knew the exact moment they left the cool air-conditioned building for the hot, summer night. She smelled rain in the air. The scent made her feel alive—made her want to live more than anything. She sucked in a lung full, hoping it wouldn't be her last.

"FBI. Freeze!"

Her eyes shot open in time to see Hart stiffen in front of her. Her heart sped up in her chest like the motor on a deluxe model Hoover vacuum. Were they going to have a show-down? A quick glance over her shoulder showed her they were surrounded by at least a half-dozen men.

"Ah, I see the cavalry has arrived." McKnight didn't sound too worried. Shouldn't he have been quaking in his boots? God only knew she was. "Tell them to back off . . . toss their pieces this way, or she's dead." The thug holding her sounded pretty damn insistent . . . and just a little too cocky.

Agent Hart hesitated. The muscle ticked in his jaw again. Robyn wondered if he was weighing his options. To her there was one decision to make—the one that would keep her alive to see another day.

"Please, Agent Hart?" she whispered. She wasn't above begging for her life.

The agent's hands clenched at his sides, then loosened as if he was relenting. "Dan, tell them to throw down their weapons."

After a moment of silence that seemed to last an eternity, the sound of clinking metal hitting the pavement rang out one after another, until Robyn counted eight different guns no longer in use. She let out a deep breath, feeling as if she'd given death the brush-off for a few more minutes.

Or did this mean death was inevitable?

Never more confused in her life, she glanced up into the sky. She'd walked through this parking lot hundreds of times. Funny how she'd noticed how dark it was before. Now the darkness seemed as pitch-black as her future.

"Lay on the ground and put your hands behind your

heads," McKnight ordered everyone.

"You heard him, Dan," Hart bit out.

Robyn listened to the other agents' muffled curses. No, they couldn't lie down. None of them could lie down. If they got on that ground, Robyn would end up in the van as a hostage. Weren't they giving up way too easy? She wanted to open her mouth and start giving them fifty different reasons why they shouldn't obey that order. Instead, she bit her quivering bottom lip. Maybe they knew something she didn't. Maybe they had a plan.

"Good," the scumbag growled when all the agents complied. "Now stay there. I've got an itchy trigger finger and the littlest movement might set me off. Open the doors to the van. Now!" he shouted when Agent Hart hesitated. "There's a length of rope lying in there. Give it to the woman."

The agent yanked the squeaky door open and reached inside. Grabbing the rope, he turned and walked back toward her. When he stood in front of Robyn, he stopped. She had to tilt her head to look up at him. She'd never realized until now how tall he was. He held out the rope. She tore her gaze from his dark eyes and stared at the object in his hand. He held his death warrant. Hers, too.

"Take it," the man behind her hissed.

She wanted to yell and scream and curse in typical Robyn fashion, but with the barrel of a gun gouging into her temple, all she could do was comply with his wishes. She reached out and curled her fingers around the corded threads. Her hand brushed up against the agent's. He felt warm and solid and alive. How long would that last? With her heart pounding a rapid beat, she looked into his eyes, which were all but hidden by the brim of his FBI ball cap. What little she could see of his gaze seemed to say trust me.

At this point, she had nothing to lose. She gave an almost

imperceptible nod of her head. She could tell he'd seen it when his hand squeezed hers.

"Tie him up. Don't make it loose, or I'll freakin' kill you right here."

Even though she half-suspected she would be the one to do this, the words still threw her. "Me? Oh, but—"

"Turn around, Hart, and put your hands behind your back."

Hart looked like he wanted to say something, but, instead, muscle ticking in his jaw, he turned. Robyn took the rope and began weaving it around his hands, tying knots as she went.

"I don't make a habit of this, I hope you know," she whispered behind him. "Not on a first date anyway."

"Of what?"

"Tying men up."

He chuckled, a deep sound that touched off a warm spot inside her—gave her hope. She clung to that emotion. "Well, now, I don't *let* women tie me up very often, so we're even."

"How touching," their kidnapper barked. "Hurry up." She watched him glance from the men on the ground back to her again.

Robyn tightened one last knot. "I'm done."

"Crawl in the back of the van, Hart, and lie down."

His hesitation was visible to Robyn. She could see it in the set of his jaw, his rigid stance. If he got into that van, he was a dead man. If she knew it, he sure as hell knew it, too.

"I'm not afraid to pull the trigger. Time is wasting. Do what I say."

"Mr. Hart, I've got a lot of living to do, if you know what I mean. Could you please get in?" She could hear her own voice shaking. The cold steel of the gun pressed harder against her temple, and the chill filled her entire body. Stars swam in her eyes. What was the agent waiting for? Sure, the whole kidnapping thing was, no doubt, her fault, but they could have warned her and Charlie of what was going down. The two of them would have gladly stayed out of the way. Why hadn't they told them? Why?

"It's Killian."

"What?" She couldn't think straight.

"My name." The federal agent moved a few steps. Climbing in, he lay face first on the dirty carpeted floor.

From behind them, Robyn heard movement. It all happened so fast. One of the agents tried to make a move. Before Robyn could even turn around to see what was going on, a gun went off and the agent was as still as death on the ground. Blood pooled around him.

"Take the other rope and tie up his feet." The bad guy shoved her from behind. He was acting like he killed people every day. For all she knew, he did. Her hands were shaking so badly, she didn't know if she could even finish the job. After Robyn did as he demanded, he tied her up as well, and shoved her into the back beside Hart. Grabbing a roll of duct tape, he ripped off a piece, leaned into the back of the van and pressed it over the agent's mouth.

"Dammit." Backing out, he threw the empty spool on the ground, obviously frustrated he wouldn't be able to seal Robyn's mouth. "Keep your trap shut. I don't want to hear a peep out of you, or you're dead. Got it?"

He didn't need to tell her twice. Robyn swallowed a lump in her throat and nodded. The doors slammed closed behind them. Never had she heard a more final sound. She imagined it sounded worse than a coffin lid closing.

The engine roared to life. The man stepped on the gas, sending the vehicle flying down the road, and Robyn sailing across the back of the van into the solid form of Agent Killian Hart.

Bullets pinged against metal. Robyn cringed and scooted closer to the agent. Scared half out of her mind, her body shaking out of control, she instinctively curled against him, using his body as a shield. She held her breath, waiting for the bullet that would take her life.

Killian cursed under his breath. What the hell was Dan thinking? A stray bullet could easily rip through the metal and kill him or the woman. When the van drove far enough away that bullets were merely wasted, he noticed the feminine body pressed close against him. She had to be terrified. It was his job to offer her comfort, protection, and a way out of this mess. Tied up as he was, he couldn't do any of those things.

Instead, he tried to concentrate on the path the vehicle took. They were heading north. He was sure of it. Left at about a half-mile. Right for a couple blocks.

"We're gonna die, aren't we?" The woman shifted her body toward him. Despite the darkness, as close as she was, he could see her somber eyes filled with fear.

He couldn't talk with the tape over his mouth, so he shook his head instead. They'd been traveling straight for several miles. By his estimation, they were on Colorado Boulevard.

"Damn, I really should have pushed that button. The red one that Charlie warned me about at least a hundred times."

Killian wrinkled his brow. What button was she talking about? Who was Charlie? And how was he supposed to concentrate on the path they were taking if she kept talking to him? The woman couldn't have been much over five feet tall. The top of her head rested right underneath his chin. She fit against him like she belonged—which was ludicrous, because no woman belonged, not with his dangerous lifestyle.

"Where is he taking us?"

Good question. One he couldn't answer. He shrugged his

shoulders. The farther they drove away from the scene, the harder it would be for the authorities to track him. Killian wondered if Dan, and the rest of the agents, were following. Had he called for more backup? If he had, it was sure taking them long enough to find one black van, traveling at what felt like speeds well in excess of the posted limits.

The absence of sirens bothered him. They should have been tailed from the beginning. Killian wiggled his hands against the tight bindings. The abrasive rope burned his skin. For such a little thing, the woman tied a knot as well as any sailor.

"I didn't mean to kick the gun out of your hand. This kidnapping is all my fault."

Killian shook his head emphatically. Civilians shouldn't have been in the bank. He didn't know whose fault that was, but he would damned sure find out, just as soon as he got them out of this mess.

"You could have warned me and Charlie." She sent him an accusing glare. "Why didn't the FBI let us know they suspected something like this was going to happen?"

Why, indeed? He'd asked himself the same question. Holgate, his boss, was going to be pissed about tonight's bizarre turn of events. The tape sealing his lips angered Killian. He wanted to rip it off and talk—set her straight. Instead, he had to resort to shaking his head again.

"Are you trying to tell me you couldn't tell us?" Her voice had risen slightly. She glanced toward the front of the van as if half-expecting a reprimand from the driver. "Oh, God, I understand it all now," she whispered. "You think it was an inside job. Why didn't I realize that sooner? Who could the guilty party be?" she asked herself. "My one employee insisted on having the night off, but I don't think Doug could help rob a bank. Good God, he's only seventeen."

Even in the darkness, penetrated by the occasional flash of a streetlamp, Killian could see questions dancing in her eyes. "Jane Landry hasn't been a teller very long, it couldn't be her. Charlie Clark is too honest. Despite the fact that Randy Cooper is a sleazy playboy, with the worst come-on lines in history, he's harmless. Clifford Barnes loves the money when it stays in the bank, not when it's taken out."

He watched her mouth as she rambled on, throwing out employees names at random from the bank president all the way down to the lowliest teller. One of the names rang a bell, but the way this woman kept rambling, he lost his train of thought.

If it weren't for the damn tape, Killian could have told her to be quiet. He should have been paying attention to the directions the van was taking. Disgusted with himself for allowing this woman to sidetrack him from his duties, he rolled his eyes.

She misinterpreted his actions. "Dammit, I'm way off base, aren't I?"

Not only did she tie knots like a sailor, she talked like one, too. He shrugged his shoulders again.

"Well, I can't think of anyone else at the bank." She gasped. Her eyes widened. "Except me."

Chapter 2

Silence filled the air as the getaway van continued speeding down the highway, mile after mile, for destinations unknown. After a while, the smooth road turned into a mass of bumps, ditches and potholes, that tested the vehicle's shocks and Robyn's patience—which, at this point, was hanging by the proverbial thread.

Where was he going?

Where was he taking them?

Was she really a suspect?

Every so often, Robyn found herself scooting backward a few inches. She was cold. Which was weird, because it had been a typical sultry June evening when they'd gotten into the van. Denver was a desert climate. It always got cooler at night, but this felt different. Could they be heading up into the mountains? It would explain the drastic drop in temperature. More than the mild discomfort of being cold, she was afraid of what would happen when the vehicle stopped. Agent Hart provided a small measure of safety her brain desperately needed. At least she wasn't alone. She moved closer to him, sucking up his warmth, clinging to the hope that he had a plan to rescue them from this hell. That's what FBI agents did. It was their job to come up with rescue plans.

As if her thoughts prompted his actions, the van screeched to a halt. Robyn closed her eyes, a whimper escaping her trembling lips. God, she wasn't ready to die yet. She still had a lot of living to do.

The front door opened, then slammed shut. Within seconds, the back doors squeaked open, sending a blast of cold air rushing in. The warmth from Hart's body evaporated in an instant.

What was happening? The unknown factor was driving her insane. Fear snaked down her spine. Robyn wriggled over on her side, her heart pounding in her throat, her arms still bound behind her. Their kidnapper reached in and manhandled the agent out of the van.

Through a flash of lightning, she saw Hart on the ground, his body motionless. Her mouth went dry. Fear licked at her insides. Had he been shot? Had the growing thunder disguised the sound of gunfire? Would she be next? She wanted to do more than whimper, but numbness held her immobile. She couldn't move a single finger if she'd wanted to.

Cold, damp hands grabbed her. Pain shot up her arm, and she winced as her kidnapper dug his fingers into her skin and dragged her across the carpeted van. The brutal grip was sure to develop into bruises by morning . . . if she lived that long.

Her heart tripped in her chest.

With a shove against her back, he sent her flying. The rope shackling her legs prevented her from stepping out to break her fall. She landed on top of the agent, causing a moan to leak through the tape on his mouth.

He was alive! Agent Hart . . . Killian—he'd told her his name—was alive.

The man sauntered up to them like he hadn't a care in the world. Through a tangled mass of hair, Robyn watched him reach inside his coat pocket. Her breath came out in jagged gasps. Was he reaching for a gun? A knife?

Too frightened to want to know the cause of her early mortality, she squeezed her eyes shut. Thunder punctuated the silence. The smell of impending rain filled her nostrils. Killian shifted beneath her. In an instant he'd rolled her off him, his body a barrier between the kidnapper and Robyn.

In the stillness, Robyn heard a distinct click. Was it the hammer of a gun being cocked? Squinting one eye, and peering around the agent's broad shoulders, she saw a tiny gun pointed straight at them. Too mesmerized to close her eyes, Robyn could only stare. A click sounded again, and she winced on instinct, expecting to feel intense pain, or see blood pouring out of an ugly bullet hole. Instead the gun shot out a tiny flame at the end.

A half-laugh, half-cry dodged her compressed lips. Robyn sagged in relief, tears pricking her eyes. The jerk had a warped sense of humor.

He took his time lighting the cigarette. It dangled from the hole ripped in the nylons that still concealed his identity. Seeming unconcerned, the thief blew a puff of smoke into the air. A few drops of rain splattered against Robyn's cheek. She shivered.

"I should kill you right now, Hart. I should kill you both. The problem is no one has ever come close to stopping me, except you. I was almost a goner in Vegas, I'll give you that, but I still got away, didn't I? It would be a shame to lose the only worthy adversary I've ever had." He took another drag on his cigarette, inhaling deeply. He blew the smoke out into rings that drifted up into the cloudy sky. "The excitement is in the chase, don't you think?"

He didn't wait for an answer he knew wasn't coming. Tape still covered Killian's mouth. "Worthy adversary or not, I will have to kill you just the same. Eventually. My theory is when you least expect it, expect it." His words were followed by a macabre grin that Robyn longed to smack off his face, if her hands hadn't been shaking, not to mention tied together.

"Too bad I need your sorry asses alive to make my plan

work." He took a last hard puff on his cigarette, then flicked it on the ground, snuffing the embers out with his heel.

Robyn could tell Killian wanted to get up from the ground and rip this man to shreds with his bare hands. His tied-up hands were balled into two fists. The muscles in his upper arms corded with strain. She was glad this man was on her side. Pushing off the ground, he got up on his knees.

The rain grew harder minute by minute, soaking them to the skin. "Worthy adversary or not, you got too close this time. Too damn close." Striding forward, he gave Killian a mean right hook that, as defenseless as he was, sent him reeling to the ground.

"Oh my God. Are you all right?" Robyn peered at the angry red mark on Killian's jaw. The jarring blow had also knocked the tape off his mouth. It hung by a sliver on the side of his lip. The agent wiped his mouth against his shoulder, stripping the tape off his face completely.

"Just what plans do you have?" Hart said. His eyes were narrowed and focused on his assailant. He barely blinked against the driving rain hitting him square in the face. All Robyn could think was that he looked lethal.

"Wouldn't you like to know?"

Robyn couldn't have cared less what the creep's plans were. Her brain had focused in on the fact that he needed them alive . . . even if it was only for a little while. Every second longer that she remained alive was a damn good second.

McKnight sneered at Hart where he sat on the ground. "We've still got a long drive ahead of us. Get back in the van."

This toying with her emotions was starting to drive Robyn crazy. Get in the van. Get out of the van. Get in the van again. She didn't know how much more she could take. The cavalry wasn't coming over the hill in the next thirty seconds. That much was obvious. She was sure Killian Hart was a very responsible, dependable agent, but the way things were going she didn't see how he alone could get them out of this nightmare. It was every man, woman and child for themselves.

"I have to relieve myself."

"Women!" McKnight scoffed. "Fine. Go. Make it fast." He was close enough that even in the darkness and the deluge of rain she could see the sneer on his lips through the nylon still disguising his face.

He turned his back, expecting Robyn to comply with his demands on the spot.

"Damn compassionate, dirty low-down—"

"Robyn, just do it. We're going to be lying in the back of that van in discomfort as it is. We don't need to make it worse," Hart said.

Yeah, death on a full bladder would really suck.

Men. They just didn't get it. He thought it would be more comfortable for her if she just dropped her drawers and squatted with two strange men standing not ten feet away. Yeah, she was totally digging this day. "I'd love to comply, but I'm kind of tied up." She held out her bound hands as evidence. "Can you please untie me?" She had to yell over the pounding rain.

McKnight muttered a curse, then strode over to her, roughly untying the ropes around her wrists and her ankles. "Make it fast."

She frowned. "Turn around."

Robyn was scared. She was cold. And she'd be damned if she was going to pee in public. She was a kidnapping victim, stripped of her dignity, and not sure if she was going to live or die. Worst of all, she'd forgotten to top off her cat's food bowl before she'd left for work this evening. That, more than anything, made her tiptoe backwards for about two feet, then pivot on her toes and make a mad dash for the woods about seventy yards away.

She could make it.

She knew she could.

Her heart pounded, her arms pumped as fast as they could trying to keep up with her legs. Freedom lay within the cover of the trees. She knew it. She was banking on it.

"Robyn, no!" Hart yelled out behind her.

She kept running. Fifty more feet. Almost there. She could make it. Above the sound of her own breathing thundering in her ears, she heard McKnight. His feet hit the wet earth behind her.

Growing closer.

Louder.

She pumped her arms faster. Forced her stride beyond endurance. Her legs hurt. Her lungs stung. The trees beckoned. Almost there. A few more steps.

She passed the first tree. It felt like victory, but she could still feel McKnight behind her.

His anger.

His hot breath.

She forced herself to keep going, not knowing how much longer she could keep up the pace. If she stopped, she'd be dead.

Lungs ready to burst, she was forced to slow her pace or give up altogether. Her foot slipped on the wet underbrush. As she was going down, arms tackled her from behind, knocking her to the ground. She hit hard, McKnight's body landing on top of her, knocking what little air she had left out of her lungs.

Face first in the wet terrain, panting heavily, she was too exhausted to move. She refused to give in to the tears stinging the backs of her eyes. Air spent, she wheezed out, "Just let me go. Just freaking let me . . . go."

"Never. You're a means to an end."

The tangle of brush in front of her face moved when she expelled a rush of air, then bent back and tickled her nose. "You don't need me."

McKnight laughed.

Robyn glanced over her shoulder. The damn nylon still hugged his features, though now wet and soggy. He looked so ridiculous that if she'd had the energy she would have laughed.

He pushed his body off her, then grabbed Robyn by her damp hair and yanked her off the ground.

Tears stung her eyes, but she refused to give him the satisfaction of giving in to the debilitating emotion. Screw him. She'd find another way out. This plan had failed, but she wasn't giving up. With a hand against her back, the jerk pushed her back toward the van. Each step forward felt like she was walking toward her own funeral, her own grave. *Here lies Robyn. She forgot to feed her cat and killed them both.* No wonder she'd never found the man of her dreams. If she couldn't even tend to a cat properly, what would happen if she ever had children?

When they reached the van, Robyn spotted Hart on the ground. He was doubled over as if he'd been hit in the gut. McKnight had obviously used brute force in the form of a right hook yet again, to make sure Hart wouldn't leave when he went after Robyn.

Guilt wormed its way into her. His pain was all her fault. All she'd thought of was herself and getting away. Making a break for it. From where he lay, he threw her a look of reprimand that asked, without words, what the hell she'd been thinking? The two of them were in this together. Okay. So she'd screwed up. From now on all escape plans would involve both of them. What the hell, it might even come in handy to have a FBI agent along with her when she made her final getaway.

Killian was grabbed by the arm and shoved into the back of the van. He rolled over as fast as he could, anticipating Robyn being pushed in right after him. She landed with a huff, the air forced out of her lungs.

"You okay?" He couldn't help but notice the tears in the corners of her eyes, despite the drops of rain covering her. Oh hell. He hated it when women cried. Nothing worse than a woman's tears. They made him feel all awkward and useless. There was nothing a seasoned FBI agent hated more than feeling useless.

"You wouldn't understand."

The van's engine revved, then shot down the road at a fast speed, mud spraying out from the back tires. Robyn's body skidded against Killian's. "Try me." He probably understood much more than she was giving him credit for. He'd been trained in this very thing. Had years of experience.

"I just . . . I don't want to be here. I need to go home. That's all I was trying to do. Go home."

"I'm sure the agency has a team after us as we speak. I'll have you home before you know it. From now on, don't try anything without warning me first. Why don't you try and get some sleep? It's been a long night." Didn't she understand that there was a code they needed to follow? One didn't break from the rules or one got killed.

Without another word, the woman shifted onto her side and closed her eyes. Killian couldn't begin to attempt sleep. His mind still raced like the bullet out of a gun barrel. What the hell had gone wrong at the bank? One second everything was going as planned, and the next all hell had broken loose.

33

He'd gone over everything in his mind, at least a hundred times. He knew he'd followed procedure to the letter. If he had to do it all over again, he would have followed exactly the same routine. Following protocol had always saved him in the past, and he wasn't about to deviate now. Miss Robyn Jeffries would do well to take a page from his playbook. She'd almost gotten herself killed with her foolish actions.

Next to him, she sighed in her sleep. He glanced down at her slight form. Her dark hair lay wet and tangled against her cheek. Had she found some sort of comfort in her sleep? The worry lines had left her forehead. He wished he could find escape in a few moments of shut-eye. It was out of the question. He didn't have time for creature comforts like sleep or warmth. His jaw hurt where McKnight had trounced him, bringing back the anger and determination with renewed vigor to best the bastard.

Even though it was June, and warm down in the city of Denver, he could tell they were climbing higher into the mountains. The air grew thinner and the temperature dropped rapidly. Springtime in the mountains could be beautiful, but it wasn't uncommon for the temperature to dip down into the forties and even thirties at night.

Minutes dragged into hours. Exhausted, Robyn continued to sleep. A few times she shivered, and Killian attempted to offer her his body warmth. He would have looped an arm around her and dragged her close, but he was limited in what he could do by the ropes binding him. He wriggled his wrist, testing the knots. Tight. Secure.

As things were right now, he couldn't see a way out of their situation. He'd have to bide his time. Wait for the right opening.

Darkness slowly gave way to daybreak, raising the temperature slightly. They'd been traveling for an endless number of miles when the van skidded to a stop. Killian tried to lift his head enough to see out the dirty back window.

"Where are we?" Coming out of her deep sleep, Robyn blinked her brown eyes and looked around.

"I don't know." The truth frustrated him, clipped his words.

The front door of the van opened, then closed. Robyn pushed back against Killian, trying to maneuver as far away from the doors as she could.

A full five minutes went by. Five minutes filled with anticipation, anxiety and dread.

"What's taking him so long?"

"I don't know."

The doors yanked open, startling them both. McKnight had said he'd needed them alive, but for how long? "Get out," he barked.

Killian urged Robyn forward before McKnight used force. He'd already noticed a bruise forming on her upper arm. The pain in his jaw throbbed again, and he vowed to avoid provoking more violence. He could take care of himself, but he was responsible for the safety of the woman.

Once standing, Killian took in his surroundings. From his vantage point, they appeared to be in the middle of nowhere. A few trees dotted the area, but where they parked was not far from timberline. A rustic cabin stood before them, nestled amongst some sparse-looking lodgepole pines that stretched right up into the sky. The rain had stopped, leaving behind nothing but clear, blue Colorado sky.

Pushing them from behind, McKnight forced them to hop toward the doorway of the tiny cabin with their legs still tied together. The door squeaked open on rusty hinges, the smell of dust, mildew and decay hitting Killian square in the face.

"Welcome to home, sweet home." McKnight laughed without a trace of humor.

"I think you need a new decorator." Robyn preceded Killian into the darkened interior, a small amount of light trickling in from a filthy windowpane hung with a tattered curtain.

"Well, let me just set up my computer and you can order from the Home Shopping Network." He all but snorted at his own joke. While McKnight was busy laughing, Killian took in his surroundings. The only door was the one through which they'd entered. One window was big enough to squeeze out of; the other two appeared too small for his frame. As tiny as Robyn was, she might be able to fit through, but not him.

A potbellied stove stood at the far end of the one-room shack. Maps and papers littered a square, wooden kitchen table. More importantly, a portable ham radio sat right in the middle. He averted his gaze, knowing the radio might come in handy. A twin-sized bed with a thin mattress sat against the far wall, unmade, the blankets rumpled. Judging by appearances, McKnight had been calling this place home for a while.

A filthy rug resided smack dab in the middle of the floor. McKnight's beefy hand settled on Killian's shoulder and, with a firm pressure, he forced him and Robyn to a sitting position on the rug.

"Sit back to back."

Killian could see the blatant fear in Robyn's eyes. He nodded to her. She turned, settling against him, the warmth of her back up against his.

McKnight grabbed a length of rope out of a crude wooden box containing wood for the potbelly stove. "Put your hands together." He then proceeded to tie Killian and Robyn together.

One thought pounded through Killian's brain. One thought that worried him more than McKnight's erratic behavior. He couldn't do this alone. Not when they were tied together. To get out of this cabin alive, he—unfortunately—was going to need the assistance of one very beautiful, but very scared young lady.

It was cold comfort to find herself tied up, back to back, with the warmth of the one man who was supposed to save her. Despite the solidity and strength she felt radiating from him, she couldn't see a way out of their predicament. Agent Hart obviously didn't have a clue what to do to save them. Not if the tight rope cutting off the circulation around her wrists was any indication. Even Maxwell Smart could have gotten himself out of this mess much sooner. Of course, 99 always came to the rescue.

Life always imitated art. Agent Killian Hart was going to need Robyn's sharp mind to save them. She'd caught a couple winks in the van. Her senses were now fresh and honed. She'd read her share of Nancy Drew mysteries growing up. If her impressions of Hart were on the money, she doubted he'd slept a wink. He seemed like the kind of man who wouldn't allow anyone to get the edge on him. "Got any brilliant plans?" Didn't hurt to double-check.

"I'm working on it."

Just as she'd thought. He was going to need her. The gruff tone to his voice said, louder than any words, that he was struggling for a scheme and still coming up empty. Just like a man not to admit it.

McKnight had just come back in the door, with a bag full of the bank's money in each hand. "Sir? May I please have some water? I'm getting very thirsty."

"Sir?" Killian whispered.

"Killing him with kindness," she turned her head and mouthed back. She couldn't see his expression, but she could see the muscles in his biceps. Corded. Rippling. Muscles like that should have been able to set them free. What was his problem? Maybe he was new at this FBI stuff.

"You're shooting blanks. Men like him don't respond to kindness."

"If you want honey from the bee, you don't kick over the hive."

With a huff, McKnight heaved the bags on top of the maps on the table, and turned toward the pair on the floor. Hesitating a second, he peeled the torn and tattered disguise off his head. "I suppose I could spare a little. I don't want you two to die of thirst just yet."

"You're too kind," Robyn replied, in the most genuine voice she could summon. She took in his blond hair and blue eyes. Swallowed past the lump in her throat, now not thirsty at all. There were a few reasons to explain why he'd taken off the nylons. They had a run in them. They'd lost their support and were sagging around his neck. Or he didn't care if he showed them his face, because they wouldn't be able to serve as witnesses after they were dead.

Robyn would have gladly planted a swift kick to his groin if she hadn't been tied and bound. Pissing off the bad guy wouldn't serve anyone's purpose, and would just get them killed sooner.

McKnight splashed a bit of water into a little tin camping cup, which Robyn suspected he'd used during his Boy Scout camping days. The cup he'd kept. The oaths, she guessed, he'd forgotten.

He held the cup to her lips and tipped it, letting a little dribble down her chin. He did the same for the agent, even though she could tell by the flash in McKnight's eyes that it pissed him off to do so. If he didn't care whether they lived or died, why was he giving them water, even if he needed them alive for a while? The signs he gave off were contradictory, and she wanted to weep from not knowing her fate, not knowing how much longer she had on this earth.

A rumble sounded deep in her tummy and she thought of Brooklyn meowing and begging to be fed with no one there to feed her. Maybe her best friend Ginger would show up. Sometimes she did that unexpectedly. Did she know Robyn had been kidnapped? If she knew, Ginger would definitely feed Brooklyn.

Of course if Ginger knew, Ginger would worry. Robyn didn't want her to worry. Not if that worry could harm Ginger's unborn baby in any way. Robyn would be fine. She knew it. She needed Ginger to know it. She threw a silent prayer up to heaven. *God, I don't ask much of you, but if you're listening, see to it that my cat gets fed. Brooklyn is pretty finicky and won't eat the food in the bottom of the bowl unless it's topped off. Could you do that for me? And make sure Ginger knows I'm going to be fine. Take care of her baby.*

After giving them a drink, their kidnapper had gone back to the table and was busy sorting stacks of money. Robyn waited for a sign from God that he'd heard her plea, but the sole answer was a pesky fly buzzing around her head. Not too promising, as far as signs went.

"Don't go anywhere." McKnight threw the comment over his shoulder. "I won't be gone long, so don't bother trying to escape." All the money had been placed back in the bags, which he now carried one in each hand. With that parting comment, he let the door slam behind him. In the reigning silence, Robyn heard what sounded like a padlock snapping shut on the outside of the door.

"Now what?" Robyn asked. Hart had been too quiet.

Maybe a solution had hit him.

"The window is one option."

"Have you forgotten that we're tied together?"

As tall as he was, back to back, the top of her head hit the nape of his neck. She could see his profile out of her peripheral vision and the brim of his hat. How he'd kept the hat on through all of this was beyond her. His warm breath fanned a lock of hair at her temple.

"I haven't forgotten. I'm just thinking through things systematically. There's no room for error. Not in a hostage situation."

The threadbare rug underneath her did little to shield her butt from the hard-packed floor. She shifted into another position. "Think faster. He said he wouldn't be gone long. What about that CB thing on the table?" She nodded toward it. "Do you know how to use one?"

"Yes," he answered, a hint of sarcasm in his tone. She could just imagine him rolling his eyes. "I think I can manage once we get untied."

Robyn wiggled her wrists around, trying to scope out how tight they were bound. Her fingers brushed up against Killian's. Warm. Strong. Alive. They sent a tingle down her arms, although in reality it could have been due to the chill in the air. McKnight must have been conserving wood because he hadn't bothered to light the little potbellied stove, despite the cooler temperatures way up here.

"Wait. Hold it. Quit fidgeting. He's tied a hatchet knot."

Robyn stopped, concerned that she'd made the status worse. She worried her bottom lip. "What's a hatchet knot?"

"A knot that will take a hatchet to get undone." Silence filled the little cabin except for tiny drops of rain—which had started up again—on the tin roof. After a while, she couldn't stand the silence anymore. She laid her head against his back.

40

"Something has been on my mind for quite some time now, and . . ." She bit her bottom lip. ". . . I have to ask. Am I a suspect in this whole bank thing?

"I have to ask because in my senior year in high school I portrayed a bank thief in the school play. The name Robyn Banks kind of stuck. I didn't think it was something the FBI would have on record, though. Would they?" She was rambling. She couldn't help it. Relief at being alive, for even five more minutes, overwhelmed her. She didn't know where to focus her turbulent emotions, so she jabbered. It was just something she did. "What's in a name anyway? I mean, look at you. Your name is Killian. Does that imply you go around killing people?"

He leaned his head back against hers. "Only when they kidnap me, or talk too much."

Robyn jerked her head upright. Of all the nerve. "You're pretty cocky for a man who's tied up."

"May I remind you, you're tied up also? And that we're in the middle of the wilderness." She could tell he looked up at the ceiling at that point. There wasn't much else to look at in their humble surroundings.

"Hey." She shrugged her shoulders. "It could be worse."

He turned his head, so she turned hers to view his profile.

Robyn favored him with a grin, whether he could witness it or not. "It could be raining." A weak rumble of thunder punctuated her sarcastic statement.

He didn't even crack a smile. She could tell. The man did not possess a sense of humor. "Quite the comedian, aren't you?" he asked. "Don't give up your day job."

"I don't have a day job. I work nights, remember. That's what got me into this mess. Didn't they teach you escape maneuvers in FBI school? Don't you have a telephone in your shoe or something? A knife in your pocket perhaps?" She looked over her shoulder at him. Still half-wet, his T-shirt clung to every sinewy muscle in his shoulder and biceps. The man was built, she'd give him that. She averted her gaze, stared straight in front of her.

"Hey, with a name like yours, you just might be a suspect. Maybe I should keep you tied up for good measure."

"A big strapping hunk of man like you, afraid of little ol' me? And if I'm tied up, you're tied up."

His humph served as his answer before he laid his head back against hers.

Out of nowhere his fingers began an exploration—or at least it felt like it anyway—of her rear anatomy. "Did you just . . . ?" Her heart tripped in her chest. He didn't just . . . did he?

"No, Banks. I didn't grab your butt. I was trying to get the blood flowing in my fingers. As close as we are tied together, your butt just happened to get in the way."

"My last name is Jeffries, not Banks."

"Whatever. Has anyone told you, you talk too much?" He shifted his position. The hard floor and the long wait must have been getting to him, too.

"I'm sorry. I can't help it." Oh God. How did she admit this? She was supposed to be strong, not weak. She didn't want to be the defenseless woman. It grated on her nerves. She took a huge breath and spit the words out anyway. "I'm scared, okay? I tend to ramble when I'm scared." She sighed and leaned her head against the support of his strong back. "Talk to me, so I don't have to say another word. Tell me about yourself. Anything at all, just so I don't have to think about the eventuality of what's going to happen to us."

Silence filled the tiny cabin. Killian shifted his position. She thought for a second he wasn't going to tell her anything, but then he started speaking. "I was born at an early age—"

"Very funny." So he wasn't a man prone to spilling his guts about his personal life . . . about anything. Even in a life-or-death situation. No deathbed statements, regrets, pardons or how-de-dos for this Secret Agent Man. "So tell me . . . are we going to die?" Angry tears welled in her eyes. She couldn't even swipe them away, which let them run down her cheeks unchecked.

"Not if I can help it." His words were quieter now, as if all the anger had spilled out of him, and the softer side was all that remained. Maybe he felt sorry for her. Hell, he was in the same boat. He might as well feel sorry for himself, too.

"I don't see you making any move to get us out of this flipping mess." He probably didn't need reminding, but she thought it couldn't hurt.

"I'm assessing the situation as we speak."

"Assess out loud. I need to be included in this. I need to know we're going to get out alive. I need to know I'm going to make it home to feed my cat in the next couple of hours." Poor Brooklyn.

"Your cat?"

"Yes." Robyn squeezed her eyes shut to stop the prick of tears. "She's all I've got, besides my friend Ginger. She's important to me."

"Okay. We're going to get home soon. Don't worry." His voice had gentled and his words soothed her.

She wanted to believe him. She did. Their circumstances said otherwise. "How?"

Chapter 3

Just how was Killian going to get them out of this mess? He'd asked himself the same question over and over, and still no answer was forthcoming. A muscle ticked in his jaw. Since no idea had broken through yet, he kept silent. McKnight wouldn't have had a radio unless there was someone to contact, give updates. This implied an accomplice. Killian would have to be careful, if he ever got a chance to use it. One wrong frequency and he'd alert McKnight's accomplice that they were trying to escape.

They both turned their heads toward the door when they heard the key in the padlock. McKnight was returning. Robyn tensed behind Killian. He tried to squeeze her hand for reassurance. Just as McKnight had promised, he hadn't been gone long. Escape plans would have to wait. "For now," Killian told her at last, "let me worry about the how—"

His words were cut short when the door creaked open. McKnight's gaze settled on them, as if reassuring himself they hadn't escaped in the short time he'd been gone. Killian assessed the man. He seemed hyper now. He came into the room and paced to and fro in front of the small kitchen table. He kept wringing his hands together. He threw glances at the ham radio often, like a man waiting for an incoming call. The bulge beneath the tail of his shirt indicated he still had his gun at the ready and wouldn't hesitate to use it. Not that Killian had doubted it for a second.

"Excuse me, sir, but I really have to go to the ladies' room." Robyn fidgeted behind Killian. She wasn't kidding

44

this time. This wasn't a plan to flee when their backs were turned.

Knees creaked when McKnight got down on his haunches in front of Robyn. Killian turned his head as far as he could to watch him. With a mud-caked hand, McKnight reached out and tucked a tangled strand of Robyn's hair behind her ear. Killian felt a slight jerk against the ropes binding them together. She was trying to be brave, he could tell. She was an innocent. Against Killian's will, his fists clenched. If McKnight hurt her, by God he'd kill the bastard with his own bare hands.

"I don't have time for bathroom breaks."

"But it's been quite a while. I'll go fast. I promise. And I won't try anything funny this time."

Killian prayed she wouldn't try to run away. Not again. Not while McKnight was agitated. He had no doubt he would pump bullets into Robyn's beautiful body if the mood struck him.

McKnight shifted his gaze to Killian and raised an eyebrow. "What do you think, buddy? Is she telling the truth?"

Teeth gritted together, Killian forced out an answer. "Of course she is. Look at her face. The woman can't lie worth a damn."

Sending a sweeping look over her strained features, McKnight capitulated. "Okay." He reached between them, deftly untying the knots binding them together. Then he untied the ropes around their ankles.

Blood rushed into Killian's fingers, and he sucked in a breath against the stinging pain, then shook his hands out. When he looked up, he was staring into the black hole of a Sig Sauer barrel. Killian froze. "Hey, man, take it easy."

"Oh, I take everything easy. No funny business from either of you, or to hell with my plans." He moved the gun toward Robyn and ran the barrel down her cheek. "You'll both be dead in a heartbeat."

Killian remained calm, hoping his demeanor would rub off on Robyn. He didn't need her freaking out, exciting McKnight any more than he already was.

"Nothing funny from me. I promise. I just need to go to the bathroom." A quiver ran through her voice, but she raised her chin in the air just a notch.

Good girl. Don't let him see you're scared. Killian felt a surge of pride for Robyn. She was one tough cookie.

In one swift move, McKnight grabbed her by the arm and yanked her off the ground. "I'm going to be watching you from the door. Don't go out of my sight. A bullet can travel a whole lot faster than my legs, and I still managed to catch up with you last time, didn't I? Death for you could happen swifter than a second. Remember that."

Killian watched Robyn to make sure she wouldn't crack under pressure. She might be one tough cookie, but he'd seen grown men snap under similar circumstances. Robyn swallowed hard, but nodded. "Fine."

They walked to the door, Robyn leading the way. The rusty hinges complained when McKnight pulled the door open. He glanced back at Killian, still sitting in the middle of the rug. "I can see both of you from here." He leaned against the doorjamb and folded his arms across his chest, the barrel of the Sig resting easily against his forearm.

Less than two minutes passed before Robyn ran back in, her dark hair sparkling with drops of rain. She swept a wide berth around their kidnapper, never taking her eyes off him until she was well past. Her gaze skittered to Killian. All color had washed from her face. He released a pent-up breath, thanking his lucky stars she hadn't tried anything. She was shaken, no doubt, but she'd be fine for now.

"Hart?" McKnight swept his hand to the door in an inviting gesture. Killian ambled up from the ground. Their gazes locked, each fighting for supremacy. He had no doubt who the winner would be. It was hard to argue when hard, cold steel was staring one in the face. For this round, the man with the gun would win. But the battle was far from over.

Killian gave the gun a once-over, then strolled out the door into the rain as if he were going for a walk in the park. Within seconds he came back in. Not wasting time, McKnight shoved him toward the rug where Robyn stood running her hands up and down her arms.

"Back to back, kiddies."

Robyn darted Killian a nervous look. "It's okay," he reassured her. He really didn't know that. Their assailant could go ballistic at any minute. It was hard telling what triggered men like him. It was hard telling how long they'd last before they snapped, and it was hard telling why they'd turned evil in the first place. Killian and Robyn both turned around, backs together, and slid to the floor in unison.

McKnight wrapped the rope around their wrists, binding them together quickly. He then strode over to the makeshift box by the door and grabbed a couple logs of wood. Tinkering with the potbellied stove, he attempted to light the thing since night was falling again, and the temperature would soon drop drastically.

"Hatchet knot?" Robyn whispered from behind, her voice soft, yet strong.

He nodded, wiggling his fingers. "Hatchet knot."

Smoke curled within the stove, embers popping. Satisfied, McKnight strode over to the bed and lay down on top of the rumpled blankets, the gun resting on his stomach.

It was going to be a long night. Keeping one eye on the

scumbag, and the other closed, Killian attempted to get some shut-eye. He'd need some sort of rest if he intended to take action tomorrow.

Robyn jerked awake, aware, by the painful crick in her neck, that she wasn't at home in the comfort of her own bed. She tried to stretch her arms over her head, but they seemed to be stuck. It all came flooding back to her. The holdup. The kidnapping. The endless drive into the mountains. The smooth steel of the gun stroking the side of her face. She shivered in revulsion.

"Did you sleep at all?" a voice asked from behind her.

"Agent Hart . . . I . . . yeah, I guess I did a little. I'm awake now, but I think my butt has gone into hibernation." She wiggled around in a futile attempt to get the blood flowing in her veins.

A voice called to them from across the room. "I see my wards have awakened."

Robyn blew hair out of her eyes. She stared at McKnight where he sat at the dilapidated table. One leg crossed over the other, he sipped coffee out of the same dented mug in which he'd given them water. His cavalier attitude made it seem like he was sipping a latte on the Italian Riviera instead of in some damn dirty shack, in the middle of freakin' nowhere, with hostages, a gun and stolen money for company.

Inhaling deeply, Robyn savored the aroma of the coffee, even if she begrudged him his. Her mouth watered. Her mind cried out for just one sip, just one mind-clearing tiny little sip. Her eyes narrowed. It would be a cold day before she opened her mouth and asked that bastard for anything.

After letting them each have some water—which Robyn pretended was the finest of coffees—and a bite of a stale breakfast bar, he gave them both a turn outside again. When he had them settled back on the filthy rug with the ropes securely in place, he wandered back to the table and picked up a newspaper.

Half the day passed, which Robyn filled alternately with dozing, and trying to come up with a foolproof escape plan. Neither activity resulted in much success.

Out of nowhere, McKnight pushed his chair back and stood. "I have to go out. I won't be gone long. Behave."

Killian grunted an unintelligible answer behind her.

"I'll take that as a yes, you will behave. How about you?"

Before he could come near her, Robyn agreed. "Of course."

McKnight drained the last of the coffee from his cup, then headed toward the door without another word. The padlock clicked in place behind him.

Robyn glanced at the table, then back at the door. "He forgot the radio." She whispered the words, afraid McKnight was standing on the other side of the door with his ear pressed to the wood.

"I noticed."

A key scraped against the padlock, and the door flew open. Striding in with a scowl on his face, McKnight stalked across the room and yanked the radio off the table. Tucking it under one arm he waltzed back out the door without even looking at them.

"How could he have heard us?" Disappointment plummeted in her empty stomach. At least something was in there, she thought.

"He didn't. He just remembered at the last second, that's all."

"Speaking of remembering at the last second, I had a dream last night and woke up with the realization I had our salvation in my back pocket. Can you believe it?" Robyn shook her head, still surprised she had forgotten all about it.

"What are you talking about?" Killian sounded somewhere between mad and stunned.

"I can't quite get my fingers at the right angle. Can you reach the back left pocket of my jeans?"

Without a word, Killian slid his fingers into her pocket. At any other time the action would have felt seductive. Who was she kidding? It felt seductive now. Despite her matted and tangled hair and dirty clothes, Robyn couldn't help the way her body responded to Hart's touch. Every single nerve she possessed was standing at attention.

His fingers slid in deeper. Robyn flinched when the weird angle tightened the rope against her already tender skin.

"You okay?"

"Yeah. Please hurry." For more reasons now than just the discomfort of the ropes.

"I'm trying. Whatever is in your pocket isn't easy to grab. Wait. I think I've got it." He pulled the item out and Robyn heaved a sigh of relief. Her body had never responded to a man's touch like that before. He hadn't even been trying anything close to sexual. Good Lord, he was trying to get them out of a hostage situation.

"What is this?" She could feel him moving the object around between his fingers.

"It's a metal fingernail file."

"Why didn't you tell me you had this in your pocket?" Exasperation laced through his words.

"I told you. I forgot. I always carry one around because I'm forever breaking nails at work. It's not a hatchet, but do you think it will work?"

For an answer, Killian started filing away at the rope. "Might take a while, the angle is awkward, but it's better than nothing. Try not to move. I don't want to cut your skin."

"I don't think I have any skin left around my wrists anyway."

"I'm sorry."

"It's not your fault."

"You're my responsibility."

She rolled her eyes. He would take it personal. She could tell he was that kind of guy. Why would a man voluntarily set himself up for a hostage situation or, for that matter, death, if he didn't take pride in and love what he did for a living? Was pride worth death?

Hart stopped what he was doing, and they both turned their heads toward the door, listening for any sign that McKnight had returned.

Since all she heard was silence, Robyn went back to her thoughts. Typical male. Thought there was no way a woman could be responsible for herself. "I can take care of myself."

"Not while I'm on duty."

"Oh, come on." This guy was unbelievable. "Admit it. You'd lay your raincoat over a puddle for some chick, wouldn't you?"

"What's wrong with a little chivalry?"

"Haven't you heard chivalry is all but dead?"

"That's because no one bothered to follow the rules. They allowed it to die."

She let loose with a dry laugh. "Who is 'they'? This is a new era, Agent Hart," she informed him over her shoulder. "Women own their own businesses, have babies out of wedlock, maintain their own portfolios. Get out of the dark ages you've been hiding in."

"Dark? Raising a baby as a single parent is considered the light years? That's warped by anyone's standards. I may never get married myself, but I happen to believe when a man and woman say their wedding vows it should be for life. Divorce is too convenient. A child should be raised by two parents, not just one."

"Wow. You're adamant about your beliefs, aren't you?" For some reason, Killian reminded her of Charlie. They were both the kind of man who would hang around with the same dame for life just because.

"Damn straight." A noise sounded outside and they both stopped talking immediately. Robyn's heart jumped in her throat, afraid McKnight had returned before they'd finished cutting through the ropes. They remained silent for a full sixty seconds before Robyn even bothered to take a breath.

"Are you getting anywhere?"

"It's hard to tell. I can't get my fingers at the right angle to test the rope. He tied it just a little too tight for most movement."

"Bastard."

Killian just grunted from behind her, and kept sawing away with slow and methodical movements. "Damn."

His muttered oath, followed by dead silence, was not a good sign. The stale power bar in her stomach churned. "What's the matter?"

"File broke."

Outside the wall-to-wall windows of the conference room, employees buzzed around like militant soldiers. Dan Stevens watched those busy little soldiers, wishing he were on the outside instead of the inside. The atmosphere carried an air of tension, unsaid accusations and downright hostile anger.

"So tell me what happened, Stevens?"

Here they went again. He had the utmost respect for Holgate, the Special Agent in Charge of the Denver Field Office, but he felt his anger simmering below the surface anyhow. He'd have to keep it in check. "I've told you a thousand times already, Agent Holgate. It all went down fast. Too fast. Before we knew it Goldsberry was dead, and Hart and the woman were taken hostage."

Silence filled the room again. One of the eight people sitting around the oval, polished-to-perfection table, coughed. They all wore standard white starched shirts and red power ties. Despite the identical blank expressions on each face, Dan could tell they didn't believe him. His right foot, where it crossed over his left knee, pumped up and down in rapid succession. He immediately put both feet flat on the floor.

Never let them see you sweat.

How many times, in all the years they'd been partners, had Hart uttered that phrase to him with a sarcastic smile on his face? Never had Dan felt the words more appropriate than right now.

"I had ten men on this assignment. Ten. You and Hart are my most seasoned, experienced officers." Holgate steepled his fingers together in front of him. "I'm a reasonable man under the best of circumstances. These are not the best of circumstances. And to top it off, I can't believe you lost track of the getaway vehicle. I could have placed rookies on this job and had a better outcome. Ten men, and you all failed miserably. I'm holding you responsible, Stevens. You let your own partner down. You let the agency down."

Dan shifted and went to tug at his tie before he realized he was the only one in the room not wearing one. Funny how a few pointed stares could make a guy feel like he had a noose around his neck. He knew he'd let Hart down in more ways than one. He hung his head. God, would Killian ever forgive him? It was going to take more than their usual six-pack to fix this one.

"You know we've been tracking McKnight for quite some time, sir. He's tricky. The craftiest con artist I've ever come across. We almost nailed him in Vegas."

" 'Almost' doesn't put the lowlife behind bars where he belongs, now does it?" The question was delivered with no inflection. They could have been discussing the weather, or the stock market.

Dan shifted, not quite feeling inflection-free. Nope, he felt every barb of that comment like a serrated knife cutting through his jugular. "No, sir." He kept his voice strong. Forceful. It was what Hart would have done. Dan knew. He'd seen him do it a thousand times.

Holgate sighed and rubbed his forehead. It was the first sign of emotion he'd shown, other than loathing, since he'd entered the room. Dan took that as a good sign.

"How is your mother, Stevens?"

Dan stiffened. "She's doing better." Surely Holgate wasn't suggesting his mother's terminal illness was affecting his job performance?

"Glad to hear it. Is it true she cancelled her insurance last year?"

All eyes in the room were staring at him. He forced himself to remain motionless. A sweat drop trickled down his temple. "She had to when the rates were hiked up after my dad died."

"That's a shame." The rest of the men in the room looked at him with pity. Holgate's gaze held empathy. Several years ago, Holgate's daughter had remained in a coma for four long months before dying. The result of a bank president who'd climbed behind the wheel drunk. Dan had heard through the grapevine the man had received a DUI and a slap on the wrist. Holgate had received an empty house since Emily had been an only child.

Dan had to get the attention off of him. He hated attention. Preferred anonymity. "I may not know much, but I do know one thing . . . McKnight may be cunning, but Hart is his equal match."

Holgate studied him. "They've been gone over twenty-four hours already, Dan. Either he and the woman are dead, or Killian has gone over to the dark side." He pushed away from the desk and stood, pointing a finger in his direction. "I don't care what it takes, how many men you need, or what rules you have to break. I want Hart found. Understood?"

"What do you mean, the file broke?"

Panic was setting in. Killian could hear it in the slight quivering of Robyn's voice.

To placate her, he tried to keep his tone on an even keel, as if nothing were wrong, and stuff like this happened to him every day. Let her think they had all the time in the world to figure out another means of escape. Never let the people you were sworn to protect see you get nervous. It always made a bad situation head south. "It snapped in half. It's useless."

"What are we going to do now?" The quiver in her voice had turned to a distinct waver. He could feel her hands trembling. If he didn't know better, he'd guess that her lips were trembling, also. He didn't know what else to do, so he slipped one part of the broken file back into her pocket.

Killian shot a glance toward the door, then scanned the room for the hundredth time. It offered damn little in the way of solutions.

The dwindling fire popped and snapped in the stove. An idea snapped into Killian's head.

"You're going to have to help me. Can you do that, Robyn?"

"Me? I think so. What do you need?"

"Together we have to move over to the door, then back over to the stove. On the count of three, we're going to push against each other's backs and stand."

"Okay." The trembling hadn't quite left her voice yet. Was it because she didn't trust him, or was she just scared?

"One, two, three." In unison they pressed their backs together. Killian dug the heels of his boots into the shabby rug and pushed. "A little bit harder, that's it. You can do it."

Robyn grunted and huffed. Killian held his breath and gritted his teeth. Within seconds, they were standing.

From behind, Robyn pulled a big breath of air into her lungs. "That was tougher than I thought."

"You did great. Now we need to shuffle and hop over to the door."

She planted her heels and refused to budge. For such a tiny thing, she had an incredible amount of strength. "The door is padlocked and we're tied together. I fail to see how shuffling over there is going to solve our problem. Shouldn't we go for a window or something?"

Killian felt the ticking time like it was a bomb in his own chest. He didn't have time to explain, but obviously the stubborn-headed woman wouldn't settle for anything less than a detailed answer. Why couldn't women just trust a man to do the right thing?

"This is where teamwork comes in. Do you see the thin stick of wood in the crate by the door?"

"Yes." Her voice lacked conviction.

"Together we're going to take that stick, then move over to the stove." They started shuffling in tandem.

"The stove? What are you going to do with the stove?"

"There are still some hot embers in there. We're going to burn our way out of these ropes."

Robyn stopped shuffling, forcing Killian to a standstill. "I want to get out of here as much as the next guy, but I don't want it at the cost of third-degree burns."

"I'm all in favor of avoiding burns." He couldn't help glancing at the door. "That's where the stick comes into play. We'll knock an ember out with the stick, then lay the rope on top of it and burn our way through."

She moved them back into the awkward shuffle. "Okay. It might work."

Killian stopped shuffling a second. Might? He knew it would work. "The clock is not our friend here."

"I'm going as fast as I can."

He refrained from commenting. Instead, he spent his energy on getting toward the door. When they managed to get across the floor, they both reached their hands out together. Killian grabbed the long stick in his fingers and tucked it between their backs.

"Okay. We're doing great. Time is ticking, though. Let's see how fast we can make it over to the stove." They huffed and puffed, using each other for balance and stability. For such a tiny little thing, Robyn kept right up with him. "Opening the door on the potbellied stove is going to be the hard part."

"We can do it."

"Thatagirl." Killian hitched the stick up so he was holding it almost at the end.

"What can I do? I feel useless letting you do everything."

"Just let your hands go loose. Move with me. It'll go faster if just one person does all the work. If we both try we'll go in the wrong directions at the same time and it will take longer. I can hear you rolling your eyes."

"Am not."

"Whatever." Feminism be damned. He had a job to do and to hell with ruffled female feathers. Killian moved the stick until it was wedged under the tiny handle, then he lifted up and pulled out. The tiny metal door popped open like magic, sending a blast of heat into their faces.

"Wow. I'm impressed, Mr. Secret Agent Man."

Killian remained silent. He needed to focus all his attention on the job at hand.

"I can hear you rolling your eyes," she said.

"Am not." He didn't know why he felt the need to defend himself, but he did. It hadn't taken long for him to discover that Robyn had a strange effect on him.

"Whatever. Just get that hot coal out."

Killian rolled his eyes. "Quit talking. You're making me lose my concentration."

"Want me to do it for you?"

"Robyn . . . just chill a minute. I've almost got . . . damn."

"What?"

"The wood moved. I have to move a little closer. It might get hot, but I promise not to burn our hands. Don't jerk your arms at all, okay?"

"Okay." Her answer was soft-spoken, like she finally realized the gravity of the situation.

Killian stuck the stick into the opening and tried again. He could move their arms just a little, until the rope cut off the circulation and made his hands shake. Three times he almost had a burning piece of tinder half out the door, and three times it fell back in. Taking a deep breath, he tried again. This time, the piece of firewood slipped out the door and landed on the floor with a hiss and a shower of embers. A tiny flame shot up, then died.

"Yes. Perfect." He tossed the stick aside. "Robyn, look down behind you. See the embers?"

"Yep. Are we going to put the ropes on there?"

"Yes, but we can't let our skin touch, or we'll get burned, too."

"Gotcha."

He moved their arms until they were right above the little piece of burning wood. "Ready?"

"I was born ready. Let's turn these ropes into toast."

Turning his head as far as he could, Killian pushed the rope around their wrists into the embers and held it steady. "This could take a while. Don't move."

It took more than a little while. They both remained silent through the entire procedure. The only sound in the tiny room was the popping of the wood in the stove and Robyn's gentle breathing. Killian could feel her back rise and fall with every breath. Her back was straight, rigid with tension, a tension he himself felt in every nerve. How much longer would McKnight stay away? Would he walk in on them seconds before the hot coals had done their job?

Robyn didn't think she could take much more. She'd never sat so still in her entire life. After what felt like hours, the rope caught fire.

"Hold still," Killian warned her. "Don't move. Let the rope burn."

She winced. "It freakin' hurts." Tiny flames were licking at her already tender skin.

"I know, I know. Just a couple more seconds." Killian pulled his wrists apart, and the rope snapped, sending it flying a few feet away from them.

Robyn turned and looked at him, rubbing her tender wrists as she did. "That took forever."

"Agreed." He scanned her face and body. Was he making sure she was all right? Or was she merely a sight for sore eyes?

"Your jaw is starting to turn a nice shade of purple," she said, drawing the attention away from herself.

He reached out and touched his own cheek. "Isn't the first time. Won't be the last. We don't have much time." He untied the ropes binding his legs, then pushed Robyn's hands out of the way and made short work of her ankle ropes. He pushed off the ground and reached out an arm to help her up.

Robyn put her hand in his. With a gentle tug she rose off the ground. When she tried to put pressure on her foot, it gave out beneath her and she flew smack dab into Hart.

"Whoa, easy there." He grabbed her shoulders to support her.

Hands flat against his chest, his heartbeat slow and steady beneath her fingertips. "I'm sorry. We've been sitting on that damn rug for so long my foot fell asleep." She still didn't move away from him. Up close, she couldn't help but notice how thick and full his lips appeared.

"Can you walk yet?" He released her, but kept his hands near her shoulders, in case she went down again.

She tore her gaze away from his mouth and looked down at her feet, her heart beating at a much faster pace than his had been. "I think I'm okay now."

"You sure?"

"Yeah. Yeah, I'm sure." She glanced around them. "I don't want to spend another minute in this place." A chill ran down her spine and she shook it off. "Let's get out of here."

"The front door is padlocked, so we'll need to go out the window."

Robyn rushed to the big window that faced the front of the cabin. She pushed against the pane, trying to open it. "It's stuck."

Killian shooed her out of the way, then used all his muscle to open the window. It wouldn't budge. Robyn stood over his shoulder, watching his every move. He tried again, desperately wanting to get them out of there. Burning the ropes had taken up way too much time. McKnight was bound to return soon. He'd been gone a long time. The sky had already gone from dusk to total darkness. The light from the little stove was all they had by which to see.

"Maybe if we both pushed together." She pressed her body next to his, her tiny hands against his large ones on the window. They both pushed to no avail.

"Damn." He yanked off his cap and rammed his hands through his hair. "We're going to have to break it." He strode over to the dilapidated kitchen table and grabbed the rickety chair. "Get across the room. Now."

When Robyn was far enough away to miss the flying glass, he raised the chair over his shoulder and swung it hard. Glass shattered everywhere. Killian tossed the chair to the ground and threw an arm up over his eyes to protect himself. The hole was big enough for them to squeeze out of, but not without risking getting cut by a sharp edge. He picked up the chair and was ready to break the window again when the sound of a vehicle outside drew their attention. He dropped the chair and ran to the little window on the back wall of the cabin. Even though he couldn't fit through it, Robyn could.

The window opened easily. "Come here. It's too small for me, but you can make it out this window. He'll see us if we go out the front." Killian glanced over his shoulder and stared at her.

Robyn stood frozen to the spot, her heart racing like a captured bird's, one hand clamped over her mouth. If she spent one more night in the shack, she'd hurl.

"Robyn . . . snap out of it. You need to come over here now, or we're dead. Look at me."

Her gaze snapped to his.

"Dead, Robyn. If you want to live, get your tiny ass over here."

That statement unfroze her. They didn't have time for trepidation right now. She fled across the room and stuck her foot into his interlaced fingers. Before he could hoist her up, he leaned forward and pressed his lips against hers in a light kiss. "You're a brave woman, don't forget it." Then he boosted her to the windowsill in one swift motion.

"You're not going to fit out this window, Killian." She huffed, the sill digging into her stomach and cutting off her wind supply.

"Don't worry about me. If I don't meet you out back in sixty seconds, run like hell."

She was so courageous, most of the time he forgot she was just a civilian and this was all new to her . . . and probably out-right scary. Robyn disappeared out the window and Killian raced to the front of the tiny cabin again. The one way out was through the broken window. The hole was small, but if he was careful he'd be all right. He knocked out as many of the broken shards as he could before he had to quit, or risk being seen. The timing was the tricky part. He'd have to go out at the same instant that McKnight was coming in. One second sooner and he'd see him on the porch. One second later and he'd shoot him in the back as he went out the window. He took off his cap and shoved it in his back pocket.

Killian stood back from the window when the van lights, which had been shining directly into the dirty window, were killed.

He listened intently. The driver's side door opened, then closed. A gentle rain hit the tin roof, every drop exaggerated and overly loud to his senses. McKnight whistled as he walked up to the front door. Killian put one foot up on the sill, ready to sail through the jagged hole. Keys jangled, then a click sounded as the key popped open the lock.

The second the door was pushed open, Killian flew out the window. When he hit the front porch, searing pain shot through his gut. In his haste, he'd misjudged the distance and ended up with a jagged piece of glass slicing into his midsection.

"What the hell?" McKnight cried out in the little cabin. The sound echoed off the rotting walls.

No time for pain. Quiet, yet swift, Killian ran off the porch and rounded the corner of the cabin. Robyn stood there wringing her hands. Even in the darkness he could see the relief wash over her face when she spotted him.

"Let's go," he whispered. He pressed one hand against his cut, trying to stop the bleeding. With the other, he grabbed Robyn's hand and pulled her along with him into the darkness of the night.

Within seconds, McKnight was running back out the door through which he'd just walked. "I'll find you," he screamed into the blackness. "Don't think you can get away from me. I'll find you." A gunshot sounded into the night air. Killian flinched. Robyn jerked behind him. He released her hand so they could run faster.

Killian fought back his instincts. He would have loved to have stayed and fought McKnight, brought the bastard to his knees. Not with a woman along for the ride. Keeping her safe was top priority.

He didn't have to tell Robyn to keep up with him. As soon as she'd recovered from the shock of hearing the gun, she was on his heels, then she overtook him.

His intent had been to head for the woods, but Robyn took off down the mountain, following the path McKnight had beaten down with his vehicle. As dangerous as it was to take to the trees when it was this dark, it was more dangerous to stay on the road.

He knew this. It was Basic Cop 101.

Robyn wasn't a cop. She hadn't taken the course.

"Can't we . . . go . . . woods?" She was running out of energy.

Killian had to admit he was, too. "Imperative." The woman was smart, he'd give her that. She could have easily panicked and froze. Blood seeped from underneath his hand and trailed down his stomach. Stars formed in front of his eyes. He kept pushing forward. Distance could save them. He fought the wave of dizziness washing over him. And luck. They needed a lot of damn luck.

Chapter 4

When Killian went down on all fours, Robyn gasped. Had he tripped? Had he been shot? She reached out and grabbed him by the shoulders. "Killian, get up. We have to run. I can't do this on my own. We're a team, remember?" She fought back a whimper. She needed to be strong. When he got to his knees, Robyn felt the sticky wetness on his shirt. She froze. "Is that blood?"

A low grunt sounded from his lips.

"Killian, look at me. Is that blood on your shirt?" Tentatively she reached out a finger and touched the stain. She jerked her hand back in revulsion and shock. "What the hell happened? Were you shot?"

"No. Glass. Window."

"Having a bad guy chasing us wasn't enough for you?" She couldn't fight the anger and fear rising in her. *Take a deep breath.* It had been an accident, but she was scared. "You felt you needed to add an extra complication to the mix?" Before he could even answer, twin headlights bore down on them. Stomach in her throat, heart beating rapidly, she tugged on his arm. "Get up!"

Behind them, the van's engine revved. Robyn whipped her head around. McKnight was going to run them down where they stood. Her heart quickened in her chest.

"Get up!" she yelled.

Struggling against the slick mud and Killian's deadweight, Robyn managed to stand. "Hart, get the hell up!"

The van's headlights sliced through the deluge of rain,

which had gone from a drizzle to an out-and-out gully washer. The engine revved again.

Tearing her gaze away from certain death, Robyn turned back to Hart. He was kneeling. With her arms around him and her shoulder braced against his side, she pushed against him in an attempt to help him stand.

Instinct made her look back. The van was barreling down on them. No time to move. No time to pray for a quick, pain-less death. She closed her eyes and waited for the moment of impact.

Nothing happened.

Her eyes shot open. Against the driving rain, she wiped a hand across her face. McKnight gunned the engine, causing the wheels to spin even faster.

"Holy crap. Now is our chance." Robyn couldn't believe their luck. The van made a horrible grinding, spinning noise when the back wheels sank deeper into the mud. "Now, Killian. We need to move now. Killian, look at me."

Killian glanced up through the rain, blinking rapidly.

"If you don't get up right now, we're dead." She used the words he'd used on her moments earlier inside the cabin.

The van's front door opened behind them. Obviously, McKnight wasn't going to bother with the stuck vehicle. Not when he had a gun.

Killian struggled to his feet.

"That's it. Way to go." Heart in her throat, Robyn turned them toward the woods.

Killian wrapped one arm around her shoulders and she grabbed his hand, keeping it firmly in place, the other arm wrapped around his waist. Together, they entered the trees, zigzagging their way around the aspens and pines. Adrenaline pumping, Robyn tried not to think. She knew McKnight would come after them on foot. He was that kind of guy.

Obsessed.

Driven.

A true killer.

Her arm still around Killian's waist, she pushed them on through trees and pitch-black darkness. Unable to see more than two inches in front of her, Robyn lost her footing. She stumbled over a rock and knocked them both to the wet ground. Robyn lay against his muscular chest and stared into his face for two seconds. Then she remembered his cut, and how any pressure on it would make it worse. Fear whipping through her, she rolled off him.

A flash of lightning threw his features into stark relief. She leaned in close to his face. "We have to do this together, Killian. You have to help me," she begged.

A look crossed over his face. Realization? Awareness? It was hard to tell. She didn't have time to analyze it.

He mumbled something, but she couldn't hear the words through the rain. Robyn had to lean in close to talk over the pounding deluge and the roaring thunder. "What?"

"You hurt?"

"Me? No, no. I'm fine." He'd been sliced and diced by the window, and all he could worry about was her? He seriously needed a vacation from his job. Not in the woods, though. She didn't know about him, but she never wanted to see a forest again. She pushed wet hair out of her face. Her clothes clung to her like a second skin. She shivered. "We have to get up. We have to keep moving. Can you do that?"

He gave a brief nod. That was all she needed. She pushed off the ground and bent down to help him up, careful not to touch his wound. As quickly as the rain washed away the blood, it just kept coming back. If they didn't get help soon, it wouldn't matter if McKnight caught them or not.

She drove herself and Killian harder than she ever knew she could. After they'd traveled for quite some time, Killian's steps faltered. She leaned him against a tree for a few moments to let him catch his breath. "We need to bandage that wound." She eyed it warily as if the wound were the enemy and not the fool chasing them. In a way it was.

"Don't have time . . . now."

Weakness was getting to him. They had to stop more often. A lump of self-pity lodged in her throat. She didn't have time for tears, though she longed to give in to a good crying jag. What purpose would it serve? She'd cry when they were safely home. When she was cuddled up on her sofa with Brooklyn on her lap, then she'd give in to emotion.

"Let's get going." She pushed off the tree and slipped her arm around him again. His body felt so cold. She was cold, too. How much of his lowered body temperature was due to blood loss, and how much to the nighttime cold mountain weather and the damn rain? They didn't have jackets, just short-sleeved shirts. But they were still alive, dammit, and if she had anything to say about it, they'd stay that way.

After a couple hours the rain slowed to a drizzle. Robyn couldn't hear their tracker over the night noises. Crickets, the gentle sound of the rain hitting the leaves on the trees and the underbrush. She knew he was out there, though. She could feel it.

They pushed onward, until even Robyn couldn't take another step. She wondered how Killian had managed to make it this far. He hadn't spoken more than a few guttural words, seemingly very content to let her take control. That wasn't the Killian she'd come to know. From what she'd observed, he liked to call the shots. This, more than anything, made her stop and help him to the ground to rest.

She pushed his hand out of the way and lifted up the hem

of his shirt. A gasp escaped her parted lips. She jerked her gaze away.

"Looks worse than it is." His words were slurred.

"No, it's worse than it looks." Robyn was no nurse. Good God . . . the one and only time she'd even attempted to play doctor was with a neighbor boy out behind his shed. He'd called her a failure. Could she help it if she'd frozen up? She felt like she was freezing up now. Blood and guts weren't up her alley. She even bypassed slasher movies because she couldn't handle gore.

Killian tried to stand, but a gentle pressure from her on his shoulders forestalled him. It was way too easy to stop him, which worried her even more.

"You're not going to make it another step until we take care of this." Her legs ached. Her head hurt. The thought of tending to his wound nauseated her. But, if their positions were reversed, she knew he'd take care of her, no questions asked.

She relied on courage she didn't know she possessed. Careful not to hurt him, she lifted his shirt up again and examined the wound. She sucked in a breath when she realized how deep the cut went. A quick glance up at his face told her he was resting. His head was back against the tree trunk, his eyes closed.

She needed something to stem the blood flow. She raked a hand through her hair and sat back on her heels, her blood-covered hands splayed against her thighs. The sight of the red handprints on her jeans made her want to gag.

Robyn scrubbed her hands into the damp underbrush, all around her, trying to remove the stains from her hands. One quick glance at Killian's wound compounded her growing worry. They were in the freaking woods. What the hell was she supposed to use as a bandage?

Despite the fact that she was cold, she ripped off the bottom half of her T-shirt, leaving her midriff bare. To hell with warmth. It would work, better than nothing, pressed against the wound. To tie it in place, she ripped off the bottom of Killian's shirt. "Good idea." He opened his eyes and gave a slight nod. "Tie it tight, but not too tight. The pressure has to be just right."

When she pressed her shirt against the wound, disillusion-ment washed over her. Blood seeped through, turning the white shirt red. "This doesn't look good, Killian."

"I've bled worse than this before." He winced when she pressed her hand flush against the wound, and her heart leapt to her throat. Gritting her teeth for him, she kept her hand there, while she wrapped the bottom of Killian's shirt around his waist and tied it in place over the wound.

It wasn't much as far as bandages went, but it would have to do. Tired herself, she rested against a tree facing Killian, her muddy and blood-splattered, jeans-clad legs caging his.

She'd allow them five minutes to catch their breath. That was all they could afford. McKnight wouldn't rest at all. And he wasn't wounded. The lowlife had the advantage. She scrubbed her hands over her face. God, this wasn't hap-pening. This wasn't real.

Killian stirred. She pushed off the tree and knelt in front of him.

"How long have we been sitting here?" he asked. His face was pale.

"Not long." She pointed to his wound. "Moving around isn't going to help."

Sparing the wound little more than a fleeting glance, he shifted. "Being a sitting duck isn't my idea of a good time." He pushed off the ground, sweat beading his upper lip.

Dammit, he was right. They couldn't afford to stay in one

spot and become targets. Grabbing his elbow, Robyn helped him stand. Glassy-eyed, he looked down on her. She went to slip her arm around his waist and he tried to push her away.

Robyn's entire body tensed. "Don't you dare get macho on me now, Hart. You've lost more blood than you think. You'll fall on your ass without me."

He didn't say a word, but didn't argue this time when she placed a supporting arm around him. She led them to the right.

Killian turned them around and led them in the complete opposite direction.

"Are you sure—" He cut her off with just a glance. Heat crept up her cheeks. Thank goodness he was paying more attention to the path his feet took than to her. She chalked it up to the fact that all the trees looked the same, and not that she was directionally challenged. They walked for hours, moving downward at a snail's pace.

The sun slowly rose above them, dappling through the trees. Robyn wiggled her fingers, welcoming the warmth she knew daybreak would bring. Daylight would also make it easier for McKnight to find them. "What's that noise?" She stopped in her tracks, whipping around to search the woods behind them. Had McKnight caught up with them?

"I didn't hear anything," Killian mumbled.

"You're in too much pain to hear anything." Robyn's senses, on the other hand, were on full alert. Her gaze swept the area, finding nothing. Maybe it was nothing. Maybe it was just a small animal or a deer or something. She turned back around. "We're at the edge of the trees, Killian. Won't we be vulnerable walking out in the open?"

"Don't have a choice." He scanned the horizon. "There are more trees across . . . clearing. We'll have to cover ground quickly."

"In case you haven't noticed, we have to cross a bunch of rocks. In your condition, it isn't going to be easy." Robyn glanced over her shoulder again and chewed on her bottom lip. He was coming. She just knew, in her gut, McKnight was hot on their trail. The hair at her nape bristled and she rubbed it with her hand.

"No one ever said life . . . fair or easy. We do what we have to do. This is no different." Jaw set, Killian started moving without her. Robyn jogged a few steps to catch up and grabbed his elbow. He would never admit to it, but he was growing weaker by the minute. His steps were sluggish, his words slurred. Traversing the rocks was not only going to be hard and unfair, she had no doubt it would prove to be a living hell. She grabbed the hat from his back pocket and shoved it on his head. While the nights were cold, the days were hot. She didn't need him to get heat exhaustion on top of everything else.

Filling her lungs with air and courage, they left the security of the woods and entered the open field. The landscape, since they'd left the cabin, stretched downward for miles and miles. While going down was faster, it was also more difficult.

The first step onto the rocks proved how cautious and slow they were going to have to take it. The rocks shifted beneath them, sliding downward. Robyn reached out and grabbed Killian, her own foothold precarious. Killian went down on his knees. Robyn landed hard on her butt. "Are you okay?" she asked.

In the ensuing silence, he sucked in a deep breath. He didn't answer for a few minutes, just held one hand over the wound in his gut. "Dandy."

Robyn could feel his pain. His face had grown more pale, and his hands were shaking. They couldn't sit here long.

They were exposed and vulnerable. They had to make it to the cover of trees.

"Let's go," he snapped.

"Are you sure you're ready?" All she needed was for him to pass out, and slide all the way down the hill, reopening his wound. A headache pounded in her temples, and she took a second to rub them.

"Yeah."

As was getting to be their habit, she grabbed him by the elbow and helped him stand. "Walk slow." It wasn't as if he could walk any other way.

"I know, Robyn."

"You don't have to be so grumpy." She knew he was holding on by a hair, using some inner force to keep moving. For a guy who thrived on control, losing it wasn't fun. She had serious doubts they'd make it to the bottom before McKnight caught up to them. Maybe Killian did, too. Anxiety clawed at her stomach. Or maybe it was hunger. She couldn't tell anymore. She didn't care anymore. Whenever she was nervous, she tended to jabber. Now was no exception. She made sure to jabber quietly, though, so the sound wouldn't carry.

"You know when you kissed me at the shack? I realize now that was just a pity kiss. You didn't expect us to live, did you?" She didn't expect him to answer. As quiet as he was, she wasn't even convinced he was listening. "It's okay, though. I just wish there had been time for me to pity kiss you back . . . or to enjoy it.

"Put your right foot forward, Killian. That's it. Yes, right there. That's it, babe."

Her stomach flipped.

Babe?

Where had that come from?

Had their forced intimacy brought them closer on an emotional level, or was it just a nurturing instinct kicking in? She couldn't even begin to rationalize her feelings. Not when their lives were at stake.

Robyn talked Killian through every agonizing inch of the way. She cried out when she twisted her ankle for the millionth time. It didn't help that every few minutes she looked over her shoulder, convinced McKnight was standing in the clearing aiming a gun at their backs.

"I'm seriously going to reconsider renewing my membership to the gym." Robyn kept talking, even though Killian never answered, other than a few grunts and groans. It was nervous chatter that helped calm her nerves. "I've had enough exercise to last a lifetime. How about you? Place your left foot a few inches to the left. There's a good spot right there. That's it."

Killian didn't seem like the gym kind of person. He wasn't sociable enough for that. She couldn't help but notice he was physically fit, though. Broad shoulders, muscular biceps and, judging by the stretch of his T-shirt, which had finally dried, an impressive set of pecs. Someone like him probably had a weight bench at home, preferring to work out in solitude instead of the party atmosphere with which some fitness centers operated.

Rocks slid underneath them again, but Robyn managed to keep them both upright. That's what she got for thinking about his physique instead of his footing. She pushed thoughts of his body out of her mind and concentrated on getting them across the rocks.

Never had she felt so joyous as when they stepped onto solid ground. "Hallelujah. We made it, Killian."

He grunted. Their pace should have quickened a little, now that they had secure footing, but Killian was moving slower. He was losing energy. Keeping up the pace would kill him. Slowing down would get them killed. Neither option held much appeal.

Anxiety had her nerves on edge. She felt like screaming. They had a few more feet to go to reach the cover of a new set of trees. Robyn glanced over her shoulder and saw movement in the trees above the rocks. Her heart leapt into her throat. McKnight pushed through the brush and strolled into the open.

"Hurry," she whispered, pushing Killian onward, praying that her own sense of urgency would make him move faster. Robyn breathed a sigh of relief when they entered the dense brush. She peeked behind them, watching McKnight behind the dense cover of bushes and trees. He didn't act like he had seen them. He scanned the entire area, then went down on his haunches, touching the ground with his fingers. He brought his hand back up, rubbing his fingers together like he was testing the consistency of something.

Robyn jolted to a standing position and glanced at Killian's wound. Good God, McKnight was tracking them with Killian's blood. They were leaving a damn trail. Robyn scoured the ground for every blade of grass, every leaf that showed even a hint of blood, and shoved them into her front pocket.

Moving as fast as she could, making little noise, she ripped the sleeves out of her T-shirt and shoved them beneath the knot on Killian's makeshift bandage. With luck it would soak up some of the blood so it wouldn't drip a trail. She wasn't going to make things any easier for the bastard than they already were.

Killian leaned his long lean frame against a tree. Robyn slipped up beside him, taking his arm and dragging it around her shoulders. "McKnight is right behind us."

"I can walk myself." He shrugged her off.

"Prove it."

Killian moved one step and stumbled. He muttered something that sounded like an oath, but she couldn't be sure and she didn't have time to ask. To hell with his pride. She slipped her arm around his waist, a sense of urgency spurring her on. She didn't bother looking back again. Didn't need to. It would waste valuable seconds. She knew who their tracker was and that he was right behind them.

Together, they pressed through the trees, Killian struggling the entire way. He kept putting one foot in front of the other, as if his unconscious mind knew there was no other choice.

They came upon a tiny clearing in the middle of all the dense brush. There in the middle of the clearing stood a bear.

Robyn's heart rate accelerated like a car stuck on high idle. What next?

The bear was big.

Hairy.

Menacing.

Four hundred pounds plus of certain death stared at them with piercing golden eyes.

Robyn didn't think she could be any more scared than she'd been for the past twenty-four hours. She was wrong, and now she had to pee.

"Why . . . stopping?" Killian managed to ask. His head hung low as he stared at the ground. He hadn't yet seen the animal.

"There's a friggin' bear in our path," she whispered out of the corner of her mouth.

"Weren't you ever . . . Girl Scout? Guidebooks say to yell. Bear . . . more afraid . . . you."

"I'd love nothing more than to yell, but there's just one problem with following that rule, big guy. If I scream, McKnight will know exactly where we are."

Chapter 5

Dan Stevens pulled up to the Victorian house and parked at the curb. He checked the address scribbled on a scrap of paper. This was the place. Instead of getting out of the car, he sat and stared out the windshield. Why did he feel so apprehensive? Like when he stood outside his mother's hospital room and dreaded opening the door? Would she be worse? Better? Would the woman he was visiting now know anything? Would she see right through him?

The weight of her forthcoming answers rounded his shoulders. It was almost as bad as facing the endless number of hospital bills that came in the mail daily. Bills he had no way of paying. He rolled his neck, stretching the muscles. That would all change soon. He grabbed the keys out of the ignition, pocketed them and stepped out of the car. Only one way to find the answers he was seeking.

The front gate opened without a sound on well-oiled hinges. The grass was freshly cut and well-manicured. The front beds hosted a riot of blooming flowers in every color.

The big brass door knocker was cold in his grasp when he banged it against the oak door three times. He heard someone moving inside, then the door swung open to reveal a very pregnant and very pretty young woman.

"Are you Mrs. Danelli?"

"Yes, I am. Can I help you with something?" She gave him a hesitant smile.

Dan reached in his back pocket and fished out his wallet.

He flashed his badge. "I'm Dan Stevens. I'm here about Robyn Jeffries."

The woman's face paled, her hand going to her chest. "Please come in." She swung the door open wide. "I've been so worried about her."

The entryway sported a cathedral ceiling and a multitude of huge green plants. She ushered him into a homey living room and offered him a seat. Uncomfortable, he perched on the edge of the sofa. Why couldn't his boss, Holgate, have done this? He reminded himself that he wanted answers, too. Fish for information, Holgate had said. If Hart is involved, then the girl might be, too.

"Mrs. Danelli—"

"Oh, please, that sounds so formal. Call me Ginger."

"Ginger, then." He forced a smile on his face, hoping it didn't look as pained as it felt. He loathed this part of his job. He'd much rather be on a stakeout. Apprehending a suspect. Exchanging gunfire. Talking one-on-one made him nervous as hell. "As I'm sure you're well aware, Robyn was taken hostage along with my partner, Agent Killian Hart."

Ginger felt for the cushion behind her and lowered herself onto the chair across from him. Good God, she wasn't going into labor, was she? How much stress could a pregnant woman take?

"Due any moment, huh?" Small talk sounded so mundane. *Get to the point, Dan. Get in, then get out.*

"As big as I am, you'd think I was overdue. I still have a month to go. And first babies are usually late . . . or so I'm told." She grimaced. "Do you have news on her yet?"

Ah, she'd steered the subject back to her friend, for which Dan was thankful. He hated small talk, he totally sucked at it, too. "Unfortunately, no."

"I feel so useless." She placed a hand on her belly and

rubbed it in a circular motion. "I mean, I go over and feed her cat every day, but I feel like there is something else I need to be doing. It's frustrating."

"The agency feels your frustration, Mrs. Dane . . . I mean, Ginger. Killian has been my partner for years. We're all worried about him. Both of them." He coughed. "I need to ask you a couple questions, if I may?"

"Fine. Of course. I'd be glad to help in any way I can."

"Has Ms. Jeffries been struggling for money lately? Acting strange. Anything out of the ordinary you can pinpoint, or put a finger on?"

The woman opened her mouth to say something, then hesitated. Dan couldn't help but notice her eyes narrowed slightly. "Robyn owns her own business. While she isn't rolling in money, she's no criminal. She leads a very happy existence. What is this about, officer? Where is this leading?"

He held his hands up in the air in surrender, and forced out a little laugh. All of a sudden small talk didn't sound so bad. "Hey, I'm just on a fact-finding mission. Don't shoot the messenger." If she acted this way about a friend, he was convinced she'd be an absolute pit bull when that baby of hers arrived.

"Well, you have wasted your time on this fact-finding mission. Robyn is honest. You won't find a more upstanding person than her. She's also loyal and giving and kind."

He nodded. "I'm sure she's all those things. That's wonderful to hear. We're just exploring all options. I didn't mean to upset you. I'm sorry."

"Well, don't talk trash about my best friend. She didn't assist in this bank robbery. She's the victim. Let's not forget that, shall we?" Ginger Danelli pushed her bulky form off the chair, stomach leading the way, and walked toward the front door.

This meeting was over. He sighed and rubbed his hand against the back of his neck, trying to ease the knot that had formed days ago and wasn't abating. He did learn one thing today. If Robyn Jeffries was involved in any way, her friend wouldn't give up her secrets in a million years.

The black bear, growing more agitated by the second if the sound of his growl was any indication, reared up on its hind legs, clawing the air with paws that looked to be the size of dinner plates. He towered over their heads, standing at least seven feet tall.

"Oh shit. We're in trouble." Robyn's mouth went dry, her hands shook, her stomach clenched. All she could see were claws and fangs. McKnight didn't matter anymore. She and Killian were going to be mauled. It would be a death much more painful than a quick bullet in the back.

"God, I hate bears." When she was seven, Herman had taken her to the zoo. She was having the time of her life when two men had shown up beside them. Herman had promised her he'd be right back after he talked to the nice men. He'd left her there for two very long hours. Just her and the stinking bears.

Robyn wasn't strong enough, or good enough, to handle this alone. All her life's inadequacies bore down on her.

Screw the past.

If she didn't deal with this, they died. She dug down deep inside of her and found the courage to handle the two very real threats to her and Killian's lives. The bear in front of them, and the bastard closing in behind them. Maybe the pair would take care of each other.

With that thought in mind, Robyn tightened her grip on Killian. "When I say three, we're going to move over to the left very slowly."

Killian didn't answer.

"Killian, do you hear me?" She didn't dare take her eyes off the bear, now down on all fours and swaying back and forth like he was thinking about charging. "We're going to move to the left. Repeat what I just said." Her heart thumped painfully in her chest. So much depended on doing this just right. If Killian stumbled, the bear just might assume they were dinner or a threat, and attack. Their movements needed to be slow and methodical.

"I'm not deaf. Move . . . left," Killian repeated.

"Good. That's right . . . I mean that's correct. We're going to move to the left. One . . . two . . . three."

She inched Killian along with her, step by painstaking step. She moved them so slowly, she hoped the bear wouldn't even know they were moving. And she thought the rocks had been difficult. This was torture. Knowing that at any second the animal could charge, and there was nothing they could do to defend themselves. All she had as a weapon was the broken nail file. Pretty damn useless against a four-hundred-pound critter with dinner on his mind.

The burly bear kept his nose pointed toward them as they moved. He growled deep in his throat, curled back his lips and bared his fangs again. Robyn's heart lurched, thinking that any second he'd charge. She kept on moving to the left. She didn't have time to stop and wait out the bear.

When they had moved far enough to the left for her satisfaction, Robyn searched the ground. When she found a couple of rocks, she released Killian, praying he'd stand on his own for a few seconds. Slowly she bent down to the ground. With her heart in her throat, a prayer on her lips, and a rock in each hand, she lobbed them at the animal, hoping she'd hurt him enough to scare him off, but no more than that.

"Go. Get out of here," she called out, as loud as she dared.

If a bear could look startled, this one did, Robyn thought. He backed up a few steps, did his swaying back and forth thing again. Robyn bent down and grabbed a few more rocks. She lobbed them, hitting him on the back and the side. He let out an affronted bear sound and spun, running in the other direction. The exact direction that would lead him straight into the path of one ugly thief by the name of McKnight.

Robyn threw her hands up in the air and screamed silently. Killian swayed on his feet next to her. She threw her arms around him, holding him steady. "I did it, Killian. I got rid of the bear."

He acknowledged her with little more than a nod. Robyn's triumph disintegrated. One danger was out of the way, but they weren't out of the woods. She slapped a hand against her forehead at her own Freudian slip. She didn't think they'd ever get out of these damn woods.

Without Killian for navigation, she had to rely on her own instincts. She moved them in a downward direction, knowing that would lead them home.

They'd gone a few feet when, through the trees, she heard a ferocious growl and a man yelling. The report of a gun caused Robyn to flinch. The two predators had found each other. That would teach them to scare the death out of her. They deserved each other. As much as she despised bears, she couldn't help but feel sorry for him. She hoped he had gotten away safely. He was just defending his territory, while McKnight was just evil.

The bear, if he had gotten to McKnight, might slow him down, but Robyn couldn't afford to wait around and see if it would stop him completely. She cringed at the thought of death by those claws and sharp teeth. God, that could have easily been her and Killian.

She tried to move Killian at a faster pace. What if

McKnight had just served as an appetizer? What if he simply whetted the bear's appetite for more people meat?

Distance, and fast, was the answer. If they could only run. If Killian could only help her. If, if, if. It wasn't going to happen. Not now. Not with his massive blood loss. She shot a sideways glance at the makeshift bandage. The sleeves she'd recently shoved in there seemed to be holding their own. They were bloody, but not totally soaked.

After a while, they came to another clearing. It had to be about noon if the high, overhead sun was an indication. She didn't see how, but Killian kept moving. Tired herself, she wondered at his stamina, his training. It must have been that which kept him putting one foot in front of the other, when anyone else would have given up. Despite checking behind her every so often, she hadn't heard any indication that McKnight still followed them. That didn't mean he didn't, though. Robyn wouldn't be able to relax until they were home, Killian's wound was stitched and she'd had about a week's worth of rest.

She eased Killian down to the ground and leaned him against a tree. Out of fear, she'd pushed them faster than she should. They wouldn't be able to go much farther. After assuring herself that Killian was as comfortable as she could make him, she walked over to the tiny stream that gurgled next to where they sat.

Cupping her hands into the frigid flow, she brought the water to her mouth and drank. God, she hadn't realized how thirsty she'd been. Hunger was another issue, but she pushed it out of her mind. They could live quite a while without food. Water was necessary.

With that in mind, she scooped another handful of water and walked over to where Killian lay, careful not to spill any along the way. Ninety percent of the water had seeped out between her fingers by the time she got to his side. "Oh, God. How do I do this?" Frustrated, she opened her hands above his mouth and just let the water drip down. His lips parted. "That's it. Good."

"I can do it, Robyn. I'm not a baby." Fingers shaking, he cupped his hands around hers.

"I never said you were a baby. I'm just trying to help. I'm doing what I know how to do in order to survive."

He leaned his head back against the tree and sighed. "I know. Sorry. You're doing a great job." His eyes slipped shut.

Exhausted. Scared. Not sure what to do next, she plopped down beside Killian. How was she supposed to keep McKnight off their trail? Better yet, how was she supposed to keep them alive when Killian kept falling in and out of consciousness? What if he developed a fever?

Florence Nightingale be damned. She had nothing on Robyn. Heart in throat, she reached out a hand and felt his forehead. No fever. Whatever she was doing must have been working. Not that she was doing much of anything. Such a feeling of relief washed over her that tears pricked her eyes. Her nose started running and she reached into her pocket to find a tissue. Instead she came back with a handful of leaves speckled with dried blood. "What the hell?" That's when the idea hit her. Instead of cleaning up the trail, she should make a new one. She jumped off the ground.

Killian opened one eye. "What are you doing now?"

"I'm going to make a false trail that will lead McKnight away from us."

"Good idea. Let me help." He tried to stand, but couldn't even make it. He sagged back against the tree.

"That's okay. I'll take care of it. We have to stay put for a while. With any luck, McKnight is as tired as we are. Especially if the bear got to him. If the bastard is wounded, we're on a level playing field for a change. If he's not, we're screwed."

"We're not screwed. You're doing fine." She could tell he hadn't been so willing to give this information by the spark of fire in his eyes. It had to annoy him to be so useless and dependent on a female.

"Hang tight." Digging the broken metal nail file out of her back pocket, Robyn ran as far away from Killian as she dared without getting lost, then took the file's sharp end and jabbed it into the fleshy part of her palm.

She flinched, shook her hand to pump the blood flow, then squeezed the wounded flesh so blood dripped on some leaves. Robyn left a trail in the opposite direction from where they really were, praying like mad that it would at least buy them some time.

McKnight was no dummy, but even a smart person could be suckered once in a while. She considered herself smart, and being suckered once was more than enough.

After scouring the area to make sure McKnight wasn't around, she headed back toward Killian. As much as she tried to keep it at bay, that same feeling of helplessness washed over her again the second she caught sight of Killian propped up a little crookedly against a tree.

Keep him comfortable. Let him get rest. That's all she could do right now. She knelt down in front of him, took off his cap and brushed a lock of wayward auburn hair off his forehead. At her touch, his eyes shot open and he stared straight at her.

"I think it will work," she whispered. Before the words had left her lips, his eyes were closed again.

Robyn glanced at the sky through the overhead trees that reached ever upward for what seemed like miles. She'd never felt so alone. She couldn't count the times she'd come home to an empty house after school and spent the evening by herself.

No time to dwell on the past. Killian was here. She wasn't alone, and there was still some daylight left. Time to move. She pushed them, but at a slower pace, for what felt like hours. When dusk started to fall, she knew they needed to settle down for the night. It may have been June, but June in the mountains still got cold when the sun dropped. With no coats—she looked down at her bare stomach and now sleeveless midriff T-shirt—they were going to be chilly. She doubted it would get below freezing, but there would be a definite nip in the air.

Helping Killian to sit again, she paused and rubbed her forehead, knowing there was nothing she could do about the weather. Her gaze drifted to the bandage around Killian's middle. The blood had dried and darkened. It appeared as if the bleeding had stopped altogether, thank God.

She wished she could wash the bandages in a creek, but it was full of icky organisms. Beside, if she took the bandages off, they risked the wound bleeding again. She placed a hand against his stomach and hung her head. Bone-tired, she sat there a minute just staring at nothing. She jumped out of her skin when Killian grabbed her wrist. His grip was tight, but not painful.

"What are you doing?" he asked.

"Relax. I'm just sitting here."

"Don't . . . touch. Leave the bandages in place."

She narrowed her eyes. "Don't rankle me, mister. I've had a very bad day. I wasn't about to remove the bandages. It looks like the bleeding has stopped."

This little weekend getaway must have been making her tough. She didn't even blink when Killian's intense brown gaze bore into hers.

Okay. Who was she kidding? She wasn't as tough as she thought. She'd been holding her breath the entire time. She was sick and tired of being in charge. Not wanting him to see the pity party she was holding for herself, she got up and scanned the area around them.

A quick peek behind some bushes showed a clearing just big enough for two bodies to curl up tight together. As cold as she knew it was going to get tonight, that's all the room they needed.

Edging that tiny little clearing was a bush with berries on it. "Score." Robyn's stomach growled. She reached for the plump little fruit, dangling all over the thin branches, like an offering from the gods.

Her hands shook from hunger as she plucked the wild currants from the branches, then popped one into her mouth, closing her eyes in ecstasy. Heaven. Sheer heaven. She chewed slowly, savoring every single taste sensation as the juice ran down her throat.

After she'd picked another handful, she walked back to Killian. "Can you open your eyes, Killian?" He needed food worse than she did. Nutrition would ease him faster on to the road to recovery.

A groan escaped his lips, and he opened his eyes, staring at her with a fixed gaze. "Of course I can. I'm not an invalid."

Robyn rolled her eyes. "Can you eat a little bit? I've found us some wild berries."

His eyes closed again for a second, then opened. His lips parted ever so slightly, and she took this as a yes. She slipped a currant into his mouth, her fingers brushing against his warm lips.

He chewed, his eyes never leaving hers. She was thrilled he appeared to be getting better, but his intense gaze unnerved her. She fed him a few more berries, then stood. "I'm going to get you some more water." They'd been following the same creek most of the afternoon. "Be right back."

Evening began to drift into darkness. Robyn helped Killian into their little hidden nest. "We need to keep going," he insisted, even though his face had paled from just moving ten feet.

"Believe it or not, Secret Agent Man, you're slowing me down. We have to rest. Tomorrow we'll move faster. Make up for lost time."

He looked affronted. "I've never slowed down anyone in my life."

"There's a first time for everything." Weary to the point of collapsing herself, Robyn curled up next to him, suppressing a shudder as the temperature had started to drop with the setting sun.

Modesty served no purpose after all they'd been through. She slipped an arm around his broad chest and spooned Killian. To hell with the fact that they'd known each other less than two days. They were two of the longest days of her life. That had to count for something. Arms lined with goose bumps, Robyn pressed a little closer, trying to suck up some of Killian's body heat. With luck they'd both be too damn tired to even feel the cold.

"Robyn?"

"Yeah?"

"I don't mean to slow you down."

She squeezed her eyes shut against a sudden prick of tears, then opened them and stared at his back. "I know."

"You're doing a good job keeping us alive."

"Thanks." It was all she needed to hear. After those words, she was able to relax her body for the first time in what felt like forever. She should have been listening for night noises that indicated someone or something approaching.

She couldn't. Despite her senses running on overload, she fell fast asleep the second her eyes drifted shut.

It must have been the middle of the night. Something had jolted Robyn awake out of a dead sleep. She tried to still her breathing so she could hear what had made her stir. A twig snapped not far from their spot. Her heart stopped, then beat a rapid pace in her chest. Out of nowhere, a hand slipped over her mouth. She glanced toward Killian. He was sitting up, one finger over his lips, warning her to be quiet.

No duh, she thought. Instead she just nodded. He slipped the warmth of his hand away, and they both sat in silence, side by side.

"Let's go back for the van," a voice said.

"Good idea." She recognized McKnight. The first voice belonged to a stranger. Great. McKnight had help. She exchanged a glance with Killian. What did this all mean?

The footsteps trudging through the brush grew farther and farther away. Robyn heaved a sigh of relief, then realized her hand was clenched upon Killian's thigh. She released her grip, then threw him an apologetic look and shrugged her shoulders. "Sorry," she mouthed.

True to his silent type persona, Killian didn't say a word.

"Are you feeling better?" She pressed her face closer to his to see him better in the darkness. "I think you look better."

He turned over and lay back down on his side. "I'll let you know in the morning. If they're going back for the van, we might as well rest. Go back to sleep." If she hadn't heard it with her own ears, she would have never believed he'd told her she was doing a good job earlier. The man was back to his gruff self.

It didn't matter if two men were after them. With a smile on her face, Robyn once again spooned Killian and wrapped her arm around him. He was going to be all right. And best of all, she wouldn't have to rely on her own company tomorrow. She'd gotten good and tired of listening to herself hours ago.

The chilly morning air faded into the hot bright sun of afternoon. They'd been walking for mile after mile, hour after hour, with only a handful of stops in between. The woman had to be starving. Lord only knew, Killian's own stomach growled so loudly the whole forest had to hear it. The wild currants they'd eaten before they'd moved on this morning hadn't lasted long.

He had to give Robyn credit. A lesser woman would have crumbled long ago. Though he'd shortened his stride, he hadn't slowed down that much. His desire to capture the scumbag who'd kidnapped them, burned within him. He had to get back to headquarters as soon as possible.

It was dangerous now, because McKnight might be in front of them instead of behind. He could easily double back and surprise them. Was one man on foot and one in a vehicle? To compound the situation, McKnight could have stopped for the night like they had. There was no way of knowing whether he was behind them or in front of them.

Killian kept his senses on red alert, scanning the area around them at all times. The pain in his midsection burned like a red-hot poker, but at least he was lucid today. The overnight rest had rejuvenated him, and he felt like he could go all day if need be.

A glance over his shoulder showed him Robyn was still trudging along behind. Dirt smudged her nose. Sweat dampened her T-shirt, or what was left of her T-shirt. Tangled hair clung to her cheeks, and her jeans were splattered in mud. All in all, Killian thought she looked pretty cute—for a woman who annoyed the hell out of him. Actually, she didn't annoy him. He annoyed himself. She'd taken care of them, kept them out of danger when he couldn't. All morning, he'd found himself not able to take his eyes off her. He'd never acted this way with a case before. He was supposed to be watching out for her, not watching her. What the hell was wrong with him? He didn't feel feverish, but who knew?

"Let's take a break for a few minutes." He sat down on a fallen log and stretched his long legs out in front of him, pressing a hand against the bandages holding him together.

Not even bothering to seek out a seat, Robyn plopped down on the ground and stretched out on her back, one arm over her eyes. After a pregnant silence, she spoke. "I'm so hungry I could eat a pine tree."

"Help yourself. I'm going to wait for steak and eggs, maybe a side of hash browns. Strong black coffee with a side of sausage and bacon sounds damn good, too." They both whispered their words, knowing sound carried in the wilderness. They were hungry, not stupid.

"Pancakes with pure maple syrup. I won't settle for anything less. What the heck, heap on a helping of strawberries and whipped cream." The tip of her pink tongue darted out and she licked her lips.

Killian sat mesmerized. He couldn't move, couldn't breathe. Food was now the furthest thought from his mind. He felt like he'd been kicked in the gut, which was the last thing he needed since his midsection already sported a huge gash. Uncomfortable with the path his body was leading him down, he jumped up. Or he tried to. Jumping now consisted of pushing himself off the ground like an old man. "Let's go."

Robyn groaned. "I thought you said we could stop for a couple minutes? It has not even been thirty seconds."

"I changed my mind."

"Slave driver."

They walked in silence for a while. The sounds of the

mountains echoed around them. Dried foliage crackled under their feet. Birds flitted from tree to tree, calling out to their mates. Occasionally, a chipmunk darted across their trail and scurried into hiding.

"You're not a man of many words, are you?"

Killian swiped an arm across his sweaty brow. "Nope."

"So what made you want to work for the FBI?"

"What made you want to be a janitor?"

"Sanitary engineer," she corrected him. "I don't know. It's pretty good money, I guess."

"Money's what drives you?"

"Not enough to make me want to rob a bank, but yes, money and security. I own the company."

The footpath was wide enough at this point that they could walk side by side. Killian shot her a glance out of the corner of his eye. "Security?"

She shoved a hand through her hair. A sad smile tugged at her lips. "Herman, my dad, wasn't around much when I was growing up. This job, my business, offered me a stable environment I wasn't used to."

For a few minutes, neither talked. "You're not going to answer me, are you?"

Killian didn't like talking about himself. It made him uncomfortable, and reminded him of his mother and father. His secrets were buried deep within him. They were going to stay that way. He coughed. "What was your question?"

Her laugh told him his play hadn't worked. She knew he was evading the question. So the woman was intuitive as well as pretty. He'd have to remember to get up early to pull one over on her. Not that he planned on being around her in the morning.

"Never mind. How much farther do we have to go?"

"I'm guessing thirty miles."

"So what you're saying is, by the time we're finished here, I could enter the Boston Marathon and treat it like a cake-walk, right?"

He laughed. "Something like that." Taking his black FBI ball cap off, he swiped a hand through his sweaty hair.

"Oh, my God!" she uttered in a theatrical whisper.

"What now?"

"You do have red hair. I thought so, but every time you had your hat off, I was too busy to look or the lighting was horrid. Granted, it's dark red, but red nonetheless."

Irritation flooded through him. "So?"

"So, that explains it."

"Explains what?" He stopped in his tracks and threw her an exasperated look.

"Your temperament."

Rolling his eyes, he started moving again. The woman was too much. "I don't have a temperament," he growled.

"Oh, yes, you do."

"Did anyone ever tell you, you talk too much? We're supposed to be quiet out here."

"People tell me that all the time. They also tell me it is part of my charm." Her voice smacked of laughter, which irritated him even more.

Killian found himself wondering what Robyn would do if he turned around and planted a wet kiss on her, just to shut her up. The more he thought about it, the more he decided he'd discard the idea. Knowing her, she would analyze his technique, judge his performance.

He turned around abruptly, following up on his plan to ignore the woman's appeal. Through the trees he spotted movement. He pushed Robyn to the ground and squatted next to her, easing a hand against his injury. It had been too easy. He knew McKnight had to show up eventually. He

94

waited with bated breath while the sounds drew closer.

When an eight-point buck pushed through the trees, Killian hung his head. He was losing his touch. He didn't even bother looking at Robyn when he pushed them forward again.

The day dragged on, yet night descended swiftly in the mountains. One second the sun set over the jagged peaks, the next it slipped behind, leaving another bone-penetrating cold in its wake.

Robyn rubbed her hands up and down her arms. "We need to find shelter. I don't think I can spend another night sleeping on that hard cold ground."

Part of Killian wanted to stop. He'd driven them hard. Another part screamed at him to continue on down the mountain. Letting McKnight and his accomplice wander around loose was a mistake he couldn't afford to make—and Killian despised mistakes. "In a little while."

He heard her deep sigh, but she kept going despite any pain or discomfort she must have felt. Thank God she had on sensible shoes instead of the high-heeled kind women often favored.

"What's that over there?"

"Where?" Killian squinted in the darkness. A dark shape loomed behind the trees. "Might be a cabin."

"Hot damn." She rubbed her hands together. "What are we waiting for?"

"Hold on a second." Stalling her, he grabbed the soft flesh of her upper arm. "You can't just barge into someone's cabin without notifying them."

"I'll send a telegram." Dark eyebrows lifted. "Do you mind loosening your clutches?"

His grip relaxed, but he didn't let go. "I'm serious, Robyn. It's called breaking and entering."

95

"Someone might be home."

"There are no lights on."

"Maybe they're sleeping. I've had enough of this outdoorsy stuff. Arrest me if you have to, but I'm checking it out."

Stubborn. Bullheaded. Obstinate. And she said *he* had a fiery temperament. The woman needed a strong man to look after her. Funny, he didn't remember volunteering for the job. What she needed was someone to put her over their lap and administer a good solid spanking. But thinking about her on his lap gave him a rush of emotion that was far from parental. With a shake of his head, he followed her silhouette through the pine trees.

She knocked on the door. After a few minutes of silence, no one answered. "Help me find a key." On tiptoe, she ran one hand over the door ledge.

"That's aiding and abetting. Can't do it." He folded his arms over his chest and leaned against the trunk of an aspen, watching her progress. He figured he'd give her five minutes to come up empty, then they'd continue on their journey.

She lifted up the doormat—looked under flowerpots—moved a dozen boulders, before she planted her hands on her hips and tapped an impatient foot against the brick sidewalk. "Well, this is just ridiculous. Don't these people know they're supposed to leave a key where anyone can find it?"

"Guess not. Come on, let's go."

"Wait, I have an idea." Bending, she grabbed a rock.

Killian straightened. His training kicked in. "Put the rock down, Robyn." In slow, soothing tones, he attempted to coax her out of her decision like he was negotiating with terrorists.

Tossing the rock into the air, she caught it and smiled. "I'm cold." She tossed it and caught it again. "I'm so hungry I could eat a horse." The rock made another trip, a little higher this time, but she palmed it easily. "I'm tired enough to sleep for a week."

"Think about what you're doing." Dread snaked along his spine. He took a tiny step forward. She wasn't rational. Why hadn't he recognized the signs? She'd been quiet for miles. If he hadn't been worrying about doing his job, keeping an eye out for McKnight, he would have realized it sooner. Quiet, for her, meant something was wrong. They could have stopped. He could have let her catch a few winks.

"Oh, there's nothing to think about. You're just acting like a lawman instead of a human being." She eyed him up and down with distaste. "You can keep going if you like. I'm staying right here."

Killian lurched forward and snaked his arms around her body, trapping her arms at her waist. "I can't let you do this." He hadn't expected his own reaction to touching her. Electric. Sizzling. Hypnotic. So much so, that not even realizing what he did, he immediately released her as if he'd been burned.

She pulled back her arm like she was going to pitch a baseball and let the rock sail. Shattering glass interrupted the hushed stillness of the summer night.

Chapter 6

"Are you nuts?"

Robyn snorted at the disbelieving look on Hart's face. "I've been a sport about all of this. I'm beyond tired, beyond hungry and beyond dirty." Glass scraped her skin as she reached through the broken pane and turned the lock from the inside. "Can you wait until I've had a decent meal and at least, oh, I don't know, ten minutes' sleep before you have me committed?" She mentally tacked "beyond cranky" to the list.

Robyn counted to three. True to form, Killian yanked off his hat and ran a hand through his hair. His habits were becoming too familiar to her. Annoyed with herself as much as with him, she withdrew her arm, then opened the door.

"Yoo-hoo . . . anybody home?"

The only sound was Killian's booted footsteps behind her. "Get real, Banks. You announced your presence the second that rock made contact with the window."

"You've got a point, Secret Agent Man." Glass crunched under her feet as she made her way across the threshold. Running her hands along the timbered wall, she searched in the dark for a switch plate. "Bingo." The cabin filled with instant light.

Robyn squeezed her eyes shut against the bright glare.

"No. Turn the damn light off."

Contrite, Robyn hit the switch. How could she have been such an idiot? "I'm sorry. I totally forgot about McKnight." He'd been in her thoughts every single breathing moment today. How she'd forgotten about him for even a second was a mystery.

"We can't forget. Ever. We need to get out of here . . . now." There was no mistaking the look of condemnation that flashed across Killian's face. "But first, look for a phone." Refusing to come in any farther, he remained by the open doorway, obviously more than happy to let her do all the law-breaking.

"What—no phone hidden in the sole of your shoe?" At his look of irritation, she swept the room with her hand. "Granted it's a nice log cabin, but it's still a log cabin, Hart. I'm sure you don't seriously think there's going to be a phone here, do you?" Robyn remained where she was, arms folded across her chest. "Why don't you just come in and make yourself comfortable on that couch? Your eyes are starting to get glassy again. I know you've got to be in pain. Maybe they've got some aspirin or something lying around."

A nerve ticked in his jaw. Hesitation flashed in his eyes. "I don't need aspirin. It's breaking and entering, not to mention theft," he reminded her. Even in the growing darkness, his eyes snapped with fire.

"You've informed me of my many violations already, officer. Get over it. We're following jungle rules now. It is called survival." Yep, Robyn thought. Red hair. Fiery temperament to go along with it.

"Since you are so intent on staying, let me search the rooms first." He strode through the cabin checking every nook and cranny.

Before the lights had gone out, Robyn had noticed a candle and book of matches on the table. Hands held out in front of her, she groped her way across the room. The smell of sulfur tickled her nose from the lit match. After the candle was flickering, she thought she'd better ask if it was okay.

He walked over and snuffed out the flame with two fingers. "A candle will be as noticeable as a bulb out here, so no lights, no candles, not even a match."

"Fine. Fine. Whatever you say. Where are you going?" She may have told him earlier he could leave if he wanted to, but her heart sank. She didn't want to be left alone. As irritating as he was, she liked Killian's company.

"I'm going to do a perimeter check. Make sure McKnight or someone else isn't lurking around the cabin."

"You're going to leave me all alone?" Too late, he'd already left. Robyn glanced over her shoulder, convinced she'd heard noises coming from some of the interior rooms, even though he'd already searched. She inched toward the door and waited for Killian to come back.

—Within minutes, his shadow emerged from the darkness and he walked through the door. Relief flooded through Robyn. He scrubbed his hands over his face, which looked pinched and tired. "All clear."

She nodded and walked back into the living room. He stayed by the door.

He'd rather go hungry, tired and cold and remain in pain than *bend* the law. She smiled to herself. The words "stuffed shirt" flitted through her mind. Trying to hide her amusement, she turned and walked into the tiny kitchen. "Can you believe this? They have a dishwasher. And a microwave."

"Too bad they don't have a phone," he grumbled.

She ignored him. The refrigerator beckoned. Robyn's stomach growled. Her mouth watered. Almost lovingly, she ran her fingers over the smooth, polished white surface. "Please, Lord, let it be stocked to the gills." Grabbing the handle, she pulled the door just a tiny crack so the light wouldn't show too much. She peeked inside. A laugh erupted from her lips. "Hallelujah! I have died and gone to food lover's heaven." She took a cellophane-wrapped steak out of the freezer and danced around the compact kitchen with the frozen package.

Killian dashed in, a scowl marring his handsome face. "Put that back!" The tiny room grew even smaller, dwarfed by the mere size of the man.

Robyn blinked. Here she was starving to death, with salvation at her fingertips, and he was denying her the right to eat? "Says who?"

"Says me," he growled. "I'm in charge here, remember?" He jabbed a thumb into his chest.

She neatly sidestepped him when he reached for the meat, placing the oak table between them. "No, I don't remember. I think, for a while there, I was the one calling the shots while you were busy bleeding to death and mumbling incoherently. Right now my stomach is in charge and it's saying, *Beef . . . it's what's for dinner.*"

She waved a hand around the room, encompassing all the luxuries within. "These people aren't going to miss some measly steaks, Killian. You need to relax. You take life way too seriously."

In a fit of defiance, Robyn marched over to the microwave, shoved the steak inside and jabbed the defrost button. Snow would fall on the Fourth of July before she let this man come between her stomach and some much-needed food.

"I want no part of this." Killian grabbed a hunk of wood he found, and a hammer and some nails out of the toolbox in the corner of the kitchen. Careful not to pound too loudly, he covered the hole Robyn had made in the windowpane. He completed the job entirely in the dark since he'd made Robyn blow out the candle. The storm appeared to be clearing since a little bit of moonlight made its way through the cracks in the drapes. When he finished pounding the last nail, he stormed back into the living room, planting himself on the couch.

It was all he could do to sit still. Even though he'd been walking all day, he fought the urge to get up and pace the room. With every second that passed, the kidnapper was getting away with his crime, and Little Miss Susie Homemaker wanted to waste time cooking a five-course dinner?

A gurgle sounded from the region of his stomach, reminding him how weak, tired and hungry he was. He sighed. Maybe Robyn was right. Maybe he did take life too seriously. But, dammit, life was serious. One wrong move and a person could be dead before they knew what hit them. He pinched the bridge of his nose, fought memories. One false move, one wrong turn was all it took to yank a person's dreams out from underneath.

Besides, he had a job to do. He sat there in the dark, listening to the sounds around him, and contemplated his life. The FBI was his entire existence. His reason for breathing—for getting up in the morning—for going to bed at night. If he couldn't do it right, if the criminals got away, what the hell was the point?

The microwave dinged. Moments later, the smell of broiling meat filled the air. A hunger pang seized his stomach and refused to subside. Hell, the woman was cooking it, he might as well eat it. "I like mine rare," he called out.

Her petite form appeared in the doorway between the kitchen and living room. With the help of the moonlight, he watched one shapely eyebrow rise, but she didn't say a word. Turning, she disappeared.

For some reason, the kiss he'd given her at the shack sprang into his mind. Even in the confusion and panic, he'd never forget the feel of her lips. Light. Soft. Perfect. Had it been a pity kiss, like she'd suggested? Not willing to go there, he pushed the thought out of his mind.

Instead, he listened to the sound of banging pots and pans as his gaze swept around the room. A stabbing pain grabbed him in the gut and he flinched. He glanced at the throw pillows, just begging for him to lay down his head. Maybe he'd stretch out on the sofa for a few minutes. He'd been complicating his injury by pushing them as hard as he had all day. It wouldn't hurt to relax a little.

Just as he lay down, Robyn appeared in the doorway again, looking domestic in a "kiss the cook" apron, one hand on her hip. Guilt swept over him. He shouldn't be touching anything in the cabin. Stretching out and making himself feel at home left a bitter taste in his mouth. "I'm letting my wound get some rest," he said in defense of his actions.

"Whatever you say." She flashed him a crooked smile, then left.

Killian felt the urge to *kiss the cook,* like the apron suggested. But, he reminded himself, she wasn't his type, or maybe he wasn't hers. Confused, he took off his ball cap, flung it to the other side of the sofa, and ran a hand through his hair. He sighed as the pain in his wound eased a little.

If he had to be honest, he didn't know what his type was—or if he even had a type anymore. The last woman he'd dated wanted him to give up his career because she thought it was too dangerous.

Instead of his career, he'd given up her. Actually, except for an occasional one-night stand, he'd divested himself of all women. They got in his way, made him lose concentration when he needed it most.

He didn't have time to worry about a wife. He couldn't take his job easy, play it safe so he wouldn't leave behind a widow. Since Killian's job demanded taking chances, initiating risks, living on the edge, he refused to get involved.

That wasn't the kind of life a woman should have to put up with.

His "hiking" partner breezed past the sofa. In a weak moment his gaze caught and followed her movement.

"Steaks will be done in a couple minutes. Can I use a candle in the bathroom since there's no window in there?"

At least she'd asked. She was finally learning who the boss was. About time. "Sure."

He watched her out of the corner of his eye, his much-needed rest forgotten for the moment. Her mere presence forced his gaze to follow her. He couldn't have stopped himself even if he'd wanted to.

He knew, because he wanted to.

A woman hadn't drawn him in like this in years. Maybe he was just fascinated by the contradictions she exuded.

She was tiny, yet her personality loomed larger than life. He took in her dirt-stained, rumpled clothing and tangled brown curls. He was starting to think of her as not just cute, but downright beautiful—sexy—desirable. Two brownish handprints dominated the denim covering each thigh. Blood? His blood? She'd taken care of him. Kept him out of harm's way when he wasn't able. He socked the pillow behind his head, trying to get rid of a lump. Lack of food was clouding his thinking.

When Robyn disappeared inside the bathroom, Killian settled down lower on the sofa, exhaustion hitting him hard. Just as his chin sank to his chest and his eyes slipped shut, a muffled oath escaped through the crack in the bathroom door. It wasn't very loud, but it awakened all of Killian's senses. What if McKnight had entered through a back window?

Heart pounding, he leapt to his feet, one hand pressed against the cut at his waist, and raced to the bathroom, yanking open the door.

He peered into the marbled interior cautiously, not knowing what to expect. "What's wrong?"

Robyn stood with her face inches from a gilt-framed mirror, a candle just as close. "Oh, my God. Oh, Lord. Why didn't you tell me?"

"Tell you what?" This slip of a woman confused the hell out of him. Heart racing like the speed of light, he moved farther into the bathroom, closing the door behind him to keep the light from escaping, and leaned against the sink to ease the stitch in his side. Searching her face, he tried to discover the problem—look for blood, or whatever had made her gasp. He half-expected to see McKnight standing there in the bathroom with her.

"Did I look like this all day?" She pointed to her face, and glared at his reflection staring back at her in the mirror. "How could you let me walk around like this all day, Hart? How could you?"

Killian jammed his fingers through his hair. "I don't know what you're talking about, Banks." He scanned her porcelain smooth skin in the candlelight. "You look fine." She looked more than fine. He grabbed the edge of the sink harder, to quell the urge to pull her into his arms, bury his face in the hollow of her neck, drown in her essence.

"Fine? You think I look fine? I look . . . I look . . . for God's sake, I look like a human unmade bed."

The thought that image invoked proved too much for Killian to handle. His body hardened with desire. She didn't look like an unmade bed—she looked like a woman who'd just been loved.

Disheveled hair. Naked, pouty lips. Sleepy bedroom eyes.

He suppressed a growl. It shook him to the core to discover he wanted to be the one who'd just made love to her.

Setting the candleholder by the sink, she wrenched open a

drawer. Rummaged through it. "There's got to be something around here. Lipstick. Powder. God, I'll take anything."

Killian rolled his eyes. Women. "Makeup isn't going to change anything. I've seen you naked for the past forty-eight hours." He realized his mistake the second the words left his lips.

She stopped in mid-search and glanced at him, her brown eyes wide with surprise. "Why, Killian Hart, is it possible that you're blushing?"

His cheeks grew hot. He averted his gaze. Studied the jungle print on the shower curtain. "Special agents don't blush. And I meant naked as in . . . your face free of all that . . ." He moved his hand in a circular motion, trying to find the correct word. ". . . goop females find so necessary."

A mental picture of Robyn popped into his head. Naked. Writhing under him as he drove his hardened body into her welcoming warmth.

Get a grip on reality, Hart. Smack dab in the middle of a case is not the time to get involved with a woman. Killian spun on his heel and left the room. "Don't burn my steak, Banks. And blow out that candle before you leave the bathroom."

Robyn couldn't dig up a single lick of makeup from the bathroom. She tried to fluff her hair, but threw her arms up in the air and gave up when the unruly curls just bounced back to where they'd been in the first place. Like Killian had said, he'd already seen her naked, so what did it matter if she looked like hell?

Even if he was devastatingly cute, he obviously placed his job before his women. Not that she was his woman. Not that she wanted to be his woman. She doubted he even had a woman. Not that she cared.

Leaving the bathroom moments after Killian had, she

marched past him with her head held high and her chin in the air. Plates, cups and utensils in hand, Robyn went from the kitchen to the dining room, purposely decorating the table with two place settings. Yes, she was using the cabin owner's dishes. She threw a surreptitious glance at Killian out of the corner of her eye, half-expecting him to make a scathing comment. Instead she found his eyes closed, one hand dangling over the edge of the sofa, his chest falling and rising with each deep breath that he took. The stiffness in her shoulders left. The sound of gentle snores escaped him, and Robyn couldn't fight the smile that flitted to her lips.

Now that she was in charge again, she went to each window in the cabin and scanned the perimeter outside, making sure she didn't see any shadows or mysterious forms moving about in the woods. When all looked clear, she went back to the kitchen and rescued the steaks before the oven broiled them to a crisp.

She had the table all set with the food before she went to wake up Killian. Kneeling down in front of the sofa, she hesitated before she reached out to tap his shoulder. "Secret Agent Man, it is time for dinner."

He shot to a sitting position, awake in less than a split second. "What's the matter?" She couldn't help but notice his hand went straight to the wound at his side. His laceration must have still been bothering him.

"Nothing's the matter," she said, noticing the way his long black lashes swept across his cheeks when he blinked the sleep out of his eyes.

"How long was I out? Why did you let me sleep?"

"You just had a quick cat nap." The word "cat" made her think of Brooklyn. She pushed the thought out of her mind. Worrying about her cat wouldn't help, and she knew Ginger was taking care of her. "I let you sleep because you needed it.

Dinner's ready. Why don't you come to the table?"

They sat down opposite each other, Killian's long legs caging hers beneath the small table. The moonlight lent the room a romantic atmosphere. She wondered if Killian thought so, too. He kept avoiding her gaze. Or maybe guilt was worming its way throughout his system because he had a stolen steak sitting smack dab in front of him.

"What are you waiting for? Dig in."

Killian cleared his throat. Glanced around him, as if he half-expected someone to slap him in handcuffs the second he cut into the meat. His stomach growled in the quiet room. He threw her an apologetic smile, picked up the knife and fork, and attacked the food in front of him.

Silence served as the main topic of dinner conversation. Killian couldn't help notice that Robyn ignored him, and instead concentrated on savoring every bite of the melt-in-your-mouth steak into which she bit.

What kind of game was she playing? "Do you have to do that?"

Robyn returned his scowl with equal hostility. "Do what?"

"Make those . . . noises?" She was driving him crazy.

"What noises?" She bit into another piece of steak and moaned with the sheer pleasure of breaking her daylong fast.

He pointed a fork at her. "That noise. That's what I'm talking about."

"Sorry. I didn't know my enjoyment of this *stolen* steak would upset you so much." She shot him a saccharine smile. "I'll try to keep it down."

"Good." Infernal female.

After eating in strained silence, Killian pushed his plate away. He stared at her a second, trying to figure her out. She looked uncomfortable with his fixed focus, since she toyed with the food on her plate, curled a lock of hair around her finger, shifted her gaze everywhere but at him. She opened her mouth to speak when a loud banging noise sounded outside.

Killian jumped up and ran around the table. "Get down," he ordered, pushing her underneath the table and out of the possible line of fire, just in case shots rang out. Here was something he could handle, he thought, while his heart settled down and his mind went to work.

Action.

Danger.

Females, like Robyn, only managed to confuse him. She served up the wrong kind of danger.

"Stay put."

"Where the hell are you going?" Robyn shot him a pleading look from those big eyes of hers, and grabbed his arm.

"I have to check it out."

"Don't be a damn hero. Remember you're still hurt, and he's got a gun."

Killian reached on top of the table and palmed a steak knife. He grunted. When would she realize he knew how to do his job? "Just do what I say. Don't move, and don't worry about me." He shook off her hand. For a second, he wanted to run a finger down the softness of her check. Just to reassure her. There was no other reason. He resisted the urge, and moved to the front door.

The knob cold in his grasp, he turned it, opened the door a crack and slipped out. His eyes had already adjusted to the dark. He skimmed the area, keeping to the shadows. A shuffling noise drew his attention around the corner of the cabin. He followed the front porch around, adrenaline rushing through his veins.

He rounded the corner, knife poised in front of him, ready

for anything. Ready to do battle with McKnight.

Instead of McKnight's tall frame, two little furry critters dumped over a garbage can in their haste to get away from a human. Killian expelled a rush of air, ran a hand through his hair and fought back a laugh. "Damn raccoons."

He walked around the entire perimeter of the cabin to make sure the raccoons were the only unwelcome trespassers. When he was satisfied all was well, he strode back inside, closing the door as quietly as when he'd gone out.

"Well?" Robyn was still under the table, hugging her knees to her chest. She'd chased away bears, staved off criminals, and tended to his wounds. He could tell by the way she was chewing on her bottom lip that she didn't even understand the breadth of her own bravery.

"All's clear. It was just a bunch of coons trying to get a free meal."

"You're telling me a little animal made all that noise?" She emerged from under the table, her arms wrapped around herself.

Killian drew his hands into fists, fighting the urge to hug her himself. "We have a long day ahead of us tomorrow." He headed for the bathroom, knowing he couldn't stay in the same room with her for a second longer without wanting to kiss her. "I'm taking a quick shower. Maintain a lookout and remember, no lights."

Cold water pounded down on Killian. It did nothing to alleviate his pain. Why couldn't he stop thinking about her? Since when did watching a woman eat, or pretty much just stand there, become such a turn-on?

He had to get her out of his head right now. Concentrate on a plan to get them back to Denver as soon as possible. He'd ignore her tomorrow. Not because he wanted to, but because he had to.

His career came first. He closed his eyes against the sting of the shower pulsating on his wound, and the memory of her pearly white teeth biting into the steak.

It would take every ounce of his training, but he'd forget about his unwanted response to her. He was on a case, dammit, and the case always came first. He couldn't allow himself to break the rules now.

Chapter 7

While Killian showered, Robyn poked around the cabin, discovering a washer and dryer tucked in a laundry room on the side of the house. Since her own clothes were mud-covered and sticking to her like a second layer, she stripped them off and borrowed an oversized T-shirt from one of the bedroom dressers.

Before she dumped her jeans into the washer, she couldn't help a shudder at the sight of her bloody handprints. That moment felt like light years away, but then again she knew she'd replay the memory over and over in her mind for years to come. Killian didn't even realize the magnitude of her fears. Nothing could scare an adrenaline junkie such as he was.

After hesitating one second, she tiptoed into the bathroom and gathered Killian's soiled clothes off the marbled floor. She left a pair of shorts and a T-shirt that looked like it might fit a man of his considerable size.

He'd been in the shower so long, she was tempted to peek behind the curtain to see if he was still alive. The mental image of his wet naked body sent her scurrying out of the room in a hurry.

Within minutes, the shower stopped. Killian's soaking wet head peeked out the door. "Where are my clothes?" he bellowed, if one could bellow in a quiet manner.

Robyn stood in the hallway, rolling her eyes at his baritone bluster. "I'm washing them. I put a clean outfit in there for you to wear."

"You're just making yourself right at home, aren't you?"

He shut the door and she heard him moving around in the small room.

"I'm sure the owners, if they knew the situation, wouldn't have wanted it any other way."

His loud hummppff served as his answer. When the door flew open a second later, she had to hop out of the way or get mowed down. "Couldn't you have found something bigger?" he demanded in evident irritation.

The "Trout Fishermen Do It In The Water" T-shirt looked two sizes too small. "It was the largest I could find." She tilted her head sideways, appreciating the way the material hugged every muscle in his broad chest. It may have been dark, but there was no mistaking the acres of rippling thigh, which the too-small khaki shorts exposed.

"Look what else I found," she said, holding out a handful of butterfly bandages. "Do you want me to put them on for you?" She reached out her free hand to lift the hem of his borrowed shirt.

He snatched the Band-Aids from her palm. "That's all right. I can handle it."

She'd been taking care of him for what seemed like forever. His immediate rebuff of her offer to help smarted. The smart-aleck comment wasn't her fault. "Sorry you have to go commando under those shorts, but I didn't think you'd want to borrow someone's underwear." Not giving him time to comment after his face turned red, she continued. "There are two bedrooms. Unless, of course, you want to take a blanket and sleep outside."

He'd already started walking down the hallway and into the living room, but at her words he stopped and turned around. "Since you've already touched, used, borrowed—"

"Don't forget stolen," Robyn added, remembering the mouthwatering steaks.

He raised one russet-colored eyebrow, still beaded with water from his shower. "—and stolen just about everything in this cabin, at this point I don't think spending a night in their beds is going to make a difference."

It hadn't made a difference in the beginning, either, but she wasn't about to tell him that. With his rigid code of conduct, he'd have a heart attack or something.

"I'll take the first watch." His voice sounded weary all of a sudden, and she wondered if he'd make it through the next couple of hours. "Get some sleep. We're getting up early tomorrow."

Her muscles groaned at the thought of more walking. "As soon as I throw the clothes in the dryer I'm hitting the sack."

"Good." His gaze roved up and down her body. "I'll wake you when I need you."

His words conjured up all kinds of images, none having to do with keeping a lookout for McKnight. The T-shirt she wore covered her almost to her knees, but she felt bare, exposed. It was almost as if he knew she had nothing on underneath. Her nipples puckered and she crossed her arms over her chest to hide the evidence from his all-seeing gaze.

She was too late. Passion heated his eyes. His nostrils flared. Scared all of a sudden, she turned on her heels. "I've got to check the laundry," she reminded him.

After dumping the load of clothes in the dryer, she padded to bed. Killian followed, close on her heels. "What are you doing? There are two bedrooms." She didn't want to sleep in the same room with Mr. Temptation.

"I can't protect you from a different room."

"I don't need protecting." Her hands found her hips. "I seem to remember me protecting you not too long ago."

"That was then. I was out of commission. This is now. I'm not."

Men like him didn't take no when they uttered commands. If she'd been too tired to even shower before bed, she was certainly too tired to argue with a man who insisted things always went his way. "You're not getting in the same bed."

"Wouldn't think of it."

Sleep. Now there was something with which she had no argument. Robyn crawled under the covers and sighed deeply. Sleep should have come easily. She flipped onto her stomach, punched the pillow into a different shape, and cursed the red-haired, hot-tempered, rule-toting Secret Agent Man keeping watch three short feet away. Would he ever need her the way she longed for him?

She stared at the ceiling for at least a good hour. It was all his fault she couldn't sleep. Why did Killian have to make sexual references? Why did he have to seduce her with his eyes? Why did he have to be so close, yet so damn far away?

Just when she was ready to drift off, a weird, unearthly sound filled the room. Robyn lifted her head off the pillow and strained her ears. Coyotes? Wolves? She swallowed. Bears? Chilled, she snatched the log cabin quilt from the end of the bed, and pulled it up to her chin.

There was no doubt about it; the noise, which now sounded like a moan, came from inside the cabin.

McKnight?

An unhealthy dose of horror movies from her youth prompted her to get up and investigate. While her mind screamed, "Don't go in there!" her body crept forward, one foot out from under the covers and onto the floor. Just then a moan ensued, followed by the mumbled word "no." Robyn was surprised to discover the ruckus coming from the chair right next to the bed. As tired as Killian had looked, he could have drifted off to sleep during his shift. Working on the assumption if she were having a bad dream she'd want someone to wake her up, she decided to rouse the sleeping man.

A shaft of moonbeam spilled in through the parted drapes, outlining Killian's form in stark relief. Her breath caught in her throat. The covers were tangled around his waist and legs. The tight T-shirt had ridden up on his chest.

"No, don't go. Please, don't leave me again," he begged in his sleep.

A woman? Not that it was any of her business—or that she gave a fig. She was just . . . curious. What would give a strong, stare-danger-in-the-face type of man like him nightmares? Why would a hunk like him have to beg anyone to stay? He wouldn't have to ask her twice.

Her bare feet made no sound on the hardwood floor as she moved to the side of the chair. Killian's head twisted from side to side. His legs kicked out, tangling the quilt further.

She needed to wake him, but hesitated. She cleared her throat, and called out in a loud whisper, "Killian?" He didn't respond. *Oh, God. I'm going to have to touch him, aren't I?* She'd been touching him for days, but this was a violation somehow. He didn't need help. He was asleep, not unconscious.

Her hand shot out, her finger jabbing him in the shoulder. "Killian?" Her voice wavered.

He turned on his side to face her, his brows knit together in worry.

Sighing, she gripped his shoulder and shook him. Heat radiated from his skin. Primal heat. Earthy heat. The kind of heat a woman could respond to, given half an ounce of encouragement.

Angry at the unwanted stirring of her emotions, she yelled in a stage whisper, "Killian. Wake up."

Out of nowhere, he jerked up, grabbed her and pulled her

down to the chair with him, one hand at her throat. "What are you doing here?"

His grip wasn't tight, but she had difficulty speaking anyway. "You were . . . dreaming. Nightmare, I think . . . trying to wake you up . . . that's all. Could you please . . . loosen grip?" He released her, and she scurried back to stand by her bed, tugging down the hem of her nightshirt. "Care . . . to talk about it?"

"No."

She didn't think so, but he could have at least hesitated with his answer. "Were you dreaming about a bear?"

"No, Robyn, I wasn't dreaming about a bear."

"McKnight?"

"You're not going to leave me alone until I tell you, are you?"

"Probably not. Was it a woman?"

His hand slid through his hair, taming the sleep-tousled locks. He fell back against the pillows, his eyes blinking heavily. "It wasn't about another woman, okay? That's all I'm going to say about the matter. Why didn't you wake me for my turn at watch?"

"You fell asleep during your watch. I was waking you. I'm thinking you were tired."

"Get back to bed, Robyn."

"Okay." This was her cue to stop looking at him. Climb back into bed, pull the covers up to her chin, and sleep.

She didn't move.

Despite all his brawn, despite what he did for a living, despite the animal attraction hovering between them, at that moment he reminded her of a little boy. There was no way she could leave him alone. "I'll keep watch if you need to keep sleeping."

"I'm not a kid."

"No one said you were." She glanced at his body, delineated by the tight clothing he wore. Thank God it was dark in the room, because her face felt twenty shades of red.

"Good night, Banks. I'm going to do a perimeter search. Don't leave this room."

She sighed and crawled back into bed. "Good night, Secret Agent Man."

A gentle breeze lifted a lock of Robyn's hair, tickling her nose. Slowly, she stretched her arms above her head, turned on her side and lay there, still half in and half out of sleep.

As she drifted further away from sleep and into the land of the living, she felt another presence in the room. Her heart gave a hard thump against her rib cage. Had McKnight entered without her knowledge while she slept? Without opening her eyes, her hand inched up and found the knife tucked under her pillow. She sprang into a sitting position, knife held menacingly in front of her. She scanned the room in the same instant she pulled the blankets up to her chin.

There, across the room, sitting in the uncomfortable-looking chair, she found Killian. In daylight the chair looked too small for his large frame, and one leg was draped at a weird angle over the arm. Feeling silly but relieved, Robyn tucked the knife back under the pillow.

Killian shifted from one side to the other, the quilt falling to the floor. Robyn bit her nails, fighting the urge to run her fingers across the hard planes of his body.

She found herself wondering about his life. Did he spend his days off at a pool somewhere, slathering suntan lotion on the back of some blond vixen? Or did he prefer brunettes? Her gut wrenched at the thought of him with another woman. She pushed the covers aside and got out of bed. Turning to the window she parted the drapes to peek out.

It was none of her business what he did. He was none of her concern. His life was none of her concern. And his preference in female partners, be they blond, redheaded or bald, was none of her concern, either.

His purpose in her life was to return her to safety. End of story. He'd go back to chasing crooks and dodging bullets, and she'd go back to . . . to what? Oh, hell, as much as she felt attracted to Killian, they were wrong for each other. She was from a different class. A different world.

A blue jay flitted in and out of the trees, demanding her attention, while he squawked in the early morning air. Her father had never been around when it mattered. He took a mile and gave less than an inch. Herman Jeffries's job, whatever it happened to be at that particular moment, always came first. Killian's job always came first, too. After a couple days with him, that much was obvious. When she fell for a man, he was going to be a younger version of Charlie, the security guard, not Herman, the throwaway dad.

She'd fight this attraction that drew her to Killian. It was based on survival anyway. As soon as they got back to the real world, she'd forget about him quicker than it took to switch on a vacuum cleaner.

Cool air rushed against Killian's skin, where seconds ago warmth had resided. Confused for a second at his surroundings, he scanned the cozy room. Masculine in design, antique furniture filled the space from the heavy walnut dresser to the four-poster bed.

Inspecting the room further, his heart jumped into his throat when his gaze stopped on the petite form looking out the window. She looked so sad, he fought the urge to leap out of bed and comfort her. She was a vivid contrast to the Robyn he'd grown used to so far. The woman he knew made a joke

119

out of everything, broke every rule in the book, and proved about as unconventional as a person could get.

He had to remind himself that he slept in her room because he was worried about her, and for no other reason. He half-suspected McKnight would find them. No matter how attracted to her he was—and the blood rushing to his groin told him he was—it couldn't lead anywhere.

"My life is too dangerous to include a woman." He hadn't realized he'd spoken aloud until she dropped the curtain and spun from the window, a hand against her chest.

She collected herself quickly. "I never *asked* to be included."

The recollection was foggy, but he remembered the way she'd tried to stay with him after his nightmare. He couldn't think of another time someone had bothered to comfort him. It was a little thing, but it sparked a spot deep down in his heart he'd thought long dead.

God, he hadn't dreamed about his parents in years. Why was the vision returning now? Was it because he felt something for this woman that he hadn't felt in ages? He glanced at her out of the corner of his eye. He wouldn't do to anyone what his parents had done to him. No one deserved to be left behind. Alone. Forgotten. How could he explain to her what he didn't understand himself? "I felt I could protect you better if we were together. I slept here in your room in case McKnight found us. There was no other reason."

She took a step toward him, then stopped. Her eyes filled with a sadness he couldn't decipher. "Thanks for protecting me." She glanced at the bed and he followed her gaze. A knife peeked out from underneath her pillow.

"Right." Disappointment settled in his gut. Why did that bother the hell out of him? Wasn't that the way he wanted it? She wasn't supposed to need him. She could take care of herself when all this was over. She'd done it before he came along, and she'd continue to do it after he left. "I just didn't want you to think—"

"Oh, I don't. And I didn't want you to think—"

"I never think before I've had my coffee."

"Good." She nodded.

"Great." He rubbed a hand against the area of his injury.

"Mind if I take a shower before we leave?" she asked. "I was too tired last night."

"Go for it."

"Your clothes are in the dryer." She shot her gaze up and down his body, taking in the ill-fitting, tight clothing that left nothing to the imagination.

"Make it fast. We've got a lot of ground to cover today." He smiled at the flush staining her cheeks, then frowned. She wasn't immune to his charms as she pretended, and he wasn't sure whether that was good or bad.

A shower had never felt so good, Robyn decided, squeezing the dampness out of her long hair with the thick towel. When she reached for her clothes, she realized she'd forgotten to retrieve them from the dryer before entering the bathroom.

That's what she got for letting Killian's smile disarm her. Which was crazy. The man had said her nearness meant nothing. Why did she still go all fuzzy inside whenever she glanced his way?

Genetics. Simple genetics. The man was as appealing as apple pie a la mode. Any woman would die for a taste of him. Hanging the towel back on the rack, she threw on her nightshirt and exited the bathroom to retrieve her clean clothes.

Killian sat on the living room floor wearing his borrowed clothing, a pile of unfolded laundry in front of him. "I believe these are yours," he said, extending a pair of black, flimsy, thong underwear toward her.

For the second time that day, and it wasn't even seven in the morning, Robyn's face burned. She snatched the revealing garment from his hand, grabbed her jeans and shirt out of the pile, and rushed back to the bathroom, the sound of his deep chuckle following on her heels.

Sufficiently recuperated five minutes later, she ventured back to the living room. "You ready to go?" she asked.

"In a minute. I want to leave a note for the owners first. Explain everything that happened."

"Do you think that's necessary? We straightened up pretty darn good. I can't even tell we've been here . . . except for the broken window, which we fixed as well as we could, given the supplies at hand," she added when she noticed the censure in his glance.

"There are certain rules a person must follow."

"What is it with you and rules?" she snorted. "Admit it, you've never even told a little white lie, have you?"

"Those who don't live by the rules, die by the rules." The look he shot her made her tremble. She couldn't help but sense the power he exuded. It wasn't that she was afraid of him. Quite the opposite. But she discerned that his words had something to do with his nightmares.

"Okay," she agreed. "We'll leave a note."

He expelled his breath in a rush. "Look, I'm sorry."

"Hey, don't worry about it." She convinced herself that when Killian fell in love, if he ever allowed it to happen, he would love with all his heart. It was something she'd dreamed about, but knew she'd never have—a man who cherished her to the point of no return. A man who stuck to his beliefs, his convictions, loved a woman until the day she died and beyond. It was a pipe dream that would never come true for her. It wasn't in the cards. For some reason Robyn attracted the wrong kind of men. Men she had no intention of ever settling for.

She strode to the table and grabbed a notepad and pen, then shoved them against his chest, forcing him to take them. Her own wasted hopes and dreams made her words as clipped as his. "Write them a love letter for all I freaking care."

Chapter 8

Two hours after they'd started on their journey, Robyn had had enough. Enough of the silent treatment. Enough of Killian's brooding, dark glances. Enough of feeling like he'd rather be anywhere than with her. Even McKnight had gotten more of a rise out of him than she had. Damn man was married to his job.

When he slowed his pace, she fell into step beside him. "So . . . are you going to keep this up all day?"

"What?" he growled, refusing to meet her glance.

"I'm tired of talking to myself. If you don't want to carry on a conversation, how about if we sing instead? We can do it quietly. Anything to break this awful silence." She didn't want to admit that half the silent treatment had been her own doing. If she spoke, she might let it slip that she had a crush on him. Crush? That sounded so juvenile. Okay, she was wildly attracted to the man.

He threw her a sidelong glance, and grunted something unintelligible that sounded like a string of curses. He'd been doing that since he'd written the note to the cabin owners. She'd been dying to know what he'd written, but refused to read it. That would have been admitting she cared. Then he'd straightened up the cabin she'd already straightened, as if he were trying to prove they'd never been there—never shared a bedroom. Not that it meant anything. He'd sat in a chair across the entire expanse of the room.

"Fine." She threw her hands up in the air. "If you won't sing, I will." She pretended to hold a microphone to her mouth and dredged up her best imitation of a lounge singer.

"How about an FBI rendition of an old Roberta Flack favorite?"

Killian rolled his eyes.

Robyn held back a snicker, and began singing, off-key, a twisted version of "Killing Me Softly," substituting Killian's name for the words "killing me."

He whirled to face her. "Robyn?"

"What?"

He blocked her path, forcing her to stop. He stuck his face inches from hers—spoke through his teeth. "If a woman gets silenced in the forest, and no one is around to hear her screams, does she make a sound?"

Her jaw dropped. She pointed at him, shaking her finger. "This is crazy. Can we start acting like adults? What's my silence worth to you, Killingthem?" She slaughtered his name on purpose.

His eyes narrowed to two tiny slits. "I'm warning you, Banks."

"Jeffries, not Banks." Through the veil of her lashes, she watched Killian turn and continue walking. The puddles under his feet sent little splashes of mud against his pant legs. Despite the fact that he made her feel safe, he was rude and sarcastic. She didn't even want to like him. So why, then, did he make her feel all squishy inside? She had nothing to worry about where he was concerned. It was plain to see she didn't inspire the same carnal feelings in him. In fact, she'd bet odds, if they were the only two humans on a deserted island, he'd still pretend she didn't exist.

Killian stopped for a second to remove a pebble from his shoe. He bent over and the rear view was a sight to behold. Robyn drank it in like a thirsty woman.

"What are you looking at?"

Heat filled her cheeks. "Nothing." She averted her gaze

and waved her hand down the road. "Weren't you in a hurry to apprehend our suspect?"

"*My* suspect." He stood glaring at her with one hand on his hip. "Right. Let's go." Setting an unrealistic pace, he marched down the road.

Robyn jumped over a rut in the mud and hurried after him. After jogging for ten minutes just to keep up, she stopped and panted for breath. "Ah, excuse me," she yelled to his retreating back. "Short-legged woman here." She tapped her chest.

He stopped, spun around, and threw his hands in the air. "We've been walking for five minutes and you're already complaining?"

Air filled her starving lungs. "Jogging. I've been jogging. And it's been ten minutes, not five. There's no way I can keep up this grueling pace." She pressed fingers to the stitch in her side.

"Maybe I should leave you behind."

"I would appreciate that." Bent at the waist, her hands on her knees, she gulped in more air. "But, as a special agent, sworn to uphold the law and protect innocent citizens, I don't think you'll do that. It's that rule thing you covet so well."

"I'd like to stand here and argue with you all day, but I've got places to go—"

"I know, I know," she held up a hand, warding off the rest of his sentence. "And thieves to catch. Just slow down a little, *capische?*"

He growled, his gaze dropped from her eyes to her lips. He growled often. She still wasn't sure whether it was a good thing, or bad.

His growl turned into a scowl, then he yanked off his hat and raked a hand through his hair. "Let's get going." Despite his clipped words, his mood seemed to shift. The tight lines around his mouth softened.

Robyn's heart melted. He was too handsome for his own good—or hers. A sigh escaped her lips. "Ready when you are." Not bothering to answer, Killian set off down the road. Robyn smiled to herself when she noticed his gait had slowed. This tough, hardened Secret Agent Man was a pussycat in disguise.

They walked in silence for a while. A companionable, comfortable silence. By accident, her hand brushed up against his. Her heart skittered to a halt, then rushed at a pace that rivaled the bear encounter.

When she dared to peek at Killian, he acted like he'd never even noticed. She would have believed it, except he'd widened the gap between them a tiny bit. Enough so that unexpected touches wouldn't happen again.

She frowned. Was she that offensive?

Killian stopped in front of her. Lost in her thoughts, she banged into him. Her hands automatically grabbed his waist to keep from falling.

"What are you stopping for?"

He turned and put a finger to his lips. "Ssshhh."

Her fingers dug into his skin, refused to let go. The kidnapping, the fear she'd experienced, seemed like a distant memory. Now that memory rushed back to haunt her. Fear kept her lips sealed together.

Pushing her behind a tree, he pointed at her. "Stay put," he warned on a stern whisper.

Robyn nodded, then sat on a huge rock to await his return. Danger seemed to always find her. She'd be damned if she'd go looking for it this time. She fidgeted on the hard seat. Peered through the dense foliage. As much as she didn't want to admit it, she was worried about her Secret Agent Man. He had no weapons. No bulletproof vest. No form of defense, other than his two fists and his quick, intelligent wit.

And lips.

Now there was a weapon against which a woman had no protection.

Minutes ticked like hours. Nervous, she bit off the tip of one fingernail. What was keeping him? Determined to avoid trouble, she leaned back against an aspen tree—stared at the blue sky through the dappled leaves overhead.

A hand dropped on her shoulder and Robyn about jumped out of her skin. "Geez, Killian, what took you so long?" she whispered, remembering the need to be quiet. She glanced over her shoulder. A scream froze in her throat.

Dripping with crimson blood, an arm pierced the heavy brush of the dense bushes surrounding her—dangled at a weird angle—touched her with the cloying scent of death.

Her eyes squeezed shut. She couldn't move. Fear held her immobile. Her chest tightened. God, was she going to hyperventilate? She knew, without a doubt, there was a dead body attached to that arm.

Can't breathe. She grabbed her throat. Fought for breath. Begged for Killian to save her. *Can't move.* Tears pricked her eyes.

"Jesus Christ!"

Robyn opened her eyes in time to see Killian rush toward her, twigs snapping under his feet. He snatched her arm. Pulled her away from the source of her fear.

"Why didn't you come and get me?" he demanded.

She sniffled. "You . . . told me . . . to stay . . . put," she stuttered. Heedless of the anger burning in his eyes, she jumped into his arms, locked her legs behind his back, wrapped her arms around his neck, and pressed her body close to his.

"Since when do you listen to what I tell you to do?" His

words were harsh, clipped.

"See? See what happens when I do? Nothing but trouble. From now on I'm sticking to my rule of breaking rules." Her heart still beat too fast for her to think straight. "Oh my God, I forgot about your wound." She pushed against his chest. "Put me down before I hurt you."

"You weigh about two pounds, Robyn. Chill. I'm fine."

The soothing pressure of his arms slipped around her waist, offering comfort, extending warmth. He rubbed the small of her back with slow circular strokes. The strength of his embrace made her wonder if he was relieved to see her unharmed. Was it her imagination, or had he kissed the top of her head?

"Who is it?" she managed to ask.

When Killian set her back on the ground, she shivered, already missing the haven of his embrace.

"I have my suspicions. I'll give you one good guess." He strode over to the rock where she'd been held prisoner seconds earlier. He parted the branches of the bush. A body fell from its hiding place, landing on the ground at Killian's feet with a thud.

Robyn peeked at the motionless form through the fingers splayed over her eyes. A startled gasp flew from her lips. She recognized the black clothing, the blond hair, and the piercing blue eyes that stared unseeing up to the sky—eyes she'd remember in her worst nightmares for years to come. Eyes that had once stared at her through the cover of stretched nylons.

"McKnight?" she squeaked, turning her back to the horror she read in the man's frozen expression.

"It appears that way." Killian pressed two fingers against the crook's throat. "He's dead. From the looks of it, not too long ago, either."

"Who did it? Was it the bear?"

"There's a superficial gash in his stomach, which looks like it might have come from a bear. My guess is the bullet that ripped through his chest did the most damage. His van is up ahead. The money's gone. Either he hid it before he died, or whoever killed him took it." He rubbed his forehead. "This doesn't make any sense."

"What doesn't?"

"I've been hunting this guy for years. He's elusive, slippery. The man knows how *not* to get caught. It doesn't compute."

"Maybe his defenses were lowered from the bear attack."

Killian shrugged, acting like he didn't buy it. "Could be. He knew the person who killed him. I'm sure of it. That still doesn't explain why his guard was down. This man's guard, from what I know, is never down." He navigated around her, making his way to the footpath.

Robyn followed behind. "Wait a minute. Are you just going to leave his body there?" She glanced over her shoulder at the body. McKnight looked as if he could be sleeping. The clump of blood staining his shirt reminded her he wasn't.

"We have to. We could disturb evidence if we try and move him."

She swallowed and kept her eyes trained on Killian's booted feet. Strong. Sure. Safe. Alive. He was in control, which, for a strange change of pace, was exactly where she wanted him.

The black getaway van, covered in layers of mud, stood in a clearing. All the doors hung open drunkenly, like someone had rummaged through every square inch. Sweat trickled down her back. She didn't want to be a victim again.

Killian rummaged through the back of the vehicle. Memories stirred. Forty-eight hours ago they had been in that exact spot. Tied. Helpless. But very much alive.

There was no need to restrain their captive. He wasn't going anywhere. He was dead, his life had met a brutal end. The forest took on sinister sounds. Leaves rustled in the slight breeze. A crow cawed once high up in the trees. Something scurried through the brush behind her.

"What are you looking for?"

"Something with which to mark the crime scene."

Always the cop. "We're going to be the crime scene if we don't get out of here." A cloud slid over the sun and Robyn shuddered, rubbing her hands up and down her arms. What if the murderer was still out there? Watching. Waiting. Hungry to taste blood again.

She rushed over to Killian—tugged on his sleeve. "Please, let's get out of here. This place is giving me the creeps."

One strong hand at the small of her back, he propelled her toward the passenger side. "Get in and wait for me. I'll be right back." Rope in hand, Killian went back to the dead body to mark the area.

Robyn flew onto the vinyl seat, slammed the door and jammed down the lock. She searched the edge of the trees, looking for movement. The hairs on the back of her neck tingled. He was close. She knew it as well as she knew her own name.

"Hurry up," she demanded, when Killian got behind the wheel.

"Damn."

"What?"

He turned and looked at her, searching her face. "No keys."

"Oh, no." Robyn shook her head, ignoring the bile rising in her throat. "I'm not hanging around here, and I refuse to walk another step. Hot-wire this baby."

"Who do you think I am, McGyver?" He pointed to her side of the dashboard. "Look in the glove box."

While she yanked it open and rummaged through music cassettes and stacks of papers, he pulled down his visor, looked under the seat and in the ashtray. "Stay put. I'll search around."

He was leaving her alone again with a killer on the loose? "Are you sure that's wise? Look what happened the last time you told me to stay put."

"Lock the doors and honk the horn if you need me." Killian was gone for less than thirty seconds, when Robyn remembered most guys shoved their keys in their pants pockets. Why didn't they think to look there first?

She opened the door to tell Killian, but the forest had already swallowed him up. She climbed out of the van, scanned the area to make sure she was alone, then paced in front of the bumper, worrying her bottom lip. She knew what needed to be done, but still she hesitated.

No one was around. She could admit it. She was little more than a coward.

A coward of the worst kind.

She couldn't even find the courage to do what needed to be done. Sure, when fear stared her in the face, she'd responded. That was just adrenaline. A natural reaction. She had no control over that. When courage called for a little more than survival instinct, she couldn't cut it.

A chipmunk darted out, stopped, scampered to her feet, stood up on his hind legs to get a better look, then, tail twitching, he scurried back into the woods.

Damn chipmunk had more balls than she had. To hell with McKnight. The bastard was dead. He couldn't hurt her anymore. Determination lengthened her stride, and she covered ground fast. She ducked under the rope and stared down at the body.

Sucking in a deep breath through her nostrils, she blew it out her mouth, shrugged her shoulders and rolled her neck from left to right. He'd deserved to die. He would have killed them, given half a chance. "Good riddance."

Robyn had no intention of disturbing the scene more than it took to search for keys. She reached toward his pants pocket. Despite every intention of being brave, she couldn't keep her skin from crawling. It was way worse than when Herman had taken her fishing and she'd had to bait her own hook with a squiggly worm, because, as usual, he'd gone off to talk business.

"Robyn . . . what the hell are you doing?"

If the forest had a ceiling, she would have hit it. She clutched her heart with both hands, certain it had just thumped its very last beat. She spun and scowled at Killian, who returned the look with one of his own. "I was checking his pockets for keys."

Killian sighed heavily. "While that was smart thinking on your part, and very courageous, number one, I told you to stay in the van. I don't think I need to remind you, we still have a killer on the loose."

Robyn glanced over her left shoulder, then her right and moved closer to Killian.

"Number two, I searched through his pockets already."

Her stomach roiled. "I touched him for nothing?"

Keys jangled when Killian pulled them out of his pocket. "Yes. Get in the van. Let's get out of here."

Relief surged through her like a powerful drug. "Cool. Let's get going." She ran back to the vehicle, threw herself in, and all but danced in her seat with the need to get as far away from this place as fast as possible.

Killian jammed a key into the ignition, shot her an irritated glance, and then threw the van into first with a grinding of gears. "You got a hot date or something?"

"Yeah, with the undertaker if you don't get this show on the road." She turned and looked out the back window, half-expecting to see *Tyrannosaurus Rex* bearing down on them.

Traveling over the rocky terrain, Robyn stared out the side window and reflected on his words. Hot date, her ass. She didn't see how she could ever date again after spending time with Killian. Why, she had no clue. The childhood chant "he loves me, he loves me not" rang through her head.

Opposites attract. Vinegar and oil don't mix. Love conquers all. Relationships built on intense emotional situations don't last.

Robyn smiled to herself, her gut clenching. Since when did they have a *relationship?* They verbally sparred more than a pair of prizefighters. The guy was egotistical, moody, inflexible, overbearing, stubborn and downright rude at times. She'd do best to keep reminding herself Killian Hart didn't fit into her neat little world.

Killian glanced at Robyn as they bumped their way down the rutted road. She was quiet. Way too quiet. He wondered what thoughts were rambling through her pretty head.

After they got back to civilization, they'd never see each other again. It was just as well. He didn't have time for a complication such as Robyn. He rubbed his forehead, beyond bone tired. He couldn't believe the turn of events in this case. Never in his wildest dreams had he expected to stumble upon McKnight's bloodied, dead body.

He'd sensed the killer had been close. Too close. He hadn't wanted to alarm Robyn, so he kept the knowledge to himself. He felt so useless without a gun. How could he protect them? How could he protect her?

He wanted nothing more than to protect her. Not just because he worked for the FBI, or because it was his duty. It went deeper than that. Was he guarding her from a madman, or from his own warring emotions? If he'd learned anything from his parents, it was to keep clear of emotional ties.

He glanced at Robyn from his peripheral vision. Watched her staring out the window, as if in a daze. She wasn't a woman a man could easily forget. Her devil-may-care attitude, her sarcastic sense of humor, her ripe, luscious lips, all added up to someone he'd like to get to know better.

More than once, he found himself biting the inside of his cheek to keep from laughing out loud at something she'd done or said. He couldn't remember the last time someone had made him smile, let alone laugh. She'd taken care of him when he couldn't take care of himself.

Allowing a woman into his life, though, no matter how she made him feel, was asking for trouble. He wasn't about to repeat the same mistakes his parents had made.

Robyn leaned forward with one slender, graceful arm and flicked on the air conditioner, lifted the wild curls off the nape of her neck, then aimed the vent at her face.

His heart lurched like someone letting off the brakes on a car parked on one of San Francisco's infamous steep hills.

Big trouble, indeed.

He cleared his throat, forced his focus back to the road. "You feeling okay?" he asked.

"As well as a person can be who has survived a kidnapping, a bear, starvation, you name it." The hand she shoved through her hair shook slightly. "I can't wait until this is all over. I want my own shower, my own bed, a pedicure, manicure, complete facial, and of course, a change of clothing." Closing her eyes, she leaned back on the headrest. "And I don't care in which order I get them."

The thought of her in a shower, slick and wet, her pink, distended nipples emerging from behind a wall of suds, kicked his body into overdrive—made him grow hard.

He shifted in his seat, searching for a comfortable position. Maybe he was trying to outrun his own desires, he wasn't sure, but something made him step harder on the gas. They hit a bump and sailed through the air.

Robyn's fingers dug into the armrest, her knuckles white with her tight grip. When they landed, she jerked backwards. "Hey, I want to get back to town as fast as the next guy, but I'd like to get there in one piece!"

Killian eased up on the gas. "Sorry." So, she was eager to get back, too? She probably couldn't wait to see the backside of him. All they ever did was argue.

Actually, that wasn't altogether true. He remembered the taste of her lips, right before he sent her out the window at the cabin, the way her body had fit against his when they'd slept out in the woods—the way they'd spooned together like a gun in a holster. They hadn't been confrontational at those moments. Of course, she'd been scared or asleep, and he'd been out of it for most of the day. She'd taken care of him. As long as he lived, he'd never forget that.

The memories intrigued him as much as they scared him. If his life were different, if he had anything to offer a woman like Robyn, he'd like to see where the relationship could lead.

Relationship? His brow puckered. Since when did they have a *relationship?* He was her protector. She was just a case. A beautiful and interesting case, but a case all the same.

Killian had never allowed himself to get attached on a personal level to any assignment; he sure as hell wasn't going to start now. He didn't know how long he'd been thinking about Robyn, but when he pulled himself out of his musing, Denver's downtown skyline came into view. He breathed a sigh of relief, then glanced at her.

Her head rested against the tinted window, her eyes closed in peaceful slumber. Pink, lush lips parted a tiny amount, as if she were waiting for a kiss from her lover. A tendril of dark hair curved across one cheek. Killian gripped the steering wheel hard, curbing the urge to brush the lock of hair away from her face.

He breathed in deeply, but instead of finding peace or answers, he inhaled her scent. Outdoorsy, yet feminine. A fragrance all its own, that curled its way into his memory, like certain smells always do. God, he'd much rather face McKnight's killer, unarmed, than explore his feelings toward Robyn.

Too busy taking in the sight of Robyn, Killian didn't notice the sedan following behind until it was bumper to bumper with the van. "Shit." His grip tightened around the steering wheel. When the first tap hit, he was ready for it. The van lurched and Robyn jolted awake.

"Who taught you how to drive?" She rubbed her eyes.

"Tighten your seat belt. We're in for a rough ride."

Her eyes widened. She whipped her head around to look out the back window. He couldn't spare her the fear he knew she was feeling, but he could keep her safe. Just like she'd kept him safe.

He watched the sedan come alongside the van. The windows were tinted darker than state regulation allowed, and he couldn't see the driver. The car swerved into them, metal scraping metal.

"I'm tired of someone trying to kill us. Do something."

Killian ignored Robyn, and concentrated on keeping the vehicle on the road as they barreled down the highway doing seventy. A couple more rounds of sidewiping and the sedan slowed down, pulling in behind them again. At the next exit, the car shot onto the off ramp.

Robyn exhaled loudly. "This is getting ridiculous. What was that all about?"

"A warning of some sort."

"Why didn't you follow them? I'm tired of their warnings. They're starting to piss me off."

"I'm not going to initiate a high-speed chase with you along. I got the plate number. Don't worry. We've got a little ways to go, try and get some sleep."

"Sleep. Yeah, that's going to happen."

Within minutes her eyes were closed, her head resting against the window again. After driving for what felt like days, they had only a couple more miles and they'd be at the FBI's Denver headquarters. Robyn could make her statement and leave. Let them both get on with their lives. If it was what he wanted, why did the thought of watching her walk out of his life bother him?

"Robyn?" He touched her, his fingers curling around the soft flesh of her upper arm. "Robyn, wake up. We're almost there."

She stretched in her seat, her arms curving above her head, her T-shirt straining taut against her firm breasts. It was all Killian could do to keep in his own lane. Desire licked at his insides like a hot flame licking at parched wood.

"Wow, that was fast. I must have been more tired than I thought." She turned her head and blinked sleepy brown eyes at him. "How long was I out?"

Long enough for me to study your face, etch it into my mind for those long nights when I have nothing to hold but your memory. "Just a little while." His answer was gruffer than he wanted. "You'll have to make a statement before they'll let you go." Was that relief that flashed across her face, or annoyance? He maneuvered the van around a group of slow-moving vehicles, and hung a right turn. He pulled into the underground parking lot of the Federal Building off of Stout Street and parked the van.

Getting out, he pocketed the keys, opened Robyn's door, and grabbed her elbow to help her out. She looked weak—which wasn't a word he thought he'd ever reserve for someone with her strong will. Inside the foyer, he pushed the elevator button, then glanced at the woman at his side. She had to be drained emotionally, despite the nap she'd just taken. She threw him a faint, weary smile that tore at his heart.

The elevator doors opened. He ushered her in and hit the button for the eighteenth floor. With a gentle, pitching motion and a whirring hum, they ascended. Neither spoke. It was as if all they had been through, the hostage situation, the guns, the endless walking, not to mention the car incident, had taken its toll. Now that it was almost over, their bodies couldn't take lack of sleep, lack of food, and everything else, another minute.

When the doors slid open, Killian, with one hand at the small of her back, ushered Robyn into the FBI's marbled foyer.

"Agent Hart!" The receptionist behind the desk stood, her face pale, her mouth dropping open in disbelief, one hand covering her heart, as if she were staring at a ghost or a figment of her imagination. "We thought you were dead!"

It had been a long three days. Killian felt half-dead. He smiled grimly. "Hope my funeral hasn't been planned yet, Jean."

The young woman's face turned bright red. She hadn't been with the agency very long, and it was plain to see she wasn't used to surprises. "No, no, of course not."

"Is Holgate in?" Killian asked, wanting to report to the Special Agent in Charge of the Denver Field Office, and no one else.

"It's Sunday," Jean answered. "I'm here finishing up a project that's due tomorrow. Everyone else is gone."

It wasn't unusual for Killian to work seven days a week, never taking time off for himself. Her answer didn't mean anything to him. Slipping an arm around Robyn's waist, he supported her weight before she fell to the floor. "Call him up and get him in here. We'll wait in Will's office. Oh, and there's a black van in the underground that needs to be processed." He pulled the keys out of his pocket and handed them to her.

"But—"

Killian raised one eyebrow.

Jean blushed. "Yes, sir." She reached for the phone. "Do you want some coffee?"

One look at Robyn's waxy pallor gave him the answer. "Black and piping hot." Coffee wasn't the only thing he wanted, but he knew he'd have to settle for that and nothing more.

William Holgate's office smelled of cigars, but offered the peaceful haven Robyn sought. She sank down onto the red vinyl sofa and rested her head against the back cushion. Two raps sounded on the door. The woman named Jean entered, a tray with two ceramic cups and a decanter of coffee in her grip.

"Mr. Holgate wasn't at home, but I was able to contact him on his cell phone. He'll be in shortly." She set the tray on the coffee table, threw them both a skeptical glance, then left. Robyn poured herself a cup and took a sip, waiting for the caffeine rush to kick in.

Killian poured himself a cup of the black liquid and took the chair across from her. "You can make a statement tomorrow if you don't feel up to doing it today."

She shook her head. Was he trying to get rid of her already? "No. I want to get it over with. Mind if I make a call, arrange for a friend to pick me up?"

He avoided her gaze. "Feel free." He pointed to the phone on the massive cherrywood desk.

So that's how it was going to be? They'd act like polite strangers? As if they'd never gone through a harrowing experience together—stared death in the eye and won? "Thanks." She set her cup down and stood. To get to the phone, she had to pass in front of Killian.

She wanted him to reach out and stop her, pull her onto his lap. Offer comfort. Solace. Warmth. Kisses. A future.

He didn't.

She picked up the receiver with tears stinging her eyes, and dialed her best friend's number. To think of calling her family was a joke. Her mom would be too busy and who the hell knew where her father was?

After three rings, someone answered. "Ginger?" She tried to stop the quivering of her voice, but couldn't.

"Robyn, is that you? Oh my God. I've been so worried. Are you okay? Where are you?"

Ginger's concern made the tears well faster. She was family, even if they weren't blood-related. Robyn turned her back to Killian and swiped at her cheek. "It's a long story." She gave a halfhearted laugh. "Can you come and pick me up?"

"Of course. Where are you?"

"Downtown somewhere. Hold on a sec." She turned to Killian. "What's the address here?" He met her gaze, with the root beer brown of his own. He remained silent for a second, looked her up and down with an unreadable expression on his face, then he gave her the address. Was that regret she saw? Pulling her gaze away, she broke the hold he had on her. She rattled off the address, said good-bye, then hung up the phone.

Shoving her hands in the back pockets of her worn jeans, she stood by the desk and stared at him. As if he felt her watching, he yanked off his cap and raked his hands through his hair. "It's over, isn't it?"

When he turned his head to her, he had his emotions under control. Neutral. Professional. The Secret Agent Man, doing his job. "For you, yes. For me, it's just beginning."

Robyn nodded, then thought about the dead body. She suppressed a shudder. "Finding the killer?"

"Yep."

He looked bushed. Robyn wanted to reach out and wipe away the frown lines on his forehead. Kiss away the grim set of his lips. Make him forget his worries with her body. She shifted her weight from one foot to the other. "Is there anything I can do to help?"

"The agency can't risk a civilian getting involved, or hurt." He took a sip of his coffee, but avoided direct eye contact.

He might as well have said he didn't want to get involved—with her. It was over, done, finished. *Yeah, right, Robyn. Sorry to disillusion you, but it never started.* Okay, if that was the way he wanted it, she could act as if nothing had ever happened between them. No lightning, no sizzle, no nothing.

"Gee, they should have informed me about the civilian involvement rule before I got kidnapped. I would have called in sick. Maybe you could have gotten one of your junior agents to fill in for me. You know, a stunt hostage double, or something." She hid her pain behind a wall of sarcastic humor.

He stood and crossed over to her, his eyes boring into hers. A touch could not have been as powerful as the look in his eyes. It branded her—reached deep into her soul. "Robyn . . ." He searched her face. "I don't want to fight anymore." One strong hand reached out and caressed her cheek. The calluses on his trigger finger were rough against her skin. He pulled her closer, their lips almost touching.

The door burst open and a man strode in, dressed in a pair of tan Dockers and a wrinkled white Izod shirt, his hair still wet as if he'd just taken a shower. Killian pulled away from her, like a bank employee caught with his hand in the till. He put his hands on his hips, his feet spread wide in a defiant stance.

"Hart! My God, man. I thought I'd never see you again." Robyn decided he must be Holgate when he rushed to Killian and pumped his arm up and down, like he was trying to get water from a dry well. "We were so worried when we didn't hear from you."

"Why weren't we followed, Will? Someone should have been on our tail from the beginning."

Holgate smoothed a hand over his wet hair. "Stevens said he tried. You guys could have been anywhere in the city, or out of the state for all we knew."

"Didn't you put out an APB?"

To Robyn's ears, Killian sounded suspicious. She wondered why.

"Of course we did. You're our best agent. How did you get away? Anything you can tell me about the suspect? Where's the money? Did you find the money?"

Killian laughed—a harsh sound that Robyn was glad wasn't directed at her. "The getaway van is already being processed."

"So Jean told me. What about the money?"

143

A muscle ticked in Killian's jaw. "McKnight is dead. I marked the crime scene as well as I could, and I can draw you a map. For the record, I didn't kill him. Someone got to him before I did. Find the murderer and chances are you'll find the money."

Holgate nodded. "Is this the other hostage?" He pointed in Robyn's direction, giving her a suspicious look. She shifted from one foot to the other, feeling as if she had something to hide.

Killian looked over his shoulder, his gaze settling on her face. Her heart lurched. "Yes. Robyn Ban—Robyn Jeffries, meet Will Holgate."

Robyn nodded. Mr. Holgate nodded back.

"Why don't you have someone obtain a statement from her, so she can get out of here and get some rest? It's been a long couple of days. Can we go somewhere private so I can fill you in on all the details?"

So he wanted rid of her that badly, did he? Robyn gritted her teeth, narrowed her eyes, and forced him to look away out of what she thought looked like guilt.

After an hour-long interview, which felt more like an inter-rogation from the Gestapo, the agents taking her statement agreed to let her go. As soon as she opened the door from Holgate's stuffy office and walked into the foyer, a familiar voice called out her name.

Never had Robyn been more relieved to see a friendly face than she was now. "Ginger!" She rushed into her best friend's arms, welcoming the hug they shared.

"God, I've been so worried about you. What happened?" Ginger scanned the area, then whispered, "They wouldn't give me any information at the front desk. The looks these people send out make me feel like a criminal."

"I know what you mean." Robyn laughed, a harsh sound

to her own ears. "Oh, you're not going to believe this story when I tell you all about it. I lived it and I still don't believe it." Her eyes rolled toward the ceiling. "And please, don't worry anymore. I'm all in one piece." She reached out and rubbed her friend's swollen, pregnant belly. "I don't want to make you and little Yahootie sick." She smiled when she used her favorite name for the unborn child.

"Yahootie and I are fine. What about you?"

"I'm okay," she reassured her. "Brooklyn?"

"Well-fed, the little pig."

Robyn heaved a sigh of relief. "Let's get out of here. I've had enough of this place to last me a lifetime." Besides, if she left now, she might be able to escape without seeing Killian again.

They headed for the elevator. Robyn reached out to push the down button when someone called her name. There was no mistaking the voice. It would be etched in her memory forever. She took a deep breath, forced a bright smile on her face, and turned to mentally photograph Killian one last time.

Despite the ordeal they'd just been through, he looked cool, aloof, ever the professional.

"Are you going to be okay?" he asked.

It was his job to ask. It wasn't a personal question. He didn't really care on an emotional level, just a professional one.

"Of course. Life goes on, Agent Hart. I'll be fine."

"Good." He nodded and drew his lips into a grim semblance of a smile. "Good." Robyn tore her gaze away and turned her back to him. With determination, she pushed the down button, praying the elevator would make a quick appearance.

As if it had been waiting for her, the bell dinged and the

doors slid open. Robyn dragged Ginger into the lift. When they turned, Killian was still standing there. She pushed the lobby button, never breaking eye contact with her Secret Agent Man. When the doors closed, she squeezed her eyes shut and took a deep sigh.

"What happened to you, Robyn? Are you okay? You had me scared half to death."

"Ginger, I will tell you everything, I promise, but right now I just can't. I don't even want to think about it. Change the subject. I don't care. Talk about anything."

"Okay. Who the heck was that man?" Ginger demanded.

"No one."

"Well, for no one—who I'm guessing is Agent Hart—in case you hadn't noticed, he's beyond handsome, and he couldn't take his eyes off you."

No kidding. Robyn opened her eyes and watched the light descend from floor to floor. "I hadn't noticed," she muttered.

"You'd have to be blind or . . . oh, my God! It's happened."

"What?" Robyn refused to look at her friend.

"Robyn, you're in love with the man, aren't you?"

Her heart froze, then plummeted to her stomach. "Don't be silly. We've never even kissed, except for that one time when he thought we were both going to die. We loathe each other."

"Yeah, I can tell." Ginger's tone held deep undercurrents of sarcasm.

"I'm serious. Besides, he's not my type."

"Oh, and what is your type?"

"You know. The guys I usually date."

Ginger laughed. "Those aren't guys. Those are laboratory specimens."

"Rats. All of them. Laboratory rats."

"That man up there," Ginger pointed to the ceiling, "is the best thing that ever happened to you. I can tell, simply by the way you're acting. Don't let him get away."

Robyn turned and studied the concern in her best friend's blue eyes. "I have nothing to do with it."

"What do you mean, you have nothing to do with it? A relationship takes two."

She rubbed a hand over her forehead, exhausted in mind, body and spirit. "I'm not the kind of woman a man like him changes his life for."

"Says who?"

"Says Killian Hart. According to him, his life is too dangerous for a woman. I'm not welcome in his world." A knot lodged in her throat.

"Men always say crap like that when they're running from emotional ties. Did something happen in his past? Did a woman hurt him?"

"We didn't exchange past histories over a campfire and marshmallows. But, yes, I think you could be right."

"Of course I'm right. I'm married. I know all there is to know about men, and what goes on in their minds."

The memories were already starting to hurt. "I've just changed my mind. There are two things I don't want to talk about right now. The kidnapping or Killian."

"I see. Okay. Are we still on for baby furniture shopping next week?"

Whew. A safe topic. "Sure. Of course. Can't wait."

The elevator doors swished open, and the pair walked out onto the street. They had to stop to allow a car to pull out of the underground lot. When she looked in to make sure no other cars were coming, she spotted the black van with yellow crime scene tape all around it. Robyn suppressed a shudder and grabbed on to Ginger's arm for support.

As much as she wanted to believe Ginger, she'd already convinced herself that Killian was right. She didn't belong in his life. He thrived on danger. She couldn't wait to get away from it. For whatever dark, deep reason, he needed to follow rules. For whatever reason, Robyn needed to break them.

Ginger was right about one thing, Robyn decided as she buckled her seat belt. As much as she tried to deny it, she was already falling hopelessly in love with her Secret Agent Man.

Chapter 9

The shrill ringing of a phone jarred Robyn out of her troubled slumber. Groping blindly through the jet-black darkness, she reached for the phone. A picture frame fell to the floor, landing on the carpet with a muffled thud.

"Killian?" she breathed into the receiver, still half-asleep. Squinting, she peered at the red digital readout on her clock. Three a.m. "Killian, is that you?"

"Robyn? It's Herman. Who's Killian?"

Pushing the covers aside, she sat up. Foolish of her to think it could have been Killian Hart. It had been two weeks since she'd last seen him. Chances were good she'd never see him again. "Herman? Is that you?" Disappointment tangled with elation. "And Killian's no one. I was dreaming. Where are you? Are you here in Denver?" She twisted the curly cord around one finger, hoping he'd follow her change of subject without comment.

"No. I'm in New York, sugar."

New York . . . it figured. "When are you going to visit?" She tried to keep the longing out of her voice.

"Well, sweetcakes, I was going to come, then I got this hot tip about a surefire windfall. Pretty soon I'm going to be richer than Donald Trump." A pause filled the static over the line. "There's just one little catch."

Robyn closed her eyes and leaned back against the headboard. With her free hand, she rubbed her forehead. A pit of quicksand sucked up the last vestiges of her hope. It was the same old story, different verse. "How much do you need this time?"

"You know me too well, baby girl." She could hear the grin in his voice across 2,000 miles. "One grand will do . . . for now."

So much for saving up for her dream home. *Sucker.* "Sure, Herman. When are you going to come and get it?" Extending him money always guaranteed she'd see him when he came to collect.

Another pregnant pause filled the silence. "I can't come, Robyn. If I leave, I'll blow the deal. Can you wire the dough?"

Say no. Say no. Say no. Make him come and get it. Make him acknowledge you exist for reasons other than giving him money for his rip-off schemes. "Sure, Herman. No problem."

"I knew I could count on you. I'll pay you back."

Yeah, I'll just add it to the list of the money you already owe me. "I know you will. I wasn't worried. You'll never believe what happened to me the other—"

"Baby, I wish I had time to talk, but I'm late for a meeting. Next time I call, we'll catch up on everything."

It was not quite five a.m. in New York. No one had legitimate meetings that early. A sharp pain jabbed her in the vicinity of her heart. He'd gotten what he wanted. Time to move on. Foolish of her to pray things would be different this time.

She tried to laugh, but the lump in her throat prevented it. Robyn would have had his surefire guaranteed fortune if she put aside a nickel every time he'd fed her that line. "I'm going to hold you to it, Herman."

"Okay, munchkin."

Tears pricked at her eyes when he used her childhood nickname.

"Bye. I lov—" The dial tone buzzed in her ear. She stared at the phone, then slammed it down on its base. Why even bother trying? She always ended up on the receiving end of pain. A bitter laugh escaped, echoing in the dark room. One of these days, she'd just say no.

A Siamese cat sauntered from the end of the bed onto Robyn's lap. Her loud purr filled the silence.

"You love me, don't you, Brooklyn?" Robyn stroked the cat under her soft chin. "I can always trust you to be there when I need you." The animal meowed, then stretched and jumped to the floor. Reaching the bedroom door, Brooklyn turned around, sat and stared at Robyn, meowing loudly, expectation written all over her whiskered face.

"All right, already. You're not going to let me go back to sleep until I feed you, are you?"

The feline blinked, then answered with a meow that held an uncanny resemblance to the word "no." Robyn tossed aside the covers and padded barefoot across the carpet. "Well, it's your lucky night, Brooky, 'cause I can't sleep anyway." *Yeah, right, Robyn. You'd get up even if you could sleep like the dead. You can't even say no to a damn cat.*

Brooklyn trotted across the living room toward her food bowl in the kitchen. Robyn followed behind, preferring to leave the apartment in darkness instead of switching on a light. The cat ran back to Robyn, dashed in and out of her legs, then ran to the kitchen again. Halfway across the linoleum, the animal arched her back and hissed. Her long tail puffed out to twice its normal size, a ridge of spiked fur danced along her back.

Robyn stopped in her tracks. A chill raced up her spine, tingling the hairs at the base of her neck. She couldn't put her finger on it, but something didn't feel right. With the barest of movements, she turned her head, searching the shadows.

A summer breeze billowed the curtains against the west wall. It had been drizzling when she'd gone to bed. Robyn knew for a fact she'd shut that window. Hadn't she? Blood rushed through her veins. Her heart pumped obnoxiously loud in her ears.

She thought of the horror movie thing again. Her own mind screamed at her to run back to her bedroom, lock the door and call the police.

"Brooklyn . . . here, kitty, kitty. Here, Brooklyn." The cat blinked at Robyn from her spot in the middle of the kitchen. Pale light from a streetlamp shone in through the lace panel over the kitchen window. The persnickety feline ignored her master, licked her paw, and then cleaned her face.

"Fine," Robyn whispered. "You're on your own—every female for herself." On the count of three, she rushed to the window, grabbed the wooden frame and pulled it closed, then whirled to face the living room. Keeping the wall to her back, Robyn searched the apartment again.

A clock ticked. A car drove by on the street below. Her heart thumped in her chest. She swallowed. The sound echoed in her head.

Protect yourself. Get a weapon. Anything Robyn had in the way of defense was in the kitchen.

Along with whatever had spooked Brooklyn.

Robyn, Robyn, Robyn . . . you watch way too many movies. How many times had her mother told her those very words when she was growing up? *You have an overactive imagination, child.*

Okay, the cat could have been frightened by her own shadow. She chased her own tail, didn't she? Breathing came a little easier, a little slower.

Robyn reached out and switched on a lamp. Light flooded the area, and she threw a hand up to cover her eyes. When her pupils adjusted, she jumped into a karate fighting stance, even though she'd never taken a single lesson in her life. She knew watching Jackie Chan movies would come in handy someday.

Edging toward the kitchen, she kept her arms out in front of her like she could deliver a deathblow with one mighty chop. With one flick, light from the overhead lamp bathed the kitchen. The only living inhabitant walked on four legs—and she sat by the pantry, jerking her tail to and fro in irritation.

"Oh, don't look at me like I'm a few peas short of a casserole," Robyn scowled at the feline. "You'd do the same thing if you could, and you know it."

Intuition told her whoever had been in her home, if someone actually *had* invaded her domain, was long gone. She filled the cat's bowl, her mind churning. Could she have left the window open and just imagined closing it? She had been exhausted. To be on the safe side, she took a butcher knife and carried it with her while she investigated every nook and cranny in the place, turning on each lamp as she went.

She thought about calling the police, but nothing seemed to be missing or out of place. Whoever had killed McKnight didn't know who she was. Didn't know where she lived. She was safe. Totally and perfectly safe. For half a second she had thought about calling Killian, but after Ginger accused her of being in love with the man, she didn't think she could face him.

In love? Her? It couldn't be possible. Could it?

Killian eased up to the red light. His partner, Dan, sat in the passenger seat next to him. He'd come into the station when Killian had been ready to leave, and insisted on riding around with him. Rain drizzled on the windshield, turning the traffic signal into a blur of colors.

Killian had filled out endless paperwork and mapped out possible leads, all night. He should have been dead tired, but he wasn't. If he went to bed right now, he'd end up staring at the shadows on the ceiling until dawn. It was the same every night—ever since the elevator doors had closed two weeks ago, killing his view of the tormented look in Robyn's brown eyes.

On impulse, he decided to turn right when he should have gone left.

"Where are we going?" Dan asked.

"I need to check on something."

"At this time of night?" Twisting his wrist, Dan glanced at his watch. "Can't it wait?"

"It will take less than a second." The building Robyn lived in sat at the end of the block, enshrouded in darkness from the cloudy, moonless night. All the lights were off with the exception of one apartment—second story, southwest corner. Robyn's apartment. It appeared as if every lamp in the place was on. Disappointment settled in his gut. Was she throwing a party? No. That was crazy. More than likely she was still experiencing fear from their ordeal.

Did she miss him as much as he missed her?

He had the urge to go in and knock on her door, make sure she was all right.

Then he remembered her words.

Life goes on.

He needed to stay away. Needed to let her get back to her life.

"Hey." Dan cut the fog from his window with a circular swipe of his hand. "Isn't this where that Jeffries chick lives?"

"Yeah, so?" Killian reholstered his emotions and placed a blank expression on his face.

"So, why are we here? Is there something you're not telling me? Do you suspect her? Do you think she knows where the money is?" His partner leaned forward in his seat, his eyes dancing with anticipation.

"No. Of course not. She was with me the whole time."

"Ahhhh."

He didn't like the sound of that. They'd been partners for over five years—could read each other like open books—trusted each other implicitly. Opening himself up to personal observation wasn't something Killian felt comfortable with at this precise moment. His friend had something devious on his mind. "Cut to the chase, Dan."

"Well, if you don't think she's in on the crime, then there has to be another reason we're driving past her pad at three o'fricking clock in the morning." A smug smile turned up the corners of his mouth. He folded his arms over his chest. "You've got the hots for her."

Bulls-eye.

His palms sweat against the steering wheel. Denial took over in a heartbeat. Killian snorted. "Get a life, Stevens. Someone killed our notorious bank robber. That someone is still out there." He waved his hand. "This is a random safety check. Nothing more." Killian flashed a look of disgust at Dan. "Do you always think with your pants?"

"No, sometimes I resort to thinking with my wallet, but"—he waved a finger at Killian—"we're not talking about me, are we?"

"Aren't we?"

"No, we're talking about a hot little brunette—" Using his hands, Dan outlined the shape of a woman. "—with fire in her veins. The agents who took her statement can't stop talking about her."

Killian turned the corner and drove away from the building. Robyn wasn't his. Never would be. He watched the brick structure fade away in the rearview mirror. Yet, how could he explain the sudden jealousy, coming out of nowhere, that kicked him in the family jewels? "She's off-limits."

"Saving her for yourself?"

Killian didn't have time for a woman. A nerve ticked in his jaw. "She's part of a case. Rule number one, we don't mix business with pleasure, remember?"

"Man." Dan shook his head. "You've been working too hard and too long. Where women are concerned, and I'm talking gorgeous women, rules are made to be crushed." He squeezed his hand into a fist, emphasizing his point.

Killian lapsed into silence. Robyn had accused him of being too caught up in rules and regulations. A man had to have a code to live by, he reasoned. Besides, it didn't matter what Robyn thought. Even if he decided to *crush* the rules that had governed him for all of his adult existence, the only woman he'd ever consider making room for needed to forget what had happened to them. Killian hanging around would simply be a constant reminder.

Robyn peeked out from beneath the quilted covers. The midday sun threw a ray of heat across the bed, making her sweat. A talk show host rambled from the television set she'd left on the night before. Pushing aside the covers, she sat on the side of the bed and swept a tangled lock of hair out of her eyes, then stood and stretched.

She hoped last night would prove itself to be nothing more than a bad dream. Switching off every single lamp as she went through the living room, told her otherwise. In the broad light of day, though, nothing seemed as scary as it had in the wee hours of the morning.

Too much work and too little sleep left Robyn feeling delusional. This was her home—her haven. The last thing she needed to do was make it into something it wasn't—sinister, scary, and full of bad men with worse intentions. She needed to forget about last night. She needed to forget about the kidnapping, and, most of all, she needed to forget about Killian Hart.

She just had to get over her attraction for the man. The cat rubbed against her legs and Robyn absently bent down and scratched Brooklyn behind the ears. The process of weeding Killian's face out of her memory would take time—lots of time. But all it took was a first step. And the first step was to go about the normal business of everyday life.

The first job for the day was to send a money gram to her father. She rolled her eyes toward the ceiling. If her life in any way exemplified normalcy, dear old dad would be sending her greenbacks, not the other way around.

The rest of the day found her edgy and irritable—and paranoid. Whenever a car followed her for more than two blocks, she'd turn down roads she had no intention of taking, just to see if it was tailing her. Not a single vehicle ever followed, but she still had the creepy sensation someone was watching her.

Her unplanned scenic route made her late for work. The bank's security guard met her at the door, unlocking it to let her in. "I'm sorry I'm late, Charlie."

Pulling the door shut behind her, he relocked it, the hint of a scowl marring his wrinkled face. He grumbled something that sounded like "no problem," but made no other comment. The old man hadn't been acting like himself since she'd returned from the hostage incident a week ago. All he'd told her about that evening was that the thief had tied him up and shoved him in a closet. She had tried to coax more out of him, but he'd clammed up tighter than a cloistered nun who'd taken a vow of silence.

At first, she wanted to believe the events of that fateful

night had scarred him somehow—made him reevaluate the meaning of life. Now she wasn't so sure. The close relationship they'd shared was missing. They'd both been victims. It should have brought them closer together, not driven a wedge between them.

It made Robyn wonder. She knew she was innocent, but did Charlie believe otherwise?

She followed him into the break room, the knot in her stomach making her feel as if she'd lost more than just a friend. She felt like she'd lost a treasured grandfather. He plopped down into a chair, drew a cigarette out of a pack of Marlboros, and stuck it in the corner of his mouth.

Robyn's eyes widened at the sight. "I didn't know you smoked, Charlie."

With a gnarled hand, he patted his breast pocket. "I've smoked off and on most of my life. Decided to take it up again. Don't tell my wife. She'd be upset. Do you have any matches? I seem to have lost my lighter."

The thought of a lighter reminded her of the gun lighter McKnight had toyed with. Thinking of McKnight reminded her of Killian. Thoughts of Killian led her to believe she would never find happiness, or contentment, or peace ever again.

She swallowed.

"Sorry, I—I don't smoke." She backed up toward the door a couple steps. She had to get out of there. Be alone. "I'm gonna start cleaning. I've got a lot to do tonight." She held up her hands when he started to get up. "No, no. You stay here and take five—enjoy your cigarette. I think there might be some matches in the silverware drawer." Turning on her heel, she rushed from the room.

Her fingers shook when she drew them up and covered her mouth. The infamous night of the bank robbery had changed everyone and everything, it seemed. She stood in the darkened lobby, alone with her misery, while her friend sat in the break room smoking. Poor, sweet Charlie. He should have been fishing, spending time with his wife, and doing whatever retired people did. Instead of enjoying his golden years, he had to continue to work just to scrape by.

If that wasn't bad enough, his days were now marred by bad memories. He'd never talked about what happened the night the bank had been broken into. Whenever she brought it up, he found an excuse to leave or changed the subject. From what she'd gathered, he'd been tied up, gagged and shoved in a closet. Now he had to be reliving the event. As a result, he'd hardened. Robyn had softened. She slumped against the wall. Somehow, she'd find a way to move on. To forget about her Secret Agent Man. An impossible task, but if life had taught her one lesson, it was that anything was possible.

Squaring her shoulders, she pushed off the wall, shrugged off the negative thoughts, and tackled her work with a bounce in her step. The trip down memory lane had robbed her energy more than she thought. Robyn would have given up wearing makeup for a month just to go home, but the night dragged on endlessly. More than once she'd glanced up to find Charlie standing in a doorway watching her, an unreadable expression on his face. She'd always trusted Charlie, yet the look made the hairs on her arms stand on end.

If the bank heist was supposed to be an inside job, could Charlie be involved?

No.

She refused to believe it. Not Charlie. He was like a grandfather to her. Grandfathers didn't help rob banks.

If her vacuum had a higher speed, she would have put it into overdrive. As it was, the belt had broken, forcing her to stop and replace it. She'd dumped over a garbage can, not once, but twice. While filling her mop bucket, she'd turned her back for a second, and it had overflowed, leaving a pile of suds on the floor big enough to swim in. Tears of frustration pricked at her eyes.

Finally, when she thought she couldn't take it another minute, she finished the last of her duties. Putting away the vacuum, the mop and pail, and the rest of her cleaning supplies in the storeroom, she nodded to Charlie. When he let her out the door, guilt refused to let her make eye contact.

What could she say to him? She didn't know if what she suspected was true, or if it was just her imagination working overtime. If she were wrong—which she had to be—he'd never forgive her. If she was right . . .

Dashing across the parking lot, she unlocked the door to her Ford Escort in a hurry, jumped inside and jammed the lock back down. Her thoughts absorbed her so completely, when she arrived home she couldn't remember having made the trip.

Exhausted, she had a hard time managing to nod at Robert, the doorman, when he opened the door for her. On a good day she took the stairs, since she lived on the second floor. Tonight she opted for the elevator. When she went to insert the key into the lock of her apartment, the door pushed open on its own.

Her mouth went slack. Rooted to the spot, her heart beating a rapid tempo against her ribs, she reached out and pushed the door open completely.

The knob banged into the wall and bounced back a couple inches. Robyn snaked an arm around the corner and flicked on the light switch.

Utter destruction met her gaze. Not a single piece of furniture was left untouched. The sofa cushions lay scattered about. Papers were everywhere. Contents from every drawer, cupboard, and nook and cranny littered the floor, hiding the carpet from view.

Blood drained from her face. Pulling the door shut against the ugly sight, she leaned against the hallway wall and ran a shaky hand through her hair. There was no way she could pass this one off as wild imagination induced by lack of sleep. The devastation inside was too real—too horrible. The open window last night had been a clue, and she'd ignored it. God, why had she done that? Stupid, stupid idiot. She wouldn't allow herself to ignore her gut instinct again.

For once, she was going to follow her intuition. Feeling nauseous and violated, she ran on wobbly legs down to the lobby and comparative safety. Ignoring the look of surprise from Robert when she practically grabbed him, she all but shouted for him to call the police.

Despite the late hour, bed was the last place Killian wanted to be. He paced the length of his living room, feeling restless and caged in. Every clue the agency had received about the killer had turned into a dead end. The long hours he worked to try and solve this case, wore him out and frustrated the hell out of him. He should have been able to sleep.

But he couldn't. Robyn kept him awake. Robyn tormented his thoughts. Robyn wouldn't leave his head, no matter what he did.

The out-of-the-blue squawking of the police radio sitting on the corner of his desk made him jump. He blamed that on Robyn, too. Listening to the radio had become second nature. He was ready to tune it out when the dispatcher repeated the address of a possible break-in.

Not just any address, but Robyn's address.

Killian's heart jumped at the thought. God, was she all

right? He steeled himself against the riot of emotions flooding him. He was losing it if he couldn't keep his feelings under control. This didn't concern him. This was simply a matter for the police. It was their job. They could handle it without him. Knowing Robyn, she could handle it much better without him.

The last thing Killian needed was to see Robyn again. Forcing her from his memory was difficult enough, he didn't need to compound it by seeing her and having to start the forgetting process all over again. It's not an FBI issue, he reminded himself again when he felt the urge to find the keys to his Jeep. The cops were more than capable. He turned back to his reports, refusing to let himself be swayed a second longer.

Chapter 10

Over the phone, the cops had advised Robyn to stay out of her apartment until someone from the force had arrived. Someone—not Killian, who was an FBI agent, and had no business working a simple robbery case. Not only did she ignore the advice to stay put until help arrived, she did it the second Robert turned his back to her. Head high and lip curled, she walked out of the lobby and waltzed back up to her apartment.

She opened the door to walk in, then stopped. Surveying the rooms that had once been neat and orderly, but now resembled a bombed-out relic from some far-off war, had her shaking her head. It would take hours to restore everything to its proper place. If she waited for help to arrive, she'd never finish before the end of this century. She had no choice. She'd been robbed. This wasn't her home any longer. Instead of giving in to the temptation to clean, she sat outside in the hallway like a good, law-abiding citizen, a person who didn't break rules, and waited for help to arrive.

The elevator doors opened, and footsteps sounded down the hall. Robyn looked up from where she sat on the floor, and sucked in a breath at the sight of the man who walked toward her. Her heart plummeted to her stomach. "Killian? What are you doing here? How did you find out? Did someone call you?" She smoothed a hand over her hair. Why did she always have to look her worst around him? She looked past him at the team of uniformed officers in his wake. This was a crime scene, not a date. Of course he wouldn't come alone.

He scowled at her, looking like he wanted to be anywhere but where he was. "You were supposed to wait downstairs." Instead of meeting her gaze, he opened the door and studied the devastation behind it.

No *hello*. No *good to see you*. No *damn, I've missed you more than life itself*. Just more rules. He didn't even notice that she had waited outside the apartment and not gone in. She was sort of following the rules, not that he cared. "My very own personal bad guy seems to prefer using a window"—she poked her head in the door and pointed to the open casement—"and not the conventional method of knocking and announcing his presence. Which explains how he got past Robert. But I will file that thought away for future reference. Thanks."

His eyes narrowed. "Who's Robert?"

"The doorman." There was no way Robyn was going to assume his look was due to something as ridiculous as jealousy. He was taking mental notes for his case, that was all. While they stood in the hallway and Killian talked to the cops, she studied him. He'd discarded his usual hat, so his dark red hair shone in the lamplight. Faded jeans hugged his muscular legs.

Lucky jeans.

The tail end of his striped blue shirt hung out the back of his waistband as if he'd dressed in a hurry and rushed over. Had he been worried about her? The possibility sent a flood of warmth through her veins.

The cops finally went into her apartment, leaving Killian and Robyn alone. "Aren't you going in there?"

"Not my jurisdiction. They can handle it."

"You didn't need to come here, did you?"

"Nope. I heard the report on the police radio." He shot her a look, which she gathered was nothing more than concern, then he sat on the floor and leaned against the wall. "Have a seat." He indicated the wall on the other side of the door. "It will be a while until they process the scene."

She was tired of scenes and crimes and cops. She took the wall opposite him, and sighed when her butt hit the ground. "Why did you come here, Secret Agent Man?"

"I just wanted to see if you were all right."

"I'm fine." She studied her hands. "Couldn't be better. You? Did you get your wounds looked at?"

"Thirty stitches. They're out already. Healing nicely."

"Thirty. Wow. I've never had stitches."

"Not fun. They itch like hell."

Since they both fell silent at the same time, Robyn guessed he thought the way she felt, that the conversation was beyond inane. They sat that way for at least an hour, before the door to the apartment opened and the cops walked out.

Killian and Robyn both stood. "All finished?"

"I think so," said one of the officers. "We've collected some evidence and taken prints." He held up a Ziploc bag.

She spotted what looked like a tiny gun inside. She peered closer to inspect it. She wheezed out a breath. She'd never forget this object in her lifetime. For a brief moment during the kidnapping she'd thought this gun was going to be the instrument of her death, before she'd discovered it was just a lighter.

Glancing up, she found Killian staring at her with a worried look in his eyes. She motioned to the bag with her eyes and his gaze followed.

"Where did you get this?"

"It was out on the fire escape."

"This lighter was used by McKnight when he kidnapped us. One has to infer McKnight's killer was the last one to touch this. How else could it have gotten here?"

"We'll make note of that."

Robyn didn't want to stand out in the hallway anymore. Actually, she didn't want to be in this apartment building. Unfortunately, it was home. She'd be damned if anyone made her feel uncomfortable in her own apartment. "Can I go in now?"

"Yes, ma'am. We're finished in there."

Robyn didn't wait a second longer. She opened the door and took in the destruction, which she would now have to put back in order. Killian followed closely on her heels.

"Why me? Why is he coming after me?"

"We don't know yet."

Having heard her voice, Robyn's Siamese cat meowed as she crawled out from wherever she'd been hiding and ambled into the room. "There you are," Robyn said. The fur ball strolled over to Killian and rubbed against his legs. "Hey, Brooklyn likes you. Weird. She hates men."

Reaching down, Killian stroked the animal under the chin. "You named your cat after a city?" Was he avoiding looking at her on purpose? It felt like it.

"Well, yeah. Herman traveled to New York often. Still does. I guess it was my way of keeping him around, even when he wasn't here." She picked up the cat and rubbed the soft fur against her cheek. "I had a tiger tom named San Diego, too, but he went out for a little action one night and never came back. Guess he was more like Herman than I thought."

With a meow, Brooklyn jumped out of her arms and trotted into the kitchen. Robyn changed the subject. "I'm not the terrible housekeeper that it appears. Wonder if the creep found what he was looking for?"

Killian brushed by her and walked farther into the room. "Can you tell if anything is missing?" Hands planted on his hips, Killian turned and met her gaze for the first time since entering the room. Whatever he saw reflected in her eyes made him walk back to her side. "Are you okay?" One callused finger brushed against her cheek with a fleeting touch.

The simple contact confused her—scared her. Robyn wanted to grab his hand, hold it there. Instead, she backed up a step, keeping an adequate distance between them. "I'm as well as can be expected, given the circumstances."

He nodded, the guarded look back in his eyes. "Judging by the lighter they found, this has to do with McKnight. Do you know anything you aren't telling me?"

Anger surfaced. And she thought he'd come because he might have missed her sparkling personality. "So that's why you're here. It had nothing to do with me. Just another lead to follow up on, huh? Killian Hart always gets his man."

His jaw ticked in obvious irritation. "It's my job, Banks."

It was a dirty job, but—"Yeah, well, I thought maybe . . ."

He searched her face. "What?"

She glanced around the room. "Nothing." She wanted to come right out and ask him if maybe he'd missed her half as much as she'd missed him. Instead, she stalked into the kitchen and pulled open the pantry door. She located Brooklyn's food dish amongst the rubble and filled it. Anything to keep busy.

"Don't get comfortable. You're not staying here. It's too dangerous. Grab an overnight bag and let's go."

"I can't leave this place in a shambles. Let me clean it up first. You're here, what could happen?" *More longing, more heated looks? Maybe they'd get around to a kiss with more heat than the one he'd bestowed on her in the cabin.*

Pausing, he hung his head, silent for a moment. "All right," he growled. She knew giving in wasn't easy for him. His gaze shifted until his brown eyes stared deep into hers.

"But just for tonight. First thing in the morning we're out of here."

"Of course. How long am I going to be gone, though? I mean, I can't leave Brooklyn here by herself indefinitely." She pouted. "She'll get lonely."

"Bring her." His voice was gruff, but Robyn watched him reach down and run a hand over Brooklyn's tan-colored back. So much for the tough guy act. He couldn't fool her. Killian had a soft streak as wide as the Grand Canyon.

"You look exhausted. Are you sure you want to do this to-night?"

Weary, Robyn contemplated the destruction around her. "I've already spent all night cleaning the bank. The last thing I want to do is drag out another vacuum cleaner, but, like my mother always says, it's not going to clean itself."

"Between the two of us, it shouldn't take too long." Grabbing a cushion off the floor, he shoved it into place on the couch.

"Oh, you don't have to help." The mental image of him wearing nothing but an apron flashed into her head. Shocked at her own depraved thoughts, she avoided his gaze.

"What do you think I'm going to do, sit here and watch you do all the work?"

Brave enough to look at Killian, she tilted her head and studied him for a moment. "You'd brandish a dust rag for me?"

Killian smiled. It was a tender, heartwarming smile that melted her insides, made her smile back. "It's my civic duty."

Would he be this helpful on a day-to-day basis with a life partner, a soul mate—a wife? Disturbed by the image of herself as his spouse, Robyn righted an overturned chair, making sure she kept her back to him. One look at her, and he'd be able to read the desire all over her unpoker-like face.

"Where would you like me to start?"

Behind the earlobe. Then, if you don't mind, blaze a trail down my jawline, toward my lips. After that, a trip to the hollow between my breasts doesn't sound like a bad idea. The room seemed to grow stifling hot all of a sudden.

She refused to look at him for the second time in as many minutes. "Oh, anywhere you want. Just dive in."

After a couple hours of straightening, folding, sorting, and cleaning, Robyn dropped onto the sofa. "I can't take this another second."

"Why don't you rest? Put your feet up. I'll run the vacuum over the bedroom floor."

The throw pillow looked inviting. Giving in to impulse, Robyn curled her feet up under her and laid her head down, reveling in the feel of the soft cushion against her cheek. "Okay, but I'm just going to relax for a minute. Don't let me fall asleep." When he turned to push the sweeper into the other room, she stopped him. "Killian?"

"Yeah?"

It was a struggle to keep her eyes open. "Thanks."

Killian watched Robyn drift off, her rich brown hair a wild contrasting halo against the cream-colored pillow upon which she rested. His heart lurched. "You're welcome."

He sucked in a breath when he entered the private domain of Robyn's bedroom. With her no-nonsense attitude and tough demeanor, he'd expected anything but the feminine atmosphere. He never would have thought so, but it suited her. An antique quilt in pale pink and white adorned the intricately carved four-poster bed.

A dusty rose–colored chair sat beneath the sill, a lacy undergarment draped over one arm. Drawn as if hypnotized, Killian walked to the chair and lifted up the fabric. It felt like

Robyn—smooth, silky, and irresistible.

God, was he nuts?

With a flick of his wrist he sent the garment fluttering back down to the chair. He was here to do a job—keep a woman safe, not ogle her lingerie in a fashion typical of some hormone-imbalanced, pubescent kid. Or worse yet, a stalker.

Grabbing the vacuum cleaner, he switched it on and attacked the floor as if it were an enemy. He refused to look at the bed, because every time he did, the idea of making love to Robyn on top of the cool, crisp sheets invaded his thoughts.

After winding the cord and putting the Electrolux aside, he reached for the furniture polish he'd placed just inside the door. A deluge of bottles, creams and makeup of every conceivable brand and color littered the top of the dresser. Odd, he'd never even seen Robyn wear a stitch of makeup, yet it appeared as if she'd bought out the entire cosmetics section at some department store. Swiping at what little of the wood surface showed through the clutter, he attempted to dust the dresser.

A tube of lipstick rolled to the floor. When Killian picked it up, he glanced at the imprinted name.

Vamp by Chanel.

Heat settled in his groin.

The color matched the vibrant teddy across the room perfectly. He closed his eyes. It was so easy to imagine Robyn wearing the lingerie, her long brown hair a wild mass of curls fanning all the way down to her cleavage, full, lush lips darkened by the lipstick. Her lids half-closed in inflamed passion.

His eyes shot open. He tossed the tube onto the dresser. Beating a hasty retreat, he exited the bedroom for the safety of the living room.

Oh, yeah, this was much better.

Not.

Robyn lay curled up on the sofa. One arm thrown above her head in careless abandon—one hand tucked under her chin.

Killian stood in the doorway, trying to decide whether to go back into the comparative safety of the bedroom or take his chances staying in the same room with one very sound asleep, but very sexy woman.

Opting for the living room, he found himself walking to the couch. An afghan hung over the back cushions. He grabbed it and spread it over Robyn's petite form.

She muttered something unintelligible and shifted. The slight movement parted her button-down shirt, revealed the curve of one breast peeking out from behind a black lace bra.

God, she was so desirable. He longed to pull her into his arms. Soothe away her worries. Throw away his inhibitions. Make sweet passionate love to her until the sun brightened the morning. As strong as she tried to appear most of the time, he'd seen the hurt in her eyes when she talked about her dad. She was vulnerable. She needed someone to take care of her.

It had felt like they were a team tonight. Like together, they could do anything. He knew better.

The happy little illusion would break the second he had to go out of town at a moment's notice. His life wasn't suited to togetherness. He wasn't the man to take care of her. If he said to hell with rules, he knew what would happen.

At first she'd say she understood when he had to leave on a case. He reached out and tucked a wayward strand of hair around her ear. The next time it happened, she'd pout, maybe shed a few tears. He traced the outline of her upper lip with the pad of his thumb. After a while she'd accuse him of never being around to help—of not caring—of ruining the last remaining threads of their relationship.

He stared at the way her eyelashes curled against her high cheekbones.

She'd accuse him of loving his job more than he loved her.

Turning away, he shoved his hands into his jeans pockets. He'd solve that problem before it ever began. He wouldn't allow a relationship to start. He'd preserve both their sanity and their hearts.

The antique clock on the mantel chimed four times. Lord, he was tired. Taking the other end of the sofa, he kicked off his sneakers and pulled the end of the crocheted blanket over his legs.

She'd thank him. If Robyn had any idea of the pain from which he was saving her, she'd thank him then and there.

Careful to keep from touching her, he stretched out his legs as best he could, and laid his head on the arm of the sofa. With Robyn living in his house on a temporary basis, he'd have to keep his resolve strong. Giving in to the emotions swarming through him would prove disastrous for them both.

Coming out of a deep, exhausted sleep, Robyn wrenched open one eyelid, blinking against the morning sun. Why couldn't she move her legs? It felt as if pillars of cement trapped them. The other eyelid opened, only for her to discover Killian at the other end of the couch, his long legs traversing the length of two cushions and intertwining with hers.

She sucked in a deep breath and studied him. In sleep, his features had softened, leaving him vulnerable-looking, child-like, endearing. Reaching out a hand, she traced his strong jawline, covered in dark stubble.

Why did she have to fall in love with him? She sighed when he rolled his head from one side to the other, as if her touch had tickled him. She watched the rise and fall of his immense chest. What would it feel like to be cradled in his arms, held tight against his rock-solid form? Moving her gaze back to his face, she gasped. His brown eyes stared into hers intently.

"Morning." She smiled sheepishly. Just how long had he been watching *her* watching him? His scrutiny moved from her face to her chest. Robyn looked down, only to discover several of the buttons on her shirt had come undone.

When she tried to sit up to button them, the covers slipped to the floor. The evidence of his morning arousal strained against the zipper of his jeans. Her gaze swung to his eyes, which were filled with heated passion.

She swallowed. Shifted her legs.

The movement did nothing more than increase the sizzling awareness between them.

Killian reached out a hand toward her. "Robyn?" Sleep thickened his voice.

Her heart thundered in her chest like a runaway train. She was ready to extend her hand to meet his when her gaze settled on the holster he still wore around his shoulder.

"I can't do this, Killian."

"Do what?"

"This. Us. It's going to lead nowhere."

He opened his mouth to comment when the doorbell rang. Robyn watched relief spread across Killian's face. *Saved by the bell.* Untangling her legs, she got up and headed for the door and glanced out the peephole. When she saw who was behind the peephole, she wrenched the door open. "Ginger! What are you doing here?"

"Baby furniture shopping."

"Oh my God. I forgot all about shopping with you today."

Robyn watched Ginger glance over her shoulder and followed her gaze. Killian stood by the side of the sofa, folding the afghan.

"Hey, I understand." Ginger winked at Robyn when he

looked away. "We can schedule our expedition for another time."

Heat flooded Robyn's cheeks. She rolled her eyes, remembering her friend's accusations in the elevator. "It's not what you think. My apartment was broken into yesterday."

"I wondered what was going on. Downstairs Robert was telling whoever would listen about the swarm of cops last night. I thought he meant out on the streets. Robyn, are you okay?" Ginger grasped her arm and looked around at the now-neat room. "Did they take anything?"

"No. It's so weird. We think it might have something to do with that guy that was killed. You know . . . the kidnapper."

Killian cleared his throat behind them.

"Oh, I'm sorry. Ginger, this is Killian Hart. He's an agent with the FBI. Killian, my best friend, Ginger Danelli."

Ginger stuck her hand out and shook Killian's. "I remember seeing you at the agency when I picked Robyn up. It's nice to meet you."

He nodded. "Same here. Can I talk to you for a second, Robyn?"

"Sure."

"If you'll excuse me, I have to use the bathroom." Ginger patted her stomach. "Not only do I eat for two, I also seem to go for two."

When she was out of earshot, Killian grasped Robyn's arm and turned her toward him. "Don't talk about the case in front of her."

"Why not? She's my best friend. I've known her forever."

"Look, at this point, we don't know who's involved. The less said, the better."

Robyn shook his hand off her arm. "Yeah," she said in an angry whisper. "You never know. That eight months' pregnant waddling woman"—she pointed in the direction of the bathroom—"might be the one that climbed up my fire escape and broke in here last night."

"That's not what I meant." A muscle ticked in his jaw.

"She can barely get up from the sofa without getting winded. But, you never know, with a little effort she probably could have torn this place apart all by herself. Forget the fact, moments ago, I wanted to—that I would have—"

He raised one eyebrow.

She'd have to watch her tongue. She almost let it slip that she was seconds from letting him ravish her body, mind and soul, before they'd been interrupted. She threw her hands up in the air. "Right now you make me so angry I could scream."

His eyes narrowed. "The feeling is mutual, Banks."

"Will you quit calling me that?"

"If the name fits . . ."

She put her balled-up fists on her hips. "Bite me, Killian."

Passion flared in his eyes.

The toilet flushed.

"Don't tempt me," he whispered as the bathroom door opened and Ginger walked out, her rounded stomach leading the way.

"Listen, Robyn, I've been thinking about it and we can do our shopping tomorrow." Ginger pointed to the baby. "This kid isn't coming for another month, anyway."

Robyn glanced at Killian. "I have to go away for a few days, Gin. It's not safe here."

"Robyn! Why didn't you say so? Where are you going?"

"I guess I'll be staying with—"

Killian coughed.

Robyn glared at him, then turned to Ginger and smiled. "The less said the better. I don't want to get you involved in this."

Ginger's gaze darted from Robyn to Killian. "Have you packed yet?"

They'd been friends forever. Could practically read each other's minds. "Why no, I haven't. Would you care to help?"

"I would love to."

There was more than one way to skin a cat—or in this case, an overimaginative, rule-oriented Secret Agent Man. Robyn turned and graced him with the sweetest, sugarcoated smile she could conjure up. "We'll be back in a jiffy." Ignoring his angry stance and the warning burning from his eyes, she linked arms with her friend and strolled into her bedroom.

"Okay, we've got a couple minutes before he barges in here demanding a blow-by-blow of every word we've exchanged." She closed the door with a decisive click.

"So . . . did you sleep with him?" Ginger asked.

"Good God . . . no!" Robyn opened the closet and dragged out a suitcase.

"Admit to me that you love him."

"What do you think I am—crazy? How can a woman love a man when all they do is fight?"

Ginger threw her purse on the end of the bed and sat down next to it. "Yes, you are crazy. Crazy in love . . . for that handsome devil waiting out there in the living room with a lovesick expression written all over him. You two are fighting because of all the unreleased sexual tension between you."

Robyn plopped the suitcase on the bed and opened it. "I think pregnancy has killed a couple million of your brain cells. You don't know what you're talking about." She paused at her dresser drawer. "Lovesick? Really? You think?"

"I know."

Robyn grabbed clothes at random. "Doesn't matter. He's not my type." She threw the wadded-up mass into the suitcase.

Ginger took them back out again and folded each garment neatly. "If he's not your type, who is?"

"You know the guys I go for." She grabbed a makeup bag and swept all the contents littering the top of her dresser into it. "I don't need to explain it to you. We've been over this a million times."

Pausing, Ginger threw her a look that only a pregnant woman could. Maternal. Motherly. "Rob, the last guy you thought was the one, is doing time behind bars right now."

Her heart pinched. "You had to bring that up, didn't you?"

"Someone needs to remind you of your mistakes."

Robyn rolled her eyes to the ceiling. "Yeah, what are friends for?"

With a groan, Ginger pushed herself up from the bed. "You are my best friend in the world. Don't ever forget it. You deserve so much more than you ever ask for."

Tears pricked her eyes. "I don't want him, Gin."

"How can you say that?"

"Because it's true. I'm just a case to him. Someone he needs to protect. His job always comes first."

"That's ridiculous. You don't even know him yet. Give him half a chance. You are giving up on the opportunity and the man of a lifetime. Go for it, Robyn. What do you have to lose?"

"Self-respect?"

"It grows back."

"My heart?"

"It'll mend. Besides, I think you've lost that already."

Robyn's heart flooded with hope. "Are you sure about this?"

"Of course. I'm a married woman. I know everything."

Catching a glimpse of lingerie out of the corner of her eye,

Robyn strolled over to the chair by the window. She scooped her scanty teddy into her grasp, flitted past Ginger and dropped it into the suitcase.

"What do you think you're doing with that?" Ginger asked, her jaw slack.

"Ammunition, Gin. Ammunition."

Chapter 11

From the outside, Killian's brick house looked neglected. Robyn followed him into the driveway, parking her Escort behind his Jeep Cherokee. Unfastening her seat belt, she opened the car door and climbed out. She concentrated on the overgrown weeds controlling what had once probably been a beautiful rose garden, so she wouldn't have to look at the FBI agents who had beat them there. The tall grass needed to be mown and sported several brown, dry patches.

"I travel a lot," Killian explained.

Robyn shrugged her shoulders, pretending she didn't care. Her dad traveled, too. Herman had always placed his job before his family. Was Killian just like him?

Standing by his front porch, Robyn turned west. "Wow, I didn't realize you could see the Rocky Mountains from way out in the boonies of Franktown." She knew she was in danger, but the FBI agents securing the property seemed to drive home the message with force.

"It's one of the reasons I moved here. That and the peace and quiet. My closest neighbor is a quarter-mile away." He pointed to a house visible through the trees.

Robyn moved to the trunk of her car and unlocked it. "Can you get these? I want to bring Brooklyn in out of the hot car."

"Sure."

The cat meowed when she pulled the carrier from the backseat. "I know, baby. You hate traveling, don't you?"

"God, Banks, I said to pack an overnight bag, not your

entire wardrobe." He lugged two suitcases out of the trunk and set them on the driveway. "What do you have in here, bricks?"

"A woman has to have her essentials." She walked up to the porch and waited for him to unlock the door. His biceps bulged with the weight of her luggage as he climbed the stairs two at a time. It was all she could do to level her gaze elsewhere. She didn't need to get attached to a man who would never be around.

This wasn't a romantic getaway weekend interlude. If she needed any further reminders of that she only needed to look around. The plainclothes agents walked the perimeter of the house, checking behind bushes, scanning the area and verifying the integrity of the security.

Shoving the key in the lock, Killian pushed open the door and indicated with a hand that she should precede him. So . . . they were back to the awkward stage again. Avoiding gazes. Polite to the screaming point. Both were trying to forget, or avoid, the awareness sizzling between them. At least she was trying to forget. Despite what Ginger had claimed, Robyn found it hard to believe Killian was enamored of her. He acted like she was just a case—and an inconvenient one at that. A fact she should have been thankful for. Instead the implication stung.

She walked into the house and stopped short. Massive floor-to-ceiling windows graced one entire wall, exposing the beautiful, crystal-clear view of Pike's Peak in the distance. The cathedral ceiling gave way to a loft on the second floor which overlooked the expansive living room. "Killian, this is spectacular."

He grinned like a little kid. "You like it?"

"Like it? I love it." She set the kitty carrier on the hardwood floor and opened the door. "Come on out, Brooklyn."

The cat stuck her face out, sniffed the air, then, low to the ground, she slunk across the floor. Her tail twitched to and fro when she stopped, sniffed again, then crawled underneath the plaid sofa for safety.

"She'll get used to it," Killian said, luggage still in hand. "Come on. I'll show you to your room."

A gallery of assorted photographs and pictures lined one wall leading toward the upstairs. One in particular caught Robyn's attention, and she felt compelled to stop and study it. It was of a war-torn town filled with rubble and debris. In the middle of all the chaos and damage was a tiny child, a waif, with a wise-beyond-her-years smile on her face.

"This is a captivating picture. Who took it?"

"My mother."

His clipped tone made her turn and look at him. Why was he so angry over one photo?

"She has a wonderful gift."

"I suppose you're right. It made the cover of *Time* magazine."

"Where is she now? Does she still shoot?"

"No. She's dead." His eyes took on a blank expression. "My parents were news photographers. They traveled all over the world to war-infested countries. On their last assignment, I begged them not to go. I was ten and tired of watching them leave on planes. I loved staying with my aunt, but I had this strange feeling I'd never see Mom and Dad again."

Robyn wanted to comfort him, wrap her arms around him and take away all the pain, but she couldn't. He had that closed look to his eyes, his shoulders were back, his head high. He didn't want to talk about it. Didn't want her pity.

"Americans were warned to leave the country as soon as possible, because it had become too dangerous. A plane was standing ready." He shook his head, as if still in disbelief.

"They just had to get one more picture. It didn't matter that I was waiting at home. They broke the rules without thinking of consequences.

"That last picture cost them their lives. A bomb exploded, killing them both." He closed his eyes and rubbed his forehead.

In a way, Robyn could imagine the horror he'd gone through. How many times had she begged Herman to stay? How many times had he ignored her? Her heart ached for the little boy in Hart, and for the little girl in her.

"They got what they wanted, though. That last picture my mother snapped became famous. I keep it here as a reminder. I always thought it ironic that the camera survived the blast and they didn't."

Without further explanation, he turned and climbed the stairs. Robyn followed him up the curving stairwell, fascinated and saddened by the story. Were his nightmares a result of his parents' deaths? She had so many questions, but knew Killian would refuse to answer a single one. Her heart went out to him.

Killian entered a sparsely decorated yet homey room, done up in pale yellows and blues. "You can sleep in here." He deposited the two suitcases on the beige carpeted floor.

"This is nice." She tossed her purse in the middle of the brass double bed, and tried to forget what he'd told her moments earlier. *And where will you be sleeping, Killian? Just in case I, ah, need you in the middle of the night?*

"What do we do now? Wait for the wacko to find me?"

A nerve ticked in his jaw. "He's not going to find you. You're safe. My room is right across the hall. If anything happens, I'll be here in a heartbeat." She flushed when he studied her face. Why did he look like he wanted to touch her?

"Good . . . great."

"I need to call the office." Twisting on his heel, he strode from the room.

Robyn spent the day wandering from room to room, feeling like the captive she was. By evening she was bored with her own company and ready to go out of her mind. Even dinner had been a solitary meal with Killian holed up in his office.

Exploring the contents of the hall closet, she discovered a jigsaw puzzle and dragged it out, blowing off a layer of dust. Emptying the contents onto the dining room table, she sat down to tackle the intricate seashell design.

"Aren't you tired? It's after eleven." Robyn jumped when Killian strolled into the room.

"I am. I've got to wind down first." She bent her head over the pieces and concentrated on finding two that fit.

Or she *tried* to concentrate, anyway. Killian made it difficult. It wasn't anything he said. Or did. It was his mere presence. His animal magnetism. His scent. Primal—earthy. Male sweat and sexual tension. The desire that had flashed across his face when he'd shown Robyn the bedroom she was to use, had been fleeting . . . but she couldn't deny that it had existed.

Was she attracted to him because they'd been in a life-or-death situation together? Or was it something stronger, deeper—something much more intense? Snapping two puzzle parts together made her wonder what it would feel like if he drew her into his arms. Would their lips fit like the two interlocking pieces of the puzzle?

She glanced at him, her gaze drawn to the hard line of his stubborn jaw, darkened by five-o'clock shadow. Despite the fact that he reminded her a bit of her father, she had to admire his dedication. When Killian Hart wanted his man, he wanted his man. Would he be that way with the woman he loved? Let nothing stand between them? Protect her? Provide for her? Devote his entire existence to her?

She shivered. Why should she care? Killian opened the refrigerator and poured himself a glass of milk, glancing in her direction when he took the first sip. Robyn directed her concentration back to the puzzle.

"You're doing that all wrong." The deep timbre of his voice lodged in her heart, trapped the breath in her lungs. He was standing right behind her. Against her back, she could feel the heat of his body.

"What are you talking about?" She smoothed a hand over the joined puzzle in front of her. "They fit together just fine."

"You're supposed to do the outside perimeter of a puzzle first."

Robyn snatched up the lid of the puzzle box and scanned it. "Well, golly, I don't remember ever reading that rule."

He moved to her side. So close she could have reached out and touched his muscular thigh, if he'd just give her half an invitation.

"It's an unwritten rule," he informed her.

Placing an elbow on the table, Robyn propped her forehead in her hands. "You know the problem with you, Killian?" She looked up at him. Stared into the chocolate brown depths of his eyes.

"What?" The look he shot back at her had "I really don't think I want to hear what you have to say" written all over it.

She ignored the warning signs. "You follow too many blasted rules."

His eyes narrowed. "No, I don't." He grabbed a flat-edged piece off the table and looked for its mate.

Just before he'd averted his gaze, she'd glimpsed something in his eyes. Pain? Regret? When would he let go of his past? "Yes, you do. If you're not in control, your world is off-kilter. Admit it."

Finding a piece that matched, Killian snapped two peach-colored parts together. His gaze locked with hers, wariness evident, and the look she'd glimpsed before concealed behind his sarcasm. "Why admit something that isn't true?"

An unruly lock of hair fell into Robyn's eye, and with an impatient gesture she pushed it out of the way. "Because it is true."

"Isn't."

"Is—and I can prove it."

He eyed her suspiciously. "How?"

The wooden chair she sat in scraped against the Spanish tile when she pushed it back and stood. "Stand right here." She placed her hands on his broad shoulders and pushed him to the middle of the kitchen. Her fingers tingled where she touched him. She moved away, breaking the intimate contact, and rubbed her hands against her pant legs.

He stood with his feet braced apart, hands on hips. He looked so male and virile, her heart skipped a couple hundred beats. Doubts flooded her. *Don't do this, Robyn. Back away right now and no one will get hurt.*

God, and she had accused him of being paranoid. She was just proving a point, she reminded herself. That was all. Nothing more. Nothing less. "Close your eyes, Killian."

After a second, his eyelids dropped. "What are you going to do?"

"Don't worry, I won't hurt you."

One lid lifted. "Promise?" The hint of a smile tugged the corner of his mouth.

Her heart raced faster than it had when they'd been running through the woods away from guns and killers and bears. She drew a cross over the left side of her chest. "Promise." Then she frowned at him. "Close your eyes." When he complied, she continued. "No matter what I do to you, you can't take over. I am in complete control. I am in charge. *Capische?*"

"Are you a throwback from some feminist movement? If we had a campfire, instead of marshmallows would we be roasting bras?"

Robyn looked down at her chest and sighed. *That blaze of glory would be little more than a tiny spark in the night.* "I sincerely doubt it. Quit trying to change the subject and pay attention."

His lips quirked. "Sorry."

One lesson Robyn had learned years ago regarding the opposite sex, was that men wanted to be in complete control. They needed to take the initiative. Be in the lead. Have the ultimate power. What they had yet to understand was that a woman could bring them to their knees with a simple touch—a heated look—a breathless whisper. First Robyn walked a slow circle around him. Close enough that he could feel her presence, yet far enough apart that touching was just a promise away.

His hands balled into tight fists at his sides. "What are you doing?"

"Just walking, Secret Agent Man. Do you want to take over already?"

His jaw tightened. "No."

Robyn stopped in front of him, took a deep breath, tried to convince herself she was doing this to prove a point. Somehow, she'd forgotten what the point was. The urge to run her fingers over his strong, muscular body transcended game playing. The female in her had to know if he felt as good as he looked. Was Killian the kind of man to fall to his knees over a woman? Or was his heart made of steel and already promised to his job?

Tentatively, she placed her hand against his chest. His

heart beat beneath her palm. Steady. Regular. Totally in control. Was he that immune to her? It hurt to think he might be. The game changed. She didn't care whether he could, or could not, maintain control—she just wanted to know whether she had the power to bring him to his knees. Not that she wanted him, she reminded herself. It was a matter of feminine pride.

"You're too tall. Bend down."

One russet eyebrow lifted above a closed eye. "Now I'm supposed to help you in your quest?"

"It takes two," she whispered.

His nostrils flared slightly, but he bent at the waist, bringing his face closer to hers.

Robyn's breath caught in her throat. Up close a faint spattering of freckles ran across the bridge of his nose. She'd never seen anything sexier in her life. A jolt of awareness zinged up her spine. Run, you idiot. Turn around and run, for God's sake. She squared her shoulders. What was she—chicken? She'd started this, and she was damn sure going to finish it. Freckles or no freckles.

Leaning toward him, she blew into his ear.

His Adam's apple bobbed.

She stuck out the tip of her tongue and traced the curve of his lobe.

The heartbeat beneath her palm quickened.

Following the line of his jaw, Robyn worked her way down to his lips. He tasted salty. Male. Her own breathing accelerated. At the corner of his mouth, she stopped, changed direction and blazed a path down his neck.

He shifted from one foot to the other.

Robyn fought the urge to press her body to his, rub her aching breasts against his chest. *He's the one who's supposed to lose control, Robyn. Not you.*

She couldn't stop. Didn't want to.

With the tip of her finger, she slipped the top button on his shirt free. Ran a hand through the dark hairs on his chest. His heat enveloped her. Surrounded her. Claimed her. She could see the tip of the scar he'd received when he'd dove through the cabin window. It brought back the feeling of danger. "Man, you weren't kidding about all those stitches." She leaned in and kissed the scar.

"Yeah."

She was in over her head. She'd heard somewhere that when one was drowning, breathing water felt like breathing air. Well, breathing Killian's essence made her feel like she was alive. He embodied danger and excitement and passion. He was everything that was missing from her normal, boring, everyday existence.

A sound very much like a growl came from Killian's throat. Robyn felt it rumble against her tongue as she made her way from his neck down to his bared chest. Firm hands grabbed her waist, held her tight, but he made no other move.

Robyn's body ignited. Blazed out of control. Why did she feel like she was the one flunking her own test?

"Robyn?" His voice came out husky.

She licked her lips, leaned back. Looked up at his still-closed eyes. "What?"

"You win. Sort of." His lids lifted. His gaze captured hers. Held on tight. Made her knees weak. Filled her with a longing so intense she almost gasped.

"I do?" She had to search to find the words.

His nod was almost imperceptible. "I'm taking over, but I have never wanted to be so out of control in my life." His head dipped. Warm lips captured hers—ground against her teeth. Demanded a response she gave with no hesitation.

Grabbing two handfuls of his shirt, she pulled herself

closer. Opened herself up to his kiss.

Killian palmed her rear and pulled her in tighter. Robyn shivered. The thought crossed her mind that they did fit like a puzzle. No outside edges, though, just curves and angles that joined like they were made for each other.

His tongue brushed across her lower lip. Robyn opened her mouth and invited him in. His erection pressed against her stomach. An answering moistness pooled between her legs. Her breathing grew erratic. She moved to press her throbbing need against him and found empty air instead.

Cold unwanted space barged between them when Killian pushed her away and stepped back. He ran a shaky hand through his disheveled hair.

Robyn stared at him in disbelief, her chest heaving, and her breathing unstable. She almost hit the ground on her knees.

He tore his gaze from hers, studied the floor, then the table behind her. "I'm sorry."

In fear that she would fall if she didn't sit, Robyn perched on the edge of the dining room chair. "No, I'm sorry." Sorry she wasn't woman enough for a man like Killian. She looked up at him. He stood there, staring down at her, one hand on his hip, a stormy look in his brown eyes. Why did she have to love him?

The portable radio at his hip bleeped and gave off static. "Agent Hart, we've got movement beyond the perimeter."

Within seconds, Killian's professional persona kicked in. Fire snapped in his eyes. Robyn realized she could never compete with the excitement that was his job.

"Send in one of your team. As soon as they get here, I'll come out."

His words confirmed her suspicions. At the least little prompting, he was ready to leave her. "Can't you stay here and let someone else do what needs to be done?"

"This is my property, Robyn. I know it better than they do. It makes sense."

Any kind of romantic involvement between her and Killian made no sense. She knew it with every fiber of her being, but her heart still ached. She nodded. "I understand."

The replacement cop strolled into the living room. "Stay safe," Killian warned her before turning and striding out of the room.

"Too late," she whispered, her heart had already been compromised.

Even though they conducted a thorough search for a good forty-five minutes that had Robyn on edge, they found one set of tracks that stopped at the edge of the woods. Whoever had made the tracks was long gone. Robyn felt too keyed up to appreciate any real sense of relief. The second Killian walked back into the house, Robyn pleaded exhaustion and went up to her room.

The next day, Robyn tinkered in the front yard pulling weeds and pruning delicate pink and yellow roses with some gardening tools she'd discovered while snooping in the garage. An officer had dogged her every step—orders from Killian, she had no doubt. Every once in a while, she'd look up to find Killian watching her out the window, cellular phone held against his ear.

She hoped they'd find the thief/murderer soon. She liked Killian's place, but it was obvious he didn't want her there, which was why she refused to go indoors until she had to.

When the sun was nothing more than a big orange glow behind the mountains, she decided it was time to go inside. She wiped sweat from her brow, anxious for a cool shower, when something brushed up against her leg.

Looking down, she discovered a little black and white

kitten staring up at her with unblinking green eyes. Her heart melted. "Oh, where did you come from, little one?"

She picked him up and held him against her cheek. He purred and rubbed his furry head against her. "You look hungry, baby." After checking to make sure he was indeed a *little guy,* she decided she'd keep him. If she couldn't have Killian, she needed something to devote her attention toward. He was too cute to resist, and Brooklyn needed a playmate.

"I was just going to come and get you," Killian announced when she walked into the kitchen. "What do you have there?"

"A kitten. I found him outside. Or I guess he found me. I'm going to keep him." She set him down on the floor next to Brooklyn. The Siamese sniffed the baby all over, then began licking his head. "Brooklyn likes him." At least somebody was getting some lovin' in this big old house.

"Looks like. Dinner will be ready in a while. Thought you might want to clean up first. I'll watch the little one for you. What's his name?"

She cocked her head sideways and studied the pair at her feet. "I'm not sure. I'll have to think about it."

"Extra towels are in the linen closet in the bathroom . . . Robyn?" He stopped her when she turned to leave.

Her heart hammered in her chest. "What?"

"You don't have to take care of my yard."

"I don't mind. It gives me something to do." How could she explain to him that it felt like she was taking care of *her* yard? He'd have her packed and out of there in no time. "I'm sure it's inconvenient to have a . . . stranger in your home. It's my way of paying you back." They shouldn't be strangers after all they'd shared. Before he could respond, she raced out of the room and headed for the shower.

Things were not going as planned, Robyn decided, as she

stood in front of the mirror blow-drying her thick hair. She needed to find a way to make him kiss her again. Last night had her craving more.

Of course, he'd never seen her at anything but her worst. No makeup, dirty hair, soiled clothing. Tonight was going to be different. Tonight he would see her at her dazzling best.

The smell of meat loaf filled the kitchen. Killian pulled the sizzling pan out of the oven and set it on a hot pad on the counter to cool.

"Wow. Smells delicious. You're going to make someone a great housekeeper someday."

Killian turned at the sound of Robyn's voice. "I was just going to come and get . . ." His words trailed off when he looked at her. This wasn't his Robyn. This was an imposter. Her hair, which he'd always loved to begin with, seemed even thicker, and the shiny, wild curls took on a life of their own.

"You look . . . different," he said. He pulled on the neck of his shirt.

Disappointment flashed in her brown eyes—eyes framed by the longest lashes he'd ever seen. Her eyelids sported a hint of color that made her look exotic and sexy as hell.

"Different? That's all?"

Was that anger laced through her voice? Why was she mad? He'd noticed a difference. Women! *Okay, Killian, say something nice to smooth this over.* "Why are you wearing all that makeup? You don't need it."

"Well, I—I just—I thought—I wanted to look nice for a change," she sputtered.

He'd never seen her looking bad. Quite the contrary, which was why he had to maintain his distance. "Oh. I see."

A crestfallen expression flashed across her face. She almost looked as if she wanted to burst into tears or flee the room, or both. Now what had he said? He'd been nice. Hell, he'd told her she didn't need makeup, how much nicer could a guy be than that? "Dinner's ready. Why don't you sit at the table."

"All of a sudden, I'm not hungry."

He tried to coax her. "Come on, it's my secret meat loaf recipe. I only feed it to special people."

"Let me guess, could arsenic be the main ingredient?" she asked, as she slid out a chair from the oak table and sat down.

Okay. She was still mad about last night, but at least she hadn't left the room. "I don't think I'd go to the trouble of trying to save you and then let you die eating my cooking."

"You've got a point, Secret Agent Man." Grabbing the napkin, she spread it on her lap. "That would be against the rules, now wouldn't it?"

Robyn may have found her misplaced appetite, but Killian lost his. All during dinner, he couldn't take his eyes off her. It was hard to eat lousy meat loaf when the best-looking dish of the evening sat across the table from him, and he couldn't even try a nibble. He didn't want to lead her on. Not when he'd have to set her free in the end. He should have never kissed her yesterday, but he couldn't have stopped for anything.

Robyn paused with her fork halfway to her mouth. "Why are you staring at me? Do I have food all over my face?" She grabbed the napkin and dabbed at her lips.

He could almost swear she was wearing the same shade of lipstick he'd picked up off her dresser the other night.

Vamp.

The color suited her. The kitchen grew warm. His jeans grew tight. He realized the color suited *him*.

"What's for dessert?" she asked, pushing her empty plate away.

She was so tiny. Where'd she put all that food? "You have room for dessert?"

"There's always room for dessert."

"Let's wait. I'm stuffed." He got up to stack the dishes in the sink when the phone rang. Arms full, he pushed the speaker button. "Hart," he announced.

"Killian, it's Will. We've got more problems." Holgate's voice boomed through the kitchen.

Killian's gaze flew to Robyn. So much for hoping she hadn't heard. She held her back rigid. The napkin in her hand shook. He threw the dishes in the sink with a clatter and grabbed the receiver, keeping the rest of the conversation private.

Robyn couldn't take any more. Pushing away from the table, she hurried into the living room. From the huge windows, she watched the stars twinkling in the dark sky. She sighed, and hugged her arms around her waist. An officer, patrolling the grounds, walked past the window, the gun in his holster reflecting a stab of moonlight.

She felt like a fugitive. Or better yet, a candidate for the witness protection program who'd already lost her name, her identity, and her place in life. As much as she wanted to stay out in the country with Killian, she wanted her old life back.

Reflected in the window, she watched Killian approach her from behind.

"What did he say?" she asked, keeping her eyes trained on the stars.

After a pregnant pause, he joined her at the window and looked up at the same constellation. "*He* knows we've hidden you somewhere."

"Yeah, but who in the hell is *he?* . . . and how does he know? And what does he want from me?" Fear made her voice more clipped than she wanted.

"We're doing our best to find out." He ran a warm hand up and down the length of her arm. "Try not to worry."

She laughed. "That's easy for you to say." An uncertain, scared meow sounded at her feet. Robyn glanced down and picked up Brooklyn, cradling her in her arms while the un-named kitten rubbed against her legs. "I know exactly how you feel, Brooky." If she hadn't picked up the cat, she knew for a fact she would have ended up in Killian's arms.

Big mistake.

She didn't want a pity embrace. She wanted it to mean much more than that. Yet, why did she want him at all when it was obvious he didn't want her?

"I need to keep myself busy." She glanced around the room looking for something to do.

"Some television?"

"I wouldn't be able to concentrate." She set Brooklyn on the floor and dashed toward the stairs. "I'll be right back." Grabbing her makeup bag off the dresser, she headed back to the living room. "Painting my nails always soothes me."

Killian had already taken one end of the sofa and was busy channel surfing with the remote.

Robyn took the other end, glad that Brooklyn and the kitten had curled up in twin tight balls on the cushion between them. They served as a safety zone. A furry barrier. Fishing through her bag, she found the shade of polish she wanted and shook the bottle. She took a tissue and pushed a section between each toe, separating them so the color wouldn't smear.

Unscrewing the cap, Robyn scraped the biggest blobs of polish off the side of the brush, then started painting her big toe. More color ended up on her skin than on the nail. "Damn. My hands are shaking too much."

"Here, let me." Killian threw the remote on the coffee table and held his hand out for the bottle.

"Discovering your feminine side?"

One eyebrow rose. "Do you want me to do it or not?"

When she thought about it, any man who would offer to paint a woman's toenails, without a gun to his head, had to be pretty damn comfortable with his own masculinity. After a slight hesitation, she handed it to him. Then, turning sideways on the couch, she lifted her foot onto his lap.

Too bad he wouldn't let *her* get comfortable with his masculinity.

Robyn studied his bent head. At first, it seemed like he didn't want to touch her. Finally, to get a better angle, he encircled her foot with his palm and twisted it a fraction.

The warm skin touching hers had her eyes slipping shut. He was so sensitive, so gentle. She had the feeling, as a lover, he'd be all that and still manage to drive her to the point of crazy.

"Quit wiggling."

She blushed. Thank God he was busy concentrating and didn't look at her. "Sorry."

"Other foot."

Withdrawing her right, she plopped her left in his lap. He attacked this foot with the same attention to detail he'd given the first. With two toes left, Robyn felt a distinct bulge beneath her heel, which hadn't been there seconds earlier. A yearning burned deep inside her. By accident, her heel pressed against the mound.

Killian fidgeted.

Robyn closed her eyes again.

A hand ran up the length of her leg, stopping beneath the knee. He pushed her foot out of his lap. The cushions shifted. When Robyn opened her eyes, the cats were on the floor nursing their wounded pride, and Killian was on his knees in the spot they'd vacated, smack dab in the middle of the sofa. Close. He was too damn close. She sucked in a deep breath.

"I can't fight this anymore, Robyn." Husky emotion filled his voice. His Adam's apple bobbed up and down when he swallowed. He cupped her face in his hands. "I need to be with you."

Robyn smiled through tears. "I thought you'd never ask."

His lips touched hers. Achingly tender, the contact was so fleeting she would have thought she'd imagined it. But she hadn't. Their eyes were both still wide open. They stared at each other like they couldn't believe what was happening. If they closed their eyes, the illusion would shatter.

He pulled her closer, one arm encircling her waist. "God, you're so beautiful," he whispered against her neck.

Robyn tilted her head, afraid to breathe—afraid to move.

"Touch me," he begged. "Touch me, so I know you're real—that this isn't a dream."

She placed her hands on the solid wall of his chest. The erratic beat of his heart pulsed beneath her palms. Her hands inched upward around his neck and plunged into the soft hair at his nape. "If you're dreaming, then I am, too." She sought out his mouth again, nipping the full bottom lip. "But this is much better than any dream I've ever had."

"Robyn?"

"Yeah?"

He pulled back, his gaze boring deep into her soul. "Did anyone ever tell you that you talk too much?"

Leaning forward, she traced the line of his jaw with the tip of her tongue. "It's part of my charm, but I'll shut up if you will."

A primal growl emanated from deep within him. Stepping off the sofa, he scooped her into his arms. "I'm taking you to my bed. We're doing this right the first time."

He kicked open the door to his bedroom and, standing on the threshold, kissed her on the lips like he couldn't get enough of the taste of her.

The mattress gave way when he laid her in the middle, and he followed her down. The length of his body trapped every inch of hers, yet he kept his weight off with the support of his hands on either side of her head. Bondage had never felt so sweet.

Shifting, he stripped his shirt over his head and threw it across the room. Through the thin material of her shirt, her nipples hardened into tight buds against the coarse hairs on his chest. She wiggled beneath him, trying to bring their bodies even closer. The curtains ruffled in the summer breeze, filling the room with the scent of the roses she'd pruned earlier.

Raising her head, she grabbed one of his nipples between her teeth and tugged. With one hand she traced the jagged scar running across his stomach.

He gave a throaty groan and ground the head of his engorged shaft against her stomach. He leaned down and kissed her again, his tongue pressing against her lips, begging for entrance.

She parted her lips, met his tongue with her own. God, she wanted him. She wanted him in her—on her—over her—and all around her. And that still wouldn't be enough.

Impatient, Robyn grabbed her own shirt and started ripping it off.

"Don't." His hands halted hers. "I'll get it." Sitting up, he pulled her onto his lap. His erection pressed against the crotch of her jeans shorts.

She drew in a ragged breath. "Killian—"

"Sshhh."

"I can't take—"

He pressed two fingers against her lips. "Ssssssshhhhh."

"Do you know what you're doing to me?"

He pulled her shirt over her head and tossed it in the corner with his own. "Yes." He licked his lips, raised his hips against her again. "I'm doing what I've wanted to do since the moment I met you." Lowering her bra strap, he slipped a hand inside the black material and cupped her breast, rolled the distended bud between finger and thumb.

She shivered as spiking heat shot through her. She couldn't take it anymore. "I need to be naked right now, Killian."

Silently, he grabbed her by the waist and raised her to her knees, his passion-filled eyes never leaving hers. His breathing whispered harsh, his need exciting her even more. With the moonlight spilling in through the window, he unbuttoned her shorts and eased them and her silky underwear down her hips until the material pooled around her knees.

He kneaded the flesh of her buttocks. Robyn arched against him, moist heat pooling at the apex of her thighs. He slipped a hand between her legs, pushing two fingers deep inside her, eliciting a throaty moan. Rapture sang through her veins.

Opening to him, craving more, she kicked free from the shorts. Robyn rode his hand, whimpering little animal noises, and he stroked deeper. "I want you naked, too." Reaching between their heated bodies, she caressed the mound pressing against his fly. Inch by tantalizing inch, she lowered the zipper, the sound mingling with their labored breathing.

He helped her push his slacks and boxers down his thighs. When his erection sprang free, her eyes drank in his splendid arousal. Tingling all over, she ached to have him inside her.

He rubbed his rapt length against her bare stomach, then kicked their clothes off the bed.

Robyn lay back against the mattress, pulling Killian along with her. He kissed her again, his tongue flicking in and out of her mouth, simulating the mating act. Her whole body tingled, caught on fire and blazed out of control.

Wanting him even closer, she wrapped her legs around his trim waist, locking them over his back. Her hips raised against his arousal, seeking release from the incredible pressure building inside her.

"I want this to last forever," he whispered, his words hot against her ear.

"If you make me wait one more second, I'll die." Grabbing his thick turgid shaft, she guided him snug against her slick heat. "Take me now. Please," she begged, clutching his back with urgent fingers.

He filled her inch by wondrous inch, until she thought she couldn't take any more—stretch any wider. When it felt as if he'd reached all the way to her womb, he withdrew with slow torturous friction, then plunged into her again. His hand slid down her belly, increasing his heated exploration of her senses, finding her wet cleft and palming her as they rode together in perfect rhythm.

Robyn couldn't think or reason. But she could taste. She ran her tongue across the rough, dark hairs on his chest, circled his nipple. He tasted salty, all heady male strength. The musky scent of their lovemaking filled the air. It was all proof that this wasn't a dream she'd wake from anytime soon.

And she could feel. God, could she feel. With the tips of her fingers, she touched every square inch of Killian's body. Discovering the texture of him. The raised ridge of his healing wound. The way his chest hairs sprang back into place when she rang her fingers through them. She ran her touch over the muscled contour of heated flesh, felt the flexing of his power bunched beneath her hands as he held her impaled. The tight straining of his biceps as he held his weight off her body.

His thickness filled her completely. Sliding in and out. The pressure building, spiraling with every thrust, until her body burst into an explosion of rapturous colors, senses and images.

Killian tensed, breathing heavily, then climaxed. Sweat glistened on his brow. He bent his head and captured her sigh in a soul-robbing kiss. Lying by her side, he drew her into his embrace, her cheek against his chest, their bodies touching all the way down to their toes.

She wanted to tell him she loved him. The words were on the tip of her tongue, ready to spill out, but for some reason she held back. How many times had she told her father she loved him? How many times had she waited in vain for the statement to be reciprocated? No. Not this time. Killian could say those three little words first.

For some reason, Robyn happened to glance down at her feet. Hunks of tissue were still stuck between several toes. "Ah, Killian?"

"Hmmm?"

She smiled. "We seem to have smudged my polish." A deep sigh escaped her parted lips, disturbing the hairs on his chest. "I think we're going to have to start all over at the beginning."

Killian refused to move. Robyn lay snuggled against his side, fast asleep. Her chest rose and fell with each breath. He kissed her temple, then tightened his hold. She wriggled even closer, throwing one shapely leg over the top of his.

They'd made love well into the night, and he'd discovered two things. One, Robyn was insatiable. Two, he couldn't get enough of her, either.

Why had he resisted his feelings for her for so long? They were perfect together. If he hadn't been so obsessed with following rules, he'd have discovered that little secret long ago. As soon as she woke up, he'd tell her how much he cared. A smile tugged at his lips. Cared? A lame word for what he felt.

He was crazy about her. Hell, he loved her. So much so that he wanted to be around her every waking minute—every sleeping one, too. Though if tonight was any example, they wouldn't get much sleeping done. ⁄

The phone on the nightstand interrupted the calm silence. Killian grabbed the receiver before it could ring again and wake Robyn. "Hart," he whispered into the mouthpiece.

"Killian? Will. Pack your bags. We've got a hot tip that leads straight to Phoenix. I need you to hop the next flight out before the trail grows cold."

His gaze shot to Robyn, who hadn't stirred at the sound of the phone. "Why me?" He wanted to stay by Robyn's side. Didn't want to leave her when his feelings were so new. No one could keep her safe the way he could. "Can't Dan go?"

"Stevens's mother has taken a slight turn for the worse. Nothing major, but I still don't have the heart to send him out of town. You're the only agent I trust to get the job done. Don't worry, I'll see to it the Jeffries woman is taken care of if I have to do it myself."

Chapter 12

The second Robyn woke up, she knew something was wrong. She was alone in the big bed. Panic threatened to surface, but she forced it away. Maybe Killian was downstairs cooking her breakfast. She smiled, then stretched her arms luxuriously over her head, reveling in the feel of the cool, crisp sheets against her naked skin.

Expanding her arms sideways across the width of the bed, her hand brushed against something on Killian's pillow that emitted a crinkling noise.

Paper. A note. Had he left her after one night? Robyn squeezed her eyes shut, then sat on the edge of the bed, her back to what had to be a "Dear John" letter. She could see this happening if they'd made love at her apartment, but this was his house. How could he walk out on her in his own place?

She dropped her forehead into her hands and sighed. Who said it had to be bad? For all she knew, it could be a gushy love note, she tried to reassure herself. And it would have worked except Killian wasn't the gushy love note kind of guy. Only one way to find out what the message said.

She'd have to read it.

Robyn tilted her head to the ceiling. Drew in a ragged breath. Reaching behind her, she ripped the dreaded piece of typing paper off the pillow, which still held the imprint of Killian's head.

Robyn, Will Holgate called. We got a hot tip on our killer. I had to go out of town. We'll talk when I get back. Killian.

A hot tip, huh? Tears pricked Robyn's eyes. She could have substituted Herman's name for Killian's. The difference was the fact Killian used the guise of his job to run away, and he hadn't asked for any money.

Where were the words of love or commitment? They'd just spent the entire night making love, and this note said they were back to playing the roles of strangers. If he were here, she'd give him a piece of her mind.

Robyn crumpled the note into a ball, walked into the bathroom and flushed it down the toilet. Turning on the shower steaming hot, she stepped under the stinging spray and tried to wash away the scent, the touch, and the memory of Killian.

When the water started to run cold, she turned it off and scrubbed a towel over her body. She didn't feel any better than before the shower. Killian's memory still clung to her. The way his touch had driven her to ecstasy. The way his lips had claimed her own. The way his heated gaze had held hers at the moment of their climax.

She grabbed her makeup bag, then flung it back onto the tile countertop. What did makeup matter? He couldn't stand her either with or without it. Why waste the energy? She pulled her wild hair back into a ponytail, her fingers shaking too much to attempt anything as elaborate as a French braid.

Dressed in her denim shorts and a pink T-shirt, she headed downstairs to feed Brooklyn and the unnamed kitten. The thought of eating food herself made her nauseous.

When she walked into the kitchen, she stopped short, grabbing the door frame for support. "Who the hell are you?" she gasped, looking at a blond-haired man sitting at the oak table reading the *Denver Post* and drinking a cup of coffee. She recognized him as the man Ginger had pointed out. She hadn't trusted him. Robyn decided not to, either.

The chair scraped across the floor as the man stood.

Robyn took a step back, one hand held to her chest.

"I'm sorry. I didn't mean to scare you. Killian had to leave." The man reached out his hand. "I'm Dan Stevens, Killian's partner. You want some coffee?"

She grabbed his hand, pumping it once before she released it. Coffee sounded unappetizing. "No, thanks. Maybe later."

She sucked in a deep breath. The sooner the killer was apprehended, the sooner they could get on with a normal life. She had to trust Killian. Now was as good a time as later. "Maybe I will have that coffee, after all." Dan wouldn't be here unless Killian trusted him with her life.

Neither uttered a word in the silent kitchen. She remained wary of him the rest of the day. As if she didn't quite trust him, she kept her distance. Much later, when they were halfway through a hastily thrown together dinner, Will Holgate strode into the kitchen.

Dan Stevens jumped to his feet. "Sir?"

Holgate didn't spare Dan a single glance. "This location has been compromised. We need to move Miss Jeffries to another safe house."

Moving without Killian along with her felt unsafe and very wrong. Uneasiness quivered down her spine. "Can't we wait for Killian to get back?"

Holgate fixed her with a stare. "Not if you want to live."

"Okay. Let me pack my bags and gather my cats."

"No time." He threw her an irritated look.

This man had never been married or he'd understand the female mind. Resigned, she rubbed a hand across her forehead. "Fine. Safety first."

"Where are we going, sir?" Dan asked.

"We? You're staying here in case our killer shows up. I'll take her someplace where no one will find her."

With a hand at the small of her back, Holgate led her outside. "We'll take your car. You can drive."

She understood now why Dan had snapped to command the second Will Holgate had entered the room. His tone brooked no argument. Whatever he wanted, he got. She slid behind the wheel. "Where to, sir?"

"You tell me. We're going where the money is."

"What money?" Robyn's gaze shifted from his eyes to the revolver aimed right at her. She tensed. This was a turn of events she hadn't expected.

"Don't play coy with me. You may have Killian suckered with your hot little body." He leered at her from head to toe. "I know better. I know all about women like you."

She raised her chin—tried to remain calm, despite a dry throat and shaky stomach. "Think whatever you like. I don't know anything about this money to which you refer. I don't *want* to know anything about the money. I wish I'd never heard about the damn money." Her foot moved from the gas to the brake.

Holgate grabbed her arm. The grip didn't hurt, but she felt the implied force behind it.

Killian's boss meant business.

"Take your hands off me." She clenched her teeth.

He responded by tightening his fingers a fraction of an inch. His voice lowered malevolently. "Keep driving. I know you've got the dough. I searched your apartment, but couldn't find it."

"You—?!"

"You're going to take me to it. Understand?"

Shocked, Robyn couldn't move. Her vision swam. Killian's boss? It couldn't be possible. Then she remembered her own words not too long ago. Anything was possible.

He shook her arm, rattling her teeth, as he demanded an answer. "You understand me?"

She swallowed, then nodded. Her foot pressed down on the gas, sending them faster down the road toward Denver.

"Good." A smile, which could have been described as evil, played across his face.

"I don't know why you insist I know where the money is. I don't."

"Whatever you say, babe. Whatever you say." Keeping his grip on her arm, he turned and looked out the window at the passing scenery.

All Robyn could think of was her cats. No wonder they'd been hiding. There wasn't a better judge of character than Brooklyn, and the little black and white kitten had the same instincts. They'd be safe at Killian's, Robyn thought. Safe until she came back to collect them.

If she came back.

Sweat trickled down her back, pasting her shirt to her skin and the vinyl seat. She had to keep reminding herself to breathe. Heading North on Flintwood, she decided she'd go back to her apartment. If Killian came home, and discovered her missing, maybe, just maybe, he'd look for her there.

It was the only hope she had.

The heat of the sun drove mercilessly through the 747's Plexiglas window. Killian grabbed the plastic shade and slid it down. He tried to stretch his cramped legs, but the confining space between him and the seat in front of him wouldn't cooperate. He shifted in his chair, anxious for the trip to end.

He'd tried to call his house from the airport in Phoenix, but the phone had rung repeatedly. No answer. He'd convinced himself they'd been outside. The closer the plane got to Denver, the more difficult it was to ignore his intuition.

As hot as the tip Holgate received had been, it turned out

to be less than nothing. If he didn't know better, Killian would almost think someone had wanted him away from his home. Away from Robyn. Out of the picture.

"Can I get you something to drink, sir?"

He glanced at the flight attendant. "No, thanks." His thoughts flew back to Robyn. Where the hell was she? Why hadn't she or Dan answered the phone? And why did his instincts tell him that foul play was involved?

When the plane landed, Killian had his seat belt unfastened and was standing with his overnight bag in hand before the jet had taxied to the gate. Ignoring the hostile looks as he all but trampled over other passengers to deplane first, he raced down the aisle.

"Thank you for flying American," a tall, dark-haired attendant chirped as he ran out the door. At the jet way entrance, two security personnel met him.

"Sir, can you come with us?"

"What is this about? I'm in a hurry." He didn't have time for interruptions.

"The flight attendants said you were acting a little suspicious. Nervous. Agitated. We just have a few questions for you, if you don't mind."

Killian stood with one hand braced on his hip, all set to argue. Hell, yes, he minded. He shook his head, instead. Arguing would delay him longer. The interrogation lasted as long as it took for Killian to flash his badge.

Racing out of the airport, he found his Jeep, hopped in and sped down the highway in no time. The hour trip to his house seemed to take days.

After thinking he'd never get there, he pulled into his driveway. Robyn's car was missing. Dan's yellow Corvette sat in the same spot where he'd parked it this morning. Killian's heart leapt into his throat as he hurried into the house.

"Robyn?" he called. The door banged against the wall.

"Dan . . . are you here?"

The Siamese cat stretched on the living room couch, then hopped to the floor and strolled over to rub against Killian's legs. The kitten followed suit. "Hey, what are you doing back so soon?" Dan asked.

"Where are all the guards? Where is Robyn?"

"Holgate sent them home when he moved Robyn."

Killian's heart leapt to his throat. He knew he should have stayed here. "Why did he move her?"

"He said this location was compromised, made me remain behind in case the killer showed up here."

"Has anyone?"

"Hell, no."

Just like he'd suspected. "No one's going to, either." His niggling hunch burned the lining of his stomach. Killian reached down and absently scratched each cat behind the ears.

"I tried calling twice. No one answered, then my phone ran out of juice."

"I stepped outside for a second to do a perimeter search."

Killian grabbed the phone and dialed his downtown office. He knew what was going to happen, but he had to hear it for himself. "This is Hart. Put me through to Holgate immediately," he snarled at the receptionist.

"He's not here, Agent Hart. He's gone on a fishing trip for two weeks."

Robyn shoved the key into the lock and opened her apartment door. She didn't know what she was going to do once they got inside. There was no money, unless she counted the old mayonnaise jar full of pennies and nickels in her pantry. Somehow she knew that wasn't going to satisfy a hardened criminal like Will Holgate.

Please, please, Killian. Come and get me even if you don't love me. Please come and save me.

"Where is it?" He shoved her farther into the room.

"Like I've been telling you all along. I don't have the money. Why won't you believe me?"

"Robyn, Robyn, Robyn. It wasn't in the van. The only other logical explanation is you or Hart. Hart is too damn honest." His eyebrows rose. "Guess that leaves you, honey."

A thought struck Robyn like a blow to the head. She didn't know why this hadn't come to her earlier. She backed up a step, twisted her hands together. "You killed that man, didn't you?"

Holgate laughed. "I enjoyed every minute of that. Little bastard. McKnight wouldn't tell me where the money was. He forced me to kill him." His hate-filled gaze shifted to her. "Don't force me to kill you." He walked a few steps closer.

Robyn took a few steps back.

"Tell me where it is." He advanced again.

Robyn shuffled backward until she met the solid wall behind her. The killer approached, taking his sweet time, clearly enjoying the fear she felt was written all over her face. He stopped right in front of her. Reaching out, he grabbed a lock of her hair and rubbed it between his fingers.

What was he going to do? Frantic, her gaze searched for a weapon, any weapon.

"You expect me to believe that load of crap? Maybe if you're real nice to me, I'll consider sharing the loot." His seedy gaze took a stroll up and down her body.

Bile rose in her throat.

"I've always admired your . . . spunk, not to mention the tight fit of your clothes." His gaze locked on her chest, which rose and fell with each fear-filled breath she took. "I watched you, you know. When I broke in here that rainy night, I went into your room and watched you sleeping. Your covers slipped off when you rolled over. You're kind of small, but more than a handful is a waste, I always say." Placing one hand on the wall by the side of her face, he trapped her. Leaning in, he cupped one of her breasts.

She shuddered, tried to flail away from him. His fingers squeezed against her flesh. Repulsed, she wanted to scream. She wanted to kick, and claw, and fight her way out of this mess. Her body wouldn't cooperate. Frozen to the spot, she whimpered. "Please, don't do this."

"Oh, come on now." He moved in closer, his breath hot on her cheek. "You can't tell me a sultry number like you doesn't like a little action now and then." He caressed her jawline.

Robyn squeezed her eyes shut and tried to think of happier things. All she could see was Killian's face. Where was he? Would he make it back in time to save her? She didn't think she had the energy to save herself again. Opening her eyes, she glanced toward the door, half-expecting Killian to race through.

"What are you looking at the door for? Killian's not coming. I took care of that. I sent him on a wild goose chase to Phoenix. Gave him enough clues to keep him out of my way."

Hope fizzled. She'd have to save herself, whether she had the wherewithal or not.

Holgate continued. "I've never had a woman complain about my . . . skills before. As a lover, I'm much better than Hart could ever hope to be." His mouth pressed against hers. Insistent. Heated. Unforgiving. Totally loathsome.

Grimacing, Robyn tightened the line of her mouth, refusing to let him in, even though he tried to force his way past with his tongue.

211

"Where's the money?" he asked, his dry lips still against hers.

She shrugged her shoulders, keeping her lips clamped together.

His hand left her breast and slid down her stomach. "One more chance . . . where is it?"

Fear ate at her insides. Tears pricked her eyes. How could she tell him something she didn't know?

He yanked her pink shirt out of the waistband of her pants. "I'm not a patient man, Robyn." He flicked open the button on her shorts, slid a finger down the zipper. "There are three things I savor in life. Money. Sex. And the joy that comes with both of them."

This wasn't sex. It had nothing to do with sex. It was just a way for him to prove he had the ultimate power. Big deal, anyone twice her size could beat her down. As far as she was concerned, it made him less of a man.

When his fingers slipped into the opening, Robyn shuddered. She couldn't get away from him. He was stronger. But she'd be damned if she'd go down without a fight. Raising her knee, she jammed it into his groin as hard as she could.

He cried out and doubled over, but grabbed her arm when she tried to run away, his grip brutal and tight.

She tried to wrench free, but he pulled his revolver out of its holster and shoved it against her stomach. The cold steel against her skin reminded her of the night of the bank heist. It didn't matter who held the offending weapon. She hadn't liked it then, and she despised it even more now.

He dragged her to the floor, still wheezing from her vicious blow to his family jewels. Then he straddled her, settling his heavy weight against her stomach.

"You won't get away with this," she spat at him.

"Maybe, maybe not." A smile slid across his face. "But I'll

sure enjoy the hell out of it." He panted as he leaned down on her. "And I'm going to make sure you do, too."

The distinct sound of a key turning in the lock filled the apartment. Her gaze flew to the door.

"What the hell?" Holgate pushed off Robyn. She yanked up her zipper and tucked in her shirt while she had the chance. Keeping the gun aimed straight at her, he walked to the door in silence. "Keep your mouth shut or die."

The door opened. Ginger walked through. Blood drained from her face when she discovered the business end of a gun barrel pointed between her eyes. Her keys fell to the carpet with a soft jingle, a hand pressed against her rounded stomach in a protective gesture. "What's going on here?" she managed to sputter.

Holgate kicked the door shut.

"Ginger!" Robyn shouted. Her trembling fingers pressed against her lips. "What are you doing here?"

"I left my purse on your bed. My prenatal vitamins are in it." Her voice trailed off when Will advanced toward her, grabbed her arm and yanked her toward the sofa. With a shove, he forced her to sit.

Robyn scrambled up from the floor and rushed to her side. "Watch it, buddy. In case you haven't noticed, she's pregnant. Are you okay, Gin?"

Ginger blinked back tears and gave a feeble nod, her eyes big and wide in her pale face.

Holgate rubbed the end of his gun up against Ginger's belly. "For all I know you're hiding the money under this dress of yours."

"Get away from her!" Robyn demanded, pushing her body between him and her best friend. "How many times do I have to tell you I don't have your damn money? Huh? How many times?"

Before she knew what had happened, he snaked an arm around her waist and wrenched her against him. Jammed the gun barrel against her temple. Robyn winced.

"Don't mess with me," he said. "I'm not in the mood." Releasing her just as abruptly as he'd grabbed her, she fell back and landed next to Ginger on the sofa.

"Which one of you wants to talk first?" Holgate waved the gun between the two of them. Silence, except for the ticking of a clock, filled the room. "You two are wasting my damn time. Last chance. Tell me now or die."

A trail of sweat trickled down Robyn's spine. She measured her words carefully. "I can't tell you what I don't know."

Will's blue eyes narrowed to tiny slits. "Then I hope you like pain. Lots of pain. Because your death isn't going to be fast, or pretty. Trust me, you'll be begging for me to kill you by the time I'm done."

"Leave her alone. I know where the money is," Ginger said.

"Gin, you're crazy. You don't know any such thing."

Ginger turned to Robyn and winked out of the eye that Stevens couldn't see. "On the key ring by the door is the key to my safety deposit box. That's where you'll find the money."

"Are you lying to me?"

"There's one way for you to find out, isn't there?" Ginger was scared, Robyn could tell from the sweat glistening on her upper lip, but she refused to back down, kept her gaze locked with Will's.

Holgate strode to the keys and grabbed them off the floor. "Which bank?"

"United Financial."

Robyn gasped. The bank she worked at? Ginger didn't have an account there. "You have to wait until morning.

The bank is closed for the day."

"Ah, but you work there. The security guard will let you in."

How did he know so much about her? Robyn hesitated, not sure she should tell him the safety deposit boxes were in a timed vault. No one could get in until morning . . . and even then, the key Ginger had given him wouldn't fit any of the locks.

"Well? He'll let you in, won't he?"

She flinched at his tone. All hope fizzled. "Yes." She'd be putting Charlie in danger, again. It was the last thing she wanted to do. She prayed he'd forgive her.

Will simply smiled. "Great. What are we waiting for? Let's go." He strode to the window and pulled the curtain aside with the barrel of his gun. "Damn. Change of plans. We're using the fire escape, ladies." He shoved them both toward the opposite window and the precarious ladder, attached to the side of the building, for emergencies.

"You can't make an eight months' pregnant woman climb down that thing."

"Watch me."

Robyn took Ginger's hands in hers. Ginger had been complaining about not being able to see her feet for months. "I'll guide you, okay? Together we can do this. Trust me."

Ginger nodded and said, "Okay. You know I trust you." Her hands shook and her eyes glistened.

They were halfway down the ladder when Robyn heard pounding on her front door. Her head jerked up and she almost missed a rung.

"Robyn! Are you in there? Let me in. It's me, Killian."

Robyn took one look at the absolute terror on Ginger's ashen face, and knew she had to keep silent. Her words, any words, would kill them all.

Chapter 13

Killian's pounding on the door gained ferocity. His heart beat in his chest like flash lightning on a summer night. Robert, the doorman, hadn't wanted to let him up. For the second time that day he'd had to resort to flashing his badge. The delays were starting to piss him off.

"Robyn! Are you okay? Robyn, answer me!" Anger flared. If the bastard hurt her, he'd kill him with his bare hands. Taking a few steps back, he rammed into the door with his shoulder. It groaned, but refused to give.

He repeated the procedure until his left side grew numb. *Dammit, this was an apartment building. Since when did they make doors so strong?* Beyond the entrance, silence reigned. Something was wrong. Panic washed over him, drowning him in thick despair. This was why he hadn't wanted to get involved with Robyn. He couldn't think straight. Couldn't reason.

At first, he thought there was no way in hell he could live with a woman like her. There was no way he could live without her. Taking a deep breath, he tried to calm himself. Panic wouldn't help anyone.

Ripping the gun out of his holster, he held it out in front of him. With one perfect aim of his foot, he kicked right next to the doorknob. The door popped open and he barged into the apartment.

Empty. He ran into the bedroom, the bathroom, and the kitchen. His palms grew clammy. They were on the second floor. Only one way out. Where could they have gone? He swept the room with his gaze.

The fire escape!

Killian dashed to the open window. Below in the parking lot, he spied Holgate shoving Robyn and a very pregnant Ginger into Robyn's Escort.

Wasting no time, he bolted from the apartment, down the stairs and headed for his Jeep. He spotted the red vehicle heading north. The Jeep's ignition refused to kick over. Killian swore under his breath. "Not now! Come on, baby."

It turned over the second time. He threw it into reverse, squealing out of the lot. Reaching the first light, he knew he was in trouble. Robyn's car was nowhere to be seen. He sped past several more lights, hoping he'd spot them.

Nothing. It was as if they'd vanished. In frustration, he pounded on the steering wheel. "Dammit. Where did you take her, Will? Where in the hell did you take her?" he shouted.

Every time Robyn tried to slow down, Holgate would jab the gun into her side and demand she accelerate. She screeched around one corner, precariously tipped on two wheels. If she continued at this pace, she'd end up killing them all.

While she didn't give a damn about the jerk next to her, she wanted to keep herself, Ginger and the baby alive. She eased up on the gas. A quick glance in the rearview mirror told her no one was following. Where was Killian? Why wasn't he coming after them?

Robyn parked in a handicapped spot at the bank, praying the defiant action would make a cop appear as if by magic. Holgate climbed out and slammed the door.

"Hurry up!" he yelled. "I don't have all day." Begrudgingly, she clambered out. Death loomed close, so close she felt she had nothing to lose. "Bully for you," she mumbled under her breath.

Will shoved his face right into hers. "What did you say?" he demanded.

She wasn't intimidated. Without her, he had nothing. He couldn't get access to the bank until morning. She opened her mouth to tell him what she thought of him, when Ginger grabbed her arm from behind.

"She didn't say anything. Not a word. Did you, Robyn?"

The imploring look in Ginger's eyes made her cave in. A ragged sigh of frustration escaped her lips. "Not a word." Ginger didn't look good, and it worried Robyn. An ashen pallor hollowed out her cheeks and her entire body seemed to tremble.

Will nudged them onto the sidewalk. "I'm watching you. Don't try anything stupid."

Robyn squashed the urge to cry. She needed to be strong to get through this. At the glass double-door entrance, she stopped. She could see the security guard inside and waved, throwing him a shaky smile. *Don't let me in. Don't let me in.*

Charlie ambled to the doors and turned the key. "A little early today, aren't you, Robyn?" He eyed her suspiciously. "The cops told me your apprentice, Doug, would be coming in for a while."

She shrugged. "Change of plans. I've, ah, got some new employees I'm going to be, ah, training. Thought it might take me a little longer to clean than usual."

"I see." He looked at the odd couple behind her with more disdain than he'd bestowed upon Robyn.

She glanced over her shoulder. A pregnant woman and a man who resembled a bodyguard. Yep, real good crew she had. No wonder Charlie looked like he didn't believe a word she said.

"Well, I think we'll get started. We've got a lot to do." Turning, she headed for the supply closet, feeling like a cheerleader trying to remain peppy when her team was down thirty-four to nothing with one minute remaining in the game. She handed a mop to each of them. "Here."

"What's this for?" Holgate looked at the tool like he'd never seen one before.

She tried to explain like she was talking to a simpleminded child. "I'm just trying to make it look good," she inclined her head toward Charlie, who was still watching them as he ambled back across the lobby.

Lip curling, Holgate flung the mop to the ground. The clatter reverberated throughout the empty room. "I'm not here to freaking clean. I want the money. Now."

"Here, here." Charlie turned around and walked back toward them. "What's all the ruckus about?"

"I'm sorry. It's nothing. The handle slipped out of my hand," Robyn said.

"Screw this. I'm tired of waiting." Will whipped the revolver out of his holster and aimed it at Charlie. "Take me to the lockboxes, old man."

The security guard raised his arms in the air. Will reached over and yanked Charlie's firearm out of the holster, then shoved it into the waistband of his own pants.

"Don't shoot me," Charlie begged, the light going out of his eyes. "My wife wouldn't make it on her own."

A rush of sympathy washed over Robyn. Charlie was too old for this.

"My heart bleeds for you," their captor rasped. "Move it!"

The security guard led them all to the room holding the boxes. "Here we are, but you can't get in there."

"Don't give me that bull."

Charlie's face paled. "It's time locked. Won't open again

until morning. No key in the world is going to make a difference."

Turning toward Robyn, Holgate's eyes narrowed to sinister slits. "You knew this, didn't you?"

"I tried to tell you."

He looked up at the ceiling. "This is just great. Freaking
great." He walked around in a tight circle, mumbling to himself. "I guess we're all camping out until morning then, aren't
we?"

What had been a long day, just grew longer.

"Sit down and keep your mouths shut."

Robyn sat on the cold marble floor, her arm around
Ginger. Charlie sat on her other side, a little farther away. It
was clear he wasn't sure whom to trust at this point.

"Ginger?" Robyn hissed under her breath.

"What?"

"Why on earth did you tell him you had a lockbox here?"

"It bought us some time, didn't it? Besides, now we're in a
public place."

"Who says pregnancy kills brain cells?" She squeezed her
closer. "That was smart thinking."

Robyn turned toward Holgate. Despite his agitation, if she
was going to die there were a few questions for which she
wanted answers. "Why are you doing this, Holgate? What do
you hope to gain? Is a little bit of money worth going to jail?"

Holgate stopped pacing long enough to fix her with a
stare. "Do you even know who you work for?"

"What do you mean?"

"Clifford Barnes. He's not just president and CEO of
United Financial Bank, he's a murderer."

Ginger and Robyn exchanged glances.

"Not just a murderer, but a damn drunk. He killed my
daughter and walked away a free man. I'm going to hurt him

like he hurt me. My daughter was my life and he took her away. Money is his life and I'm going to take it away." Explanation finished, Holgate resumed pacing. The minutes slowly ticked as they waited for the time the bank vault would open.

After a while, the shuffle of Will Holgate's pacing grated on Robyn's nerves. She was ready to hop up and hit him when Ginger squeezed her hand tightly. "What's the matter, Gin?"

Ginger's hand massaged her rounded stomach. "I'm just scared."

"Me, too," Robyn admitted.

Charlie scooted a little closer. "Robyn, remember me telling you that if anything funny ever happened you needed to push the red button? Things don't get any funnier than right now."

Squealing up to the nearest convenience store, Killian could have killed himself for letting his cell phone go dead. He was wasting precious minutes. He rooted in his pocket for a couple quarters. Shoving them into the coin slot on the pay phone, he dialed Dan's cell phone.

The first ring sounded in his ear. What had caused Will to turn bad? Ring number two. He'd been the head of this agency for five years. Why hadn't Killian seen it coming? What had caused it?

Ring number three. "Yeah. Dan Stevens."

"It's Hart," he identified himself. "I lost their trail. I need all the help I can get. Put out an APB on a red Escort." He rattled off the plate number.

"Am I glad you called. Couldn't get you on your cell phone. I think I know where they are! I just received a call that the security system has gone off at the United Financial Bank building. I'm almost there myself. I left your house as soon as they called me. Don't you dare move in before backup arrives."

Killian dropped the receiver and left it swinging by its cord. He jumped into his Jeep and sent it flying down the road toward the bank. Besides money, what was the appeal of the bank? There had to be something he was missing.

It was then that he remembered Robyn rattling off the names of all the bank employees the first night they'd been kidnapped. One name had rung a bell, but he couldn't figure out why. Clifford Barnes. Bank president. He was also responsible for killing Holgate's daughter, Emily. This crime spree was all motivated by revenge.

Robyn watched Will closely. When he started pacing away from her, she slipped around the corner and, heart pounding and hands shaking, headed for the red button in the security room. She had to hurry. She hadn't wanted to do it at all. Hadn't wanted to risk anyone's life. Ginger had insisted. Said it was their only hope.

"Where did she go?"

Robyn heard Will's deep voice bellowing all the way down the hall. On the TV screen she watched him stalk toward Ginger and demand an answer, the gun pressed to the middle of her stomach.

Scared for her friend's life, Robyn jammed a fist down on the silent red alarm and ran back to the lobby. "I'm right here. Ginger's not feeling well." She held up a wet washcloth for his inspection.

Holgate's eyes narrowed to tiny twin steel slits. "You expect me to believe that line of bull?" Pulling the gun away from Ginger, Will walked over to Robyn. "What do you take me for? An imbecile?" He waved the weapon in her face.

Robyn refused to let him intimidate her. *No. I take you for a lying, cheating, no-good piece of lawbreaking garbage.* "Of course not. You're too smart for me to try and pull one over on you. Aren't you?"

He hesitated. "Of course I am. You stay right here, do you hear me?"

"I won't move so much as a finger."

His crazed blue eyes locked with hers. "See that you don't." He moved back to his spot against the wall and paced back and forth in front of it, every so often glancing at his watch in irritation.

Charlie grabbed Robyn's arm. He looked down at her with worry in his eyes.

She nodded, answering his unspoken question. "Done."

Charlie leaned back against the wall, his face damp and ashen. With shaking fingers, he tugged at his tie as if he couldn't breathe.

Holgate's pacing quickened. Dread snaked through Robyn. Impatient as he was, he wouldn't make it to morning. The man wanted satisfaction now. In lieu of money, would he start killing them?

He stopped and pierced her with his gaze. "What the hell are you looking at?"

Terror flicked at Robyn's insides. "Nothing." She dropped her gaze. The police should have arrived already. What was keeping them?

Out of the corner of her eye, she gave a surreptitious glance at Charlie. A bead of moisture lined his upper lip.

"Charlie? Are you okay?" She started to get up to help him.

Holgate plowed in front of her, blocking her path. "Stay put."

"Look, something's wrong. I was just trying—"

"I don't care what you were trying to do." His eyes took on

a wild, crazed look. "I will not be deceived. Clifford Barnes will suffer like I've suffered." Aiming his pistol in the air, he fired.

Robyn tried to cover Ginger to protect her and the baby. Ceiling particles and dust fell to the floor, coating everything around them.

"Oh, God," Charlie gasped, clutching his heart.

Despite Will's warning, Robyn jumped up and ran over to him as he slumped down to the ground. "Charlie, what is it? I think he's having a heart attack." She turned and glared at her captor. "We need to get him help. He could die!"

Will's eyebrows rose. "So?"

Robyn unfastened the top button on Charlie's shirt. "You're going to be fine," she reassured him. "Don't worry." She brushed a hand against his cheek. He nodded and licked his dry lips. She glanced at Will over her shoulder, piercing him with her glare. "Please, don't you care about anything?"

A harsh laugh rolled from Will's twisted mouth. "Everything I ever cared about was taken from me." He kicked a piece of plaster across the open room. "When Barnes loses everything he cares about, we'll be even." He paced faster, more furious, punched at the wall with a closed fist. His knuckles bled, but he didn't seem to notice.

Robyn recited a few Hail Mary's, a couple Our Father's and a half-dozen Acts of Contrition while she stared at Charlie. She was scared and confused, and didn't know what to do. It reminded her of her days on the run all over again. If she could make it then, dammit, she could make it now.

Ginger moved beside her. "Lay him down flat. It might help." Together, they assisted Charlie to the ground.

She had to think of something to get them out of this mess. Holgate was ready to snap, and if Charlie didn't get help soon, she didn't even want to think of the consequences.

Out of the corner of her eye, she saw a flash behind Will. Praying it was Killian, but not wanting to draw attention to him, Robyn forced herself to turn around and apply the wet washcloth to Charlie's forehead. Her hands shook. She shared a glance with Ginger. Judging by her pale face and quivering lower lip, she was as scared as Robyn.

Without warning, Will grabbed Robyn from behind and pulled her to her feet. "What the . . ."

He spun her around, gun to her temple. "Don't come another step, Hart."

Robyn's gut clenched at the sight of Killian. He wore his FBI hat and looked exactly like he did the first time she'd met him. He palmed his gun easily, aiming it right at his boss. "I know why you're doing this, Holgate. You've worked hard to get where you are. This isn't going to bring Emily back."

"Sorry to blow the image you have of me, but I can't be the faithful, follow-the-rules type of man that you always are. I used to be. We'd put the bad guys in jail, you and I, and the system sets them free." He shook his head. "I need revenge, Hart."

"That's not always the case. Your thirst for revenge is going to put you behind bars."

In answer, Holgate cocked the hammer on his pistol.

This wasn't the way Robyn wanted her life to end. Panting heavily, Robyn opened her eyes and dragged her gaze to Killian. Help me, she begged without words.

Killian spared Robyn no more than a fleeting glance. He had to maintain control. If he saw her fear, he'd be liable to make a foolish mistake. He couldn't afford to do that. Not when he'd screwed the rules and gone in without backup.

"Come on, Will. You don't want to do this, do you? Your sentence will be lighter if you let her go."

"Don't use your pathetic pop psychology on me. I've repeated those same lines so many damn times I could puke."

Sweat dripped off Will's face. Killian could tell he was nervous. Any sudden move would spook him. They were in a standoff. "This is a no-win situation, Will. You don't want to harm her. You know you don't."

Will smiled.

Killian's heart lodged in his throat. Holgate had gone off the deep end.

"She means nothing to me." He grabbed Robyn's chin. "But what about you? Should I save her for you, Hart?"

A muscle ticked in Killian's jaw. Of course she meant something to him. He loved her. Good God, he'd just entered a hostage situation, alone, without cover.

Robyn held her body rigid, her hands clenched at her sides. He still refused to look at her. "She's done nothing wrong. She's an innocent victim, just like your daughter. Nothing more. Let her go."

Something flashed in Will's eyes. Regret? Sorrow?

He almost had him. "Come on, Will. Do it for me . . . do it for Emily." He didn't breathe while he waited for Will's answer. Behind them a bloodcurdling scream ripped from Ginger's throat. In the resulting confusion, Robyn deadened her body weight, slipped out of Holgate's grip and dropped to the ground. Gunshots reverberated all around. Robyn covered her ears with her hands.

When the shooting stopped, the acrid smell of smoke filled the air. Robyn peeked up and scanned the room. Ginger leaned against the wall next to Charlie. They both looked stunned but in one piece. Her gaze moved across the room. Holgate lay on the floor close to her, blood seeping from a hole in his chest.

She scanned the room for Killian, but there were cops

swarming all around, and she couldn't find him. Her heart rose in her throat. She'd die a slow death without him. Had he been shot? Killed?

"Are you okay?"

Robyn spun at the sound of Killian's voice. He was alive. She ran a quick gaze over his body. He appeared to be in one piece. She didn't see blood.

"I'm fine," she managed.

Dan Stevens interrupted them, demanding Killian's full attention. "I told you to wait for backup, partner. You broke the biggest rule of all. Were you trying to get yourself killed or something?"

Robyn's gaze snapped to Killian's. He looked away. Her heart ricocheted in her chest like the bullets off the walls moments earlier. He'd broken the rules for her?

When Dan finished with his lecture, Killian turned back to her. "Listen . . . we can't right now, but when you've got time we need to talk," he said.

"Sure." As ill at ease as he was, she dropped her gaze to the ground and studied the tips of her shoes. This awkward, polite stranger bit drove her nuts. Would they ever get past it? Somehow, she doubted it. She sighed, certain he wanted to talk to her to explain why a relationship between the two of them could never work.

He was right. Damn him.

"Say it right now, Killian." Better to get the good-byes over with. Why prolong the pain? It seemed to be the day for severing connections, anyway.

"Now?" He yanked on the neck of his shirt. "I'm kind of busy, Robyn."

She lifted her gaze and stared straight into his rich brown eyes. "Yes. Just spit it out."

"Robyn, I—"

Ginger interrupted, tugging at Robyn's sleeve. "Rob, we've got a little problem."

She tore her gaze away from Killian and glanced at her friend. "Can it wait a few minutes?"

"I don't think so." Bent over slightly, Ginger groaned. She held one hand to her back, and squeezed the life out of Robyn's arm with the other. "That bloodcurdling scream wasn't fear. It was a contraction. My water broke."

Chapter 14

"Isn't she the most precious gift you've ever seen?" Ginger asked, a pink-bundled baby cradled in her arms.

Ginger's husband, Vince, sat at her side on the narrow hospital bed, the infant's fist wrapped around his pinky finger. "I need to get some coffee, Gin," he said, regret threaded throughout his deep voice. "As much as I don't want to leave you for a second, I've been awake for over twenty-four hours. I need the caffeine." The look he exchanged with his wife was one of rapture and awe.

Robyn watched Ginger look at her husband with love radiating from her eyes. She glanced away. It hurt to watch two people so much in love. Especially when she couldn't find it herself.

Vince leaned down and kissed his new daughter's forehead, then gave his wife a tender kiss on the lips. "I'll be back before you miss me."

"Do you want me to bring you some coffee, Auntie Rob?" On his way out the door, he hugged Robyn.

"No. I'm good. Congratulations again. She looks just like you, Vince. A real chip off the old block." She mock-punched his shoulder.

"She does look like me, doesn't she?" His wide, proud papa grin was infectious.

When he left, Robyn peeked inside the pink blanket. A tuft of black hair, the same shade as her father's, covered little Sarah's head. "God. It's so amazing. I've just met her, and I love her to pieces already."

Ginger looked at her tiny baby, pride and love filling her eyes. "I know what you mean. Hey, how's that security guard?"

"Oh, I went and visited Charlie while you were in delivery. He's doing great. He'll probably be released tomorrow. I guess it was a mild heart attack, thank goodness."

"That's a relief."

"It sure is. And his wife has convinced him to retire for good. The way Charlie's always talked about her, I thought she'd be this frail, tiny woman."

"Isn't she?"

"God, no. Just the opposite. I mean, she's little, but she's got a personality that makes up for it. It's so cute to watch them together. She fusses over him like a mother hen and he's all, 'Yes, dear' and 'No, dear.' "

"Did he ever tell you why he was acting so weird?"

"He was worried about the effect the kidnapping had on me. Said I wasn't acting like myself. We laughed when I told him I was worried because he wasn't acting like *himself*, either."

"I'm glad everything worked out. I heard on the news they found the money buried out behind the shack where you were held captive."

"Yeah." She shuddered. That money and thirst for revenge had changed everyone's lives forever. They both turned to Sarah when the little girl stretched her arms out wide.

"Do you want to hold her?"

Robyn's instinct took over. "Yes." Reaching out, Robyn took the bundle from Ginger's arms. Feeling the warmth, watching Sarah's little mouth make sucking noises in her sleep, smelling the powdered scent, made Robyn want to cry.

"Spill it, Rob. You haven't been yourself lately."

"Yeah? Who have I been?" She tried to avoid the question . . . ignorance was bliss, wasn't it?

Ginger gave her a look that said, you know what I mean. "What's the matter?"

"I just . . ." Tears stung her eyes. "I want . . ."

"What? You can tell me."

"I want what you and Vince have." She drew a ragged breath into her lungs. "Is that so terrible of me?"

"Of course not. Sometimes things worth waiting for take a little while and come with their share of pain."

Robyn studied the infant's face. Marveled at the way she went from sound asleep to awake and fussy in an instant. "I think she wants dinner. Sorry, but I'm not equipped to help her with that one."

She handed her back, and Ginger adjusted her daughter to her breast to feed. "Sarah was something Vince and I both wanted very much. But it took her nine long months and sixteen hours of intense labor to get here. I'd do it again in a heartbeat. She was worth every minute."

Tears pricked at Robyn's eyes again for about the millionth time in one week. "It's amazing, you know."

"What is?"

"One minute I'm sure we're all going to die, the next I'm here celebrating the birth of your daughter. We did it, you know." Robyn concentrated on fingering a wrinkle in the bedcovers.

"We who? And did what?" Ginger cocked her head sideways.

"You know . . . *it*. Me and Killian."

"No! When?"

"The night I spent at his house."

Ginger patted the extra space on the side of the bed. Perching on the edge, Robyn let the baby grab her finger.

"It's no secret I've been with my share of men. I've even imagined myself in love a couple of times." She paused, drew in a deep breath. "But that time spent with Killian was . . . was . . . I can't even describe it, it was so magnificent."

"It's true love this time. I can see it on your face."

"If true love hurts like hell, then I guess you're right." Tears stung her eyes and she forced a shaky smile on to her face.

"Hey, I went through the same thing with Vince, remember? I thought we'd never end up together, and yet I couldn't imagine myself with any other man." She patted Robyn's arm. "If it's meant to be, it will all work out."

"That's just it . . . what if it's not meant to be? What if he hates my guts? What if he never wants to see me again? What if I was just a one-night stand?"

"Do you feel like you were just an outlet for some guy's overcharged libido?"

Robyn pushed off the bed and wandered to the window, overlooking the parking lot. "It didn't feel like it at the time, but now I'm not so sure." She dropped the shade back in place. "I have never been so confused in my life."

"Have you talked to Killian about it?"

"We started to talk at the bank, but then little Sarah here"—she pointed to the infant—"demanded to be heard. A couple hours old and she's already craving attention. You and Vince are going to have your hands full."

Ginger smiled, rubbed her finger against the baby's soft cheek. "And we're looking forward to every second of it." Her voice turned serious. "Go home and call him, Rob. You'll never know what kind of future the two of you might share unless you find the courage to ask."

And what if he said they didn't have a future? What if she *had* been a one-night stand and nothing more? That thought scared Robyn more than she was willing to admit.

When the doorbell rang, Robyn fluffed up her bangs one last time then checked her lipstick. Vamp, by Chanel. It had been lucky for her once. She crossed her fingers, hoping it would work its magic a second time. Heart in her throat, she went to answer the door.

Killian stood on the threshold in a gray Yale T-shirt and faded jeans. In his right hand, he held a cat carrier.

"Thanks for coming." She grabbed the edge of the door with one hand and ushered him in with the other.

"No problem. Here." He extended the cat carrier to her.

"Hi, guys." Robyn peered into the little door, then set the cage on the ground and released the animals. Brooklyn strolled out first, sniffed the air, then walked around the room and sharpened her clawless front paws against the back of the sofa. "I think she's glad to be home," Robyn laughed.

The kitten took longer coming out. "Come on, baby. You can do it." She dangled one of Brooklyn's toys in front of him. A white paw snaked out and batted the fuzzy fake mouse. "Come on." Like a missile coming out of a cannon, the black and white creature shot out of the cage and ran after Brooklyn's tail.

"He's been doing that for a couple days now," Killian explained. "I think he's adopted Brooklyn as his mother."

"I'm glad to see they're getting along." Robyn glanced at him, then snapped her gaze away. *Just ask him. Come on, you big chicken. Just ask him what his intentions are, get this whole thing over with and get on with your life.* "Killian?"

He tore his gaze away from the cats. "Yeah?"

"Do you want something to drink? Ice tea, maybe? Or perhaps a beer?"

"No, thanks." He shoved his hands in his back pockets

like he didn't know what to do with them.

They both stood in complete uncomfortable silence, watching the animals wrestle around the floor like a couple of kids. There they stood, two people who'd seen each other naked, yet didn't know what to do about it.

She'd had enough. They weren't strangers.

She had every inch of his body catalogued and stored in memory. She felt just as sure he knew her body as well, since he'd spent enough time studying it.

Besides, would a complete stranger do this? Propelling herself toward him, she jumped into his arms and wrapped her legs around his waist, locking them in back. He shifted his feet to regain his balance, his eyes wide in surprise.

"Damn, but I've missed you, Secret Agent Man." Not giving him time to think, assess, or evaluate the situation, she pressed her lips against his.

His hands slipped under her rear to hold her in place. Giving as good as he got, he groaned, returned her kiss with an urgency of his own, then pressed against her mouth with the tip of his tongue. She opened to allow him in, her heart beating a rapid tempo against her chest.

"Stop for a minute," she said when they drew apart. "We need to talk." Killian let her slip from his arms. She paced away a few steps, then turned and looked at him, saw the heated passion burning in his eyes.

She drew a deep breath and tugged her fingers through the curly hair at her temple. "I just want you to know, before we go any further, that Brooklyn, Sam and I will take you any way you want us to." She paced across the living room, then came back again. "We won't complain when you have to go out of town. We won't shed tears to make you feel guilty. It's part of your job. We understand that. We're willing to accept it as long as you keep us in your life, 'cause we can't live without you."

She looked up to see a grin on his face. "Sam, huh? I'm surprised you didn't name him Phoenix, or Arizona or something like that."

Men . . . they just didn't get it. Placing one hand on her hip, she explained it to him. "It's not Sam, as in Sam. It's Sam as in S-A-M."

His eyebrows rose. Clearly, he still didn't understand.

She sighed. "Sam as in Secret Agent Man. Whenever you leave, a part of you will still be here. Or if you decide you don't want to be a part of my life—"

"Wait a minute." He strode over to her and pulled her into his arms. "Who says I don't want to be a part of your life?"

"I . . . well . . . just in case . . . if you didn't want . . ."

"Robyn . . . I have never wanted anything so much in my life. Sorry, but you're stuck with me. I love you."

Robyn took a step forward and placed a hand on his chest. She searched his eyes. "I love you, too. There is no way I can*not* be involved with you. Do you understand that?" Standing on tiptoe, she leaned forward and pressed her lips to his. "I'll take you anyway I can have you. Danger or no danger. FBI job or no FBI job. Fiery red-haired temperament and all."

He shook his head and actually chuckled. "Did anyone ever tell you that you talk too much?"

"Why don't you just shut me up, then?" She tilted her lips up to his in invitation.

"Good idea." His kiss was earth-shattering. Somehow, they ended up on the couch, buck-naked and spent, but very satisfied.

"Does that tell you I want to be a part of your life?" he asked, rubbing a hand lazily up and down her bare back.

"Hmmm," she murmured against his chest, stirring the dark hairs there.

"Oh, I think I forgot to mention one thing."

"What?"

"I won't ever be leaving you. Now that I've found you, I have this strange desire to be near you every single second of every single day. I've quit the department. As of today, I no longer work for the FBI."

Robyn lifted her head, gazed deep into his eyes, her heart thumping like a herd of wild buffaloes running across the prairie. "Are you serious? Are you sure this is what you want? You're not going to regret it later, are you? What are you going to do?"

"Actually, I've wanted to quit for a long time, I just couldn't admit it to myself. Working for the FBI kept me from getting involved with anyone. I don't need or want that excuse anymore. I refuse to leave a loved one like my parents did." He kissed her lips. "Besides, the job hasn't been as rewarding as it used to be. I used to think work was everything, made my life complete. But lately, I've felt like something was missing."

He stared at her with love shining in his eyes. "You helped me make the decision whether you know it or not. I'm going to become a private investigator. Dan Stevens is opening his own agency. He asked me to be his partner. In the private sector, we'll make more money than we ever could working for the government." He tightened his grip around her. "I never thought I wanted a white picket fence existence. I thought it would drive me crazy within a week." He leaned forward and tugged on her bottom lip with his teeth. "Being around you is going to be anything but boring."

Hours later, they shared a candlelight dinner, and Killian's meat loaf surprise. "You don't have any arsenic in it this time, do you?"

He laughed. Reaching across the table, he kissed her. "No arsenic, just a couple rocks."

"Rocks?"

"I'm kidding, just eat."

Stabbing a piece of meat, she put it into her mouth, then cried out when she bit into something hard and almost cracked her tooth. "Ouch! What the heck is in here?" Fishing the object out of her mouth with her fingers, she looked at it. A sparkling dark blue sapphire in the center of two lighter blue sapphires, offset with two tiny diamonds on each side, caught the candlelight and winked at her. "Oh, my God. Killian! Rocks?"

He nodded, a sexy grin on his face. "Rocks."

"Oh, my God!" She looked at him, then glanced back at the ring. What did this mean? Her mind couldn't keep up with the rapid pace of her heart. She dragged her gaze away from the sparkling gems and met Killian's gaze. No words came.

"If this relationship is leading where I think it might be, someday there will be an engagement ring to replace this promise ring. Read the inscription, Robyn," he begged.

Eyes squinted, she turned the ring so the words were visible in the light. *Robyn, Love me, and leave me not. Killian.* She remained silent for a moment, absorbing everything. She struggled with pulling a deep breath into her lungs, then slipped the ring on her finger. "I adore it, Killian. I do love you, and I promise to never, ever leave you." She leaned across the table and kissed him tenderly, then pulled back.

He brushed a lock of hair away from her face. "It's okay with you that it's not an engagement ring?"

"Absolutely. I'm glad we're taking it slow. I've made more than my fair share of mistakes in relationships. I want to take this one moment at a time. I don't want to mess it up."

"I'm glad we both agree, because that ring comes with about a thousand million promises."

"Yeah?"

"Yeah."

"What's the first promise you're going to make to me?"

Killian rolled his eyes in a playful manner. "Oh my God, she's exacting promises already." He took her fingers in his, holding their hands up to admire how the ring looked on her. "I've thought about that a lot. You know the old saying about how you can take the man away from the job, but you can't take the job away from the man?"

"Yep."

"Well, the FBI's motto is to protect. My first promise to you is that no matter what happens, or where this relationship takes us, I promise I will never stop protecting you. No matter what, and whether you need it or not. You've proven that you can take care of yourself . . . and me . . . but it's what I do. It's the best thing that I do."

Robyn smiled, then shook her head. "Sorry, but I disagree. It's not the *best* thing that you do."

In question he raised one eyebrow. "Oh?"

For some wacky reason, despite everything they had been through, she blushed, then bent forward and whispered a heated message in his ear.

Killian's grin couldn't have been wider. An incorrigible, seductive broad smile, that promised so much more than she had ever expected, or hoped for in her life. The ring's message was already coming true. In answer to her whispered words, he pushed away from the table and held out his hand, a serious look on his face.

Her tummy flip-flopped. She slipped her palm in his, comforted by the warmth of his grip and the love in his eyes.

"Let's go to the bedroom, and I vow to show you how

much I love you all night long, and prove how good we are to-gether, and that the future is even brighter than your ring."

Robyn let him pull her from her chair and into his arms. "Now that, Secret Agent Man, is one hell of a wicked promise."

About the Author

Amy Sandrin has written short stories since she was a little girl. She never considered herself an author, though. Writing was just something she did. Many years later she tried her hand at novel-length fiction, and whether she wanted it or not, the label of author took hold and stuck. Not only does Amy pen award-winning fiction novels, as an avid quilter she's also published nonfiction quilting books. She lives in Colorado's High Plains outside of Denver with her husband, son, and two very spoiled cats.